ALSO BY MARY JANE CLARK

Let Me Whisper in Your Ear

Do You Promise Not to Tell?

Do You Want to Know a Secret?

CLOSE
— TO YOU —

MARY JANE CLARK

ST. MARTIN'S PRESS ❦ NEW YORK

www.stmartins.com

Library of Congress Cataloging-in-Publication Data

Clark, Mary Jane Behrends.
    Close to you / Mary Jane Clark—1st ed.
        p. cm.
    ISBN 0-312-26266-3
    1. Women television journalists—Fiction. 2. Television news anchors—Fiction. 3. Mothers and daughters—Fiction. 4. Stalking victims—Fiction. 5. New Jersey—Fiction. I. Title.

PS3553.L2873 C58 2001
813'.54—dc21   2001031815

First Edition: September 2001

10   9   8   7   6   5   4   3   2   1

For David
my loving and loveable son,
and
all those who struggle with Fragile X syndrome...
with great hopes and fervent prayers for a cure

ACKNOWLEDGMENTS

Over the years, working behind the scenes, producing too many news stories to count, I have often wondered what it would be like to be "on-air" talent, standing or sitting in front of the television camera. To be sure, it looks glamorous. Millions of eyes are fixed on the correspondent's face as she delivers the latest news. But as the reporter gazes into the dark camera lens and talks to the unseen audience, she has no idea just who is watching her. What could be going on in some skewed mind out there as she "exposes" herself night after night?

The premise chilled me.

Reporters I asked said they tried not to think about unstable people watching them. They couldn't do their jobs, they said, if they spent their time worrying about "the nuts." They claimed they pushed from their minds the knowledge there were viewers who became fixated on them. Yet, without exception, each had experiences with obsessive fans, some in very unlikely places, and the bizarre lengths to which those "fans" were willing to go. Some stalkers were sick, some just plain evil, but all wanted to get too close.

Newswomen and friends Liz Flock, Bobbi Harley, and Elizabeth Kaledin shared some stories with me that left me slack-jawed. I thank them for the seeds that germinated into this book.

My sincere thanks to Stan Romaine, Director of CBS Corporate Security, for taking the time to answer my questions about what a television network does to protect its threatened personnel and for being extremely generous in sharing his expertise on what steps are taken to catch a stalker. Stan recounted some mesmerizing stories, but the twinkle in his eye left me feeling that he just scratched the surface. He knows much more than he can tell. But I'm awfully glad he was willing to give me his tutorial.

Christina Weisberg, makeup artist and resplendent, delightful character herself, provided the raw makeup material and insight necessary to fashion the fictional character of Doris Brice. I could never do you justice, Christina, but I tried.

Joy Blake, once again, helped me with her knowledge of the intricacies of real estate transactions. Her professional expertise is appreciated, but her friendship is treasured.

By now, criminal attorney Joseph Hayden must be sick of the telephone calls asking what the legal ramifications of my characters' actions are, but he has the good grace not to show it. Thank you, Joe.

Linda Karas gave the world's best tour of London in record time. She is one of the fastest thinkers I know and always has helpful ideas when I run problems past her. Together, we started out in the news business many moons ago and, over the years, Linda has been a source of strength, comfort, and great fun.

Colleen Kenny worked hard to get www.maryjaneclark.com up and running. This, in addition to always being there for me and my children. How fortunate I've been to have you, Col!

For a priest, Father Paul Holmes plays an excellent devil's advocate. As the deadline loomed closer, Paul made himself available to help in ways both great and small...from brainstorming sessions to research assistance to deciphering my handwritten scrawl and enterring those last minute changes into the master document. Father Holmes is the answer to this writer's prayers...a heaven-sent independent editor.

Eva's mommy, Laura Dail, is also, lucky for me, my tireless, devoted and enthusiastic agent. Time after time, Laura goes above and beyond the job description for a literary agent. I so appreciate that

ACKNOWLEDGMENTS

you run those extra miles, Laura. Thank you, too, for your insights on the Guatemalan people and help with the Spanish language.

The input of Jennifer Enderlin, my new editor, definitely made this a better book. Jen was instrumental in ratcheting up the suspense, and I'm grateful for her focus on this project and for the special attention of Sally Richardson, Matthew Shear, John Murphy, and Linda McFall. The St. Martin's crew has been very good to me.

And finally, thank you to my patient family and dear friends. It is my great joy to be *Close to You*.

PROLOGUE

For the two years she had anchored the ten o'clock news for the Garden State Network, she had never given a second thought to entering the well-lit parking lot after work. She had been so confident, so sure of herself.

Now she lived in fear. And she hated it.

The late-October night air was cold and crisp as she hurried across the lot toward her locked car, another week of work behind her. Shivering beneath the wool coat she had just picked up from the dry cleaners', she fumbled with the shiny key, her nervousness only making her aim less efficient. She breathed a heavy sigh of relief as she got in and locked the door beside her.

She was determined not to be a victim. She had signed up for a self-defense course at her health club and had a security system installed on her condo. She forced herself to carry on with her life, determined not to be held hostage by some sick nut.

She drove home, comforting herself with the fact that her boss, the news director, while showing some concern, did not seem overly worried. He had been in the business for twenty years and had listened to dozens of stories from his on-air talent who had been targeted as objects of desire by viewers. Most of the obsessive fans were harmless.

Most.

She pulled her blue two-seater convertible into her reserved spot at the end of the row of two-story condominiums. She had been so happy to get an end unit when she bought the place, having neighbors only on one side and the yard at the end to herself. Now she wished her condo was smack in the middle of all the others.

She pulled the car key from the ignition and searched out the house keys, holding them tight in her hand. She looked out the windows on both sides and behind her before getting out of the car. It was just a few steps to the front door.

The first key slid smoothly into the top lock and she heard the dead bolt shift. But the second key got stuck halfway in the doorknob. She jiggled at it frantically.

"Linda, you've been avoiding me." The words sliced through the still night air and the hand clamped down on hers.

The next morning, an eager trick-or-treater, thrilled that Halloween fell on a Saturday that year and provided a full day of candy-gathering, made his way along the row of condos in his gorilla costume. When he got to the last door there was no answer. He shrugged, undisturbed. There were lots more doorbells to ring.

He cut across the side yard, toward the woods that led to the next housing development. He paid little attention to the woman's shoe or to the can of hairspray that lay on the dew-covered grass.

The anchorwoman's mother screamed with rage and desperation at the police. Her daughter had reported that she thought she was being followed. Why hadn't they *done* something?

The police were on the defensive. Hadn't they given her escorts for weeks? There had been no problems. No one menacing had shown up. They couldn't have gone on indefinitely, accompanying her back and forth from the studio each night. There wasn't a budget for that.

They vowed they would do everything in their power to find Linda Anderson. It was a high-profile case. The Garden State Network was breathing down the police chief's neck every day for developments in the investigation. But the suspect list was infinite.

It could be anyone with a television set.

AUGUST

CHAPTER

1

"Eliza! I've found it! But you've got to come out here and look at it right away. It isn't going to last."

Eliza Blake listened to Louise Kendall's breathless voice and felt her own heart beat faster. She glanced at her watch as she swiveled around in her high-backed leather chair and looked out the windowed wall of her office down to the studio on the floor below. She could see the stagehands readying the set for the news segment she was scheduled to pretape for this evening's broadcast.

"God, Louise," Eliza pleaded. "There's no way I can leave now."

"You *have* to." Louise was adamant. "This is your house, Eliza. I'm sure of it. My office just signed the listing agreement and it's going into multiple tomorrow. Everyone and his cousin will be looking at it in the morning and, I swear to you, Eliza, in this crazy market, the house will be gone by this time tomorrow."

If the house were as special as Louise promised it was, Eliza knew the Realtor was probably right. During the few short weeks Eliza had begun her house-hunting in earnest, she had been stunned by the dizzying speed with which prime real estate moved in Bergen County. Eliza was desperate to find somewhere peaceful she and Janie could live, out of New York City and away from all the recent unhappy memories. Their apartment was beautiful and it was certainly big enough for just the two of them. But Eliza wanted to get her little girl in a new environment, out of the city, cultural capital of the world or not.

Louise was not giving up. "And, Eliza, I almost forgot to tell you. It's an estate sale. The house is vacant, so you could close as soon as you wanted. Janie could even be enrolled in her new school by the first day of kindergarten."

It was little wonder that Louise Kendall was a consistent member of the Realtors' Million Dollar Sales Club, thought Eliza. She was an expert at enticing her customers.

"Look, Louise, here's the best I can do. Right after the broadcast, I'll pick up Janie and we'll drive out there. I should be able to meet you by eight."

"Great!" exclaimed Louise triumphantly. "We'll still have some light then. We can walk around the outside property first while we can still see and then we'll go inside. I know you are going to fall in love with this house, Eliza. I'm bringing a contract with me. Make sure to bring your checkbook."

CHAPTER

2

Not far from the Lincoln Tunnel in Moonachie, New Jersey, every seat at the bar was taken at the noisy Like It Rare steakhouse. As the clock on the wall neared six–thirty, the regulars groaned when the bartender switched the television mounted on the wall at the corner of the bar to the *KEY Evening Headlines* with Eliza Blake.

"Aw, come on, Meat. Give us a break. Leave on the wrestling."

"For Christ's sake, Meat, we come here to get away from the real world for a while. Why do you always have to watch the damned news?"

"Forget it, you guys. You should know better by now. Meat's got a hard-on for Eliza Blake. There's nothing you can say or do that is going to make him change that freakin' channel."

Cornelius Bacon appeared to ignore the comments from his customers, but in fact he didn't even hear them. He was mesmerized and then angered as he watched Eliza Blake open the newscast, as she did each evening, not sitting at her desk as the male anchormen did at the other networks, but by walking across the studio set. Though the network could deny it up and down, KEY News was obviously capitalizing on Eliza's sex appeal.

The tall, willowy brunette stepped with assurance as she welcomed her viewers and recounted the top stories of the evening. Then, as the *KEY Evening Headlines* fanfare music blared, the camera followed Eliza as she took her seat at the anchor desk.

Meat didn't like that suit she was wearing. The skirt was much too short.

Hadn't he warned her about that? He had told her what he would do the next time she dared to show so much of those shapely legs.

Why hadn't she listened?

CHAPTER

3

Even before the closing credits had finished rolling, Eliza unclipped her microphone and said a silent prayer of thanks that there was no reason to update tonight's show. The broadcast had been technically perfect. Every news piece and each live standup had been executed without a hitch. There had been no misspelled supers or misplaced graphics. A clean feed to the two hundred–plus KEY affiliates around the country.

"Nice work, everybody." Executive producer Range Bullock goodnighted the studio crew from his seat inside the control room.

As Eliza stepped down from the anchor platform, Doris Brice approached with her cosmetics case in hand, a gold–sequined baseball cap perched jauntily atop her dark head. But tonight Eliza waved off their evening ritual.

"Thanks, Doris, but don't even bother with taking off my makeup tonight. I've got to get out of here. There's a house."

Doris knew all about Eliza's real–estate quest. They had talked about it at length over the last few weeks as Eliza sat in the chair before each broadcast while Doris carefully painted, contoured and powdered the anchorwoman's face. Like almost everyone at KEY News, Doris knew Eliza's history: the death from cancer of her husband, John, a painful death that Eliza endured while she was pregnant with their first child. The battle with depression that followed the birth of her daughter and her struggle to come back to work. And just last month, the betrayal of the woman Eliza had entrusted with the care of her precious Janie. A betrayal that had ended with gunshots. Doris noticed that Eliza still winced sometimes if she turned the wrong way or too quickly in the chair, the wound in her side almost healed now, but still tender.

After all Eliza had been through, Doris could well understand that the woman who had become her friend would want to make a fresh start somewhere. She hoped this house would be everything that Eliza wanted. She deserved it.

And she could certainly afford it, now that she was the anchor of the *KEY Evening Headlines*.

"Good luck," Doris called as she watched Eliza hurry from the studio. Eliza turned, grinned and gave the thumbs–up sign.

CHAPTER

4

Since Eliza Blake had taken over as anchor of the *KEY Evening Headlines*, Jerry Walinski had scheduled his massages for the evenings, immediately after the broadcast aired. After watching Eliza Blake he was so worked up that he needed Lori's hour-long therapy to calm down.

Tonight he was especially relieved that Lori was here. In his well-appointed bedroom, Jerry lay on his stomach with his eyes closed on the massage table as the masseuse worked on his lower body. He didn't feel the expert kneading his leg muscles. His mind was on what he had just seen on television.

Eliza Blake was his dream woman. She was beautiful, intelligent and classy. That elegantly cut yellow suit she had worn tonight had set off her figure to perfection. She moved so gracefully across the studio, sat so erect in her anchor chair. Her face was enchanting and those piercing blue eyes saw into his soul. She understood him, Jerry was certain of it. When Eliza spoke, it was as if she were talking to him alone.

He could stare at her forever and never grow tired of her. In fact, sometimes he did stare at her, for hours, gazing into the framed picture of her that stood in a silver frame on the table beside his bed. The autographed photograph had been easy to get. He had simply written to Eliza at KEY News and asked for it. Sure enough, a few weeks later it had arrived in the mail.

Lori said it must be a stock picture KEY News sent out to anyone who requested one. He had been angry when she said that but he had tried not to show it. He knew Eliza had meant that picture to be special, for him alone, and he wasn't going to let Lori ruin it for him. She was just jealous, anyway, because he had never made a pass at her.

He felt Lori's strong hands rubbing his back now, pushing the tenseness out of his upper body.

"I can see you've been doing your exercises," she observed. "Your muscles are getting more defined back here."

"Mm-hmm."

Lori took the cue that her client didn't want to talk and continued her work in silence. As she rubbed the warm oils between his shoulder blades, Jerry made up his mind. He was going to call Eliza and tell her how beautiful he thought she was and how much he admired her.

He had been trying hard to control himself, but he couldn't anymore. He had to let her know how he felt.

CHAPTER

5

Motor running, the blue Lincoln Town Car was waiting at the curb in front of the building as Eliza pushed breathlessly through the revolving doors of the Broadcast Center into the steamy August early-evening air. Janie's smiling, expectant face was pressed against the glass of the backseat window. Eliza could see Katharine Blake sitting beside her soon-to-be five-year-old granddaughter. As the driver opened the car door, Janie spilled out onto the sidewalk, running to hug her mother.

"Mmmmm. That feels so good," Eliza cried as she felt the little girl's arms wrapping around her. "I missed you. Did you have a good day with KayKay and Poppie today?"

Janie nodded happily. "Yeah. KayKay took me to the zoo. We saw the monkeys. Poppie was too tired to go. He stayed home and took a nap."

Eliza glanced into the backseat of the car. Katharine was in her late sixties now and it couldn't have been a treat for her to take a child to the Central Park Zoo on a hot summer afternoon. The chocolate ice-cream splatters on Janie's yellow T-shirt testified to the good time the child had had, but now, as mother and daughter climbed into the car, Eliza could see that Katharine looked exhausted.

"What would I have done without you?" Eliza whispered to her mother-in-law as she kissed her on her soft cheek.

Katharine just patted Eliza's hand. Both women understood exactly why it had been best for Janie to spend the last few weeks with her grandparents during the day while Eliza was at work. None of them wanted to let the child out of their sight. While they knew the child-care situation was temporary, they dreaded the inevitable time when a new babysitter would be found. After the last time, how could they ever trust anyone again to take care of their precious Janie?

But trust, they had to. Eliza knew this arrangement couldn't go on forever. It wasn't fair to Katharine and Paul. Over the course of their lifetimes, they had worked hard and paid their dues, suffering the worst fate any parents can endure. They had watched their only child—John, Janie's father—die.

Then, they had faced the terror of losing Janie as well.

If Janie was traumatized over the loss of Mrs. Twomey, the housekeeper who had watched over her for as long as the child could remember, it didn't show. And that bothered Eliza. The little girl had witnessed her mother being shot by the housekeeper in a situation far too complicated for a child to understand. How could Janie be expected to comprehend that her beloved Mrs. Twomey had committed two murders and almost killed Eliza as the caretaker tried to cover up her own son's misdeeds? Janie had seemed to readily accept Eliza's explanation that Mrs. Twomey was troubled and sick and wasn't in her right mind when she hurt Mommy.

Eliza had consulted a child psychologist who was of the opinion that, while many children suffer trauma, it wasn't just one thing that scarred a child for life. It was repeated instances of abuse or abandonment or betrayal that did the psychic damage. If Janie continued to feel secure in her mother's and grandparents' love, unthreatened in her surroundings and nurtured, as Eliza had every intention of doing, the doctor was confident she would be all right. Yes, it was true, Janie did not have a father, but it was also true that since he had died before she was born, she had never known him to suffer the loss.

As time went by and Janie was exposed more to the world of other children with both parents there would be, inevitably, longings for a daddy of her own. At any point, counseling was always an option.

"I know you must be tired, Katharine, but I'm so glad you're coming out with us to see the house. I so value your opinion. And from what Louise tells me, if we want it, we're going to have to make a decision on the spot."

Katharine shook her head wearily. "I don't understand this market. In my time, you could think about things for a few days and then decide. This is crazy."

"You're right," declared Eliza, taking Janie's hand and looking out the car window at the Hudson River as they drove up the West Side Highway toward the George Washington Bridge and New Jersey. "This is crazy."

So much had been crazy and out of control. This move could bring some stability to their lives.

CHAPTER

6

If Eliza Blake were made aware of every letter that came from every crackpot obsessed with her, Joe Connelly was certain, the *Evening Headlines* anchor would never sleep again. As Director of KEY Corporate Security, Connelly maintained a policy of not telling her or any of the other on-air correspondents about letters unless there was actually something they should do to protect themselves. Part of his job was to insulate those he was responsible for protecting from unwarranted fear. Another part was weeding out the harmless letters from the ones that were truly threatening.

Eliza never even saw the crazy letters that came to her at the Broadcast Center. Her assistant opened all her mail and immediately sent on to security anything that seemed weird or menacing rather than just annoying. Over the years Eliza had anchored *KEY to America,* the morning news broadcast, Connelly had been concerned enough to send a few letters to the FBI. But now, in the short time Eliza had been anchoring the *KEY Evening Headlines,* her viewership had increased and so had the letters.

Connelly walked through the security command post buried in the basement of the Broadcast Center, scanning the dozens of video monitors along the wall. There were sixteen cameras on each chain, timed to record views of different locations. Cameras were trained on every entrance and exit of the building, outside each elevator, along each hallway. If Joe had his way, there would be cameras in the bathrooms, but, of course, that was against the law. The security monitors were not staffed at all times. That was impossible with the manpower situation as it was. But in the old days, all the camera tapes were recorded and saved for ten days—plenty of time to painstakingly replay and study each tape for any problems or signs of security lapses. Now the cameras were mostly digital, which made things much easier. Everything was saved on a disk and pinpointing time was more exact.

Still, during the hours when most of the on-air talent was in the Broadcast Center, Connelly liked to have a guard keeping an eye on the security screens.

"Everything okay?" he asked the guard now stationed in front of the monitors.

"I'm trying not to fall asleep, it's so quiet."

Unsmiling, Connelly nodded. "Good. Let's keep it that way."

CHAPTER

7

Louise Kendall stood waiting on the lawn in front of the Georgian colonial as the car carrying Eliza, Janie and Katharine Blake pulled into the driveway.

"I'm in love already!" Eliza whispered to her mother-in-law, inhaling as she viewed for the first time the house she was already certain she would buy. The gracious brick home sat well back from the street on carefully manicured grounds that Eliza estimated must be at least three acres. "Look, it has a slate roof!"

"Don't act excited in front of Louise," Katharine warned. "You shouldn't seem too anxious."

Eliza leaned over and pecked her mother-in-law's cheek. "Yes, KayKay," she said good-naturedly. "I won't give myself away."

But Janie was not good at keeping secrets. She bounded from the car, dragging her precious stuffed monkey, Zippy, by the arm, and ran straight across the lawn for Louise. "My mommy loves the house," she announced proudly.

Eliza and Katharine followed behind, the younger woman laughing. "So much for playing it cool," Eliza shrugged. "Okay, Louise, you've got me hooked. Give us the tour."

In the fading light, they walked slowly around the exterior of the house, Janie running ahead and calling back what they were about to see next.

"Mommy!" she shrieked. "It has a swimming pool!"

"Great," Katharine groaned sarcastically. "Now you'll have to worry about that, too."

Eliza chose not to respond, knowing that Janie's grandmother was at a point now where she was apprehensive about any possible thing that could pose a threat to her grandchild.

"It also has a hot tub," Louise pointed out, ignoring the negative comment. "And, as you can see, a cabana."

She opened the unlocked door and they walked through the small building. A full kitchen outfitted with a large refrigerator, double sink, oven and dishwasher was the main room. Off it was a perfectly tiled bathroom with an oversized shower stall. Beyond that was a utility room with a washer and dryer.

"Think of the great parties you can have out here," Louise enthused.

Eliza was just thinking of quietly sitting on a lounge chair watching Janie swim, or soaking in the hot tub after a long day at work, as her daughter scooted out the cabana door.

"Mommy, KayKay, come see!"

They followed the direction of the child's voice in time to see Janie climbing up the wooden slat steps nailed to a giant elm. "There's a tree house!" she called with wonder.

"Be careful, honey. You don't know if those steps are safe." Katharine hurried toward the old tree.

In that instant Eliza knew for certain that she was doing the right thing. She didn't want Janie growing up timid and afraid. She wanted her to be confident and strong. Though she wanted to shield Janie from anything that would wound her, Eliza knew that her daughter would have to take chances in life, be hurt and then learn to recover. Janie's was a strong and beautiful spirit and, painful though it might be, she would have to take life's knocks in order to learn how to survive in the world as it was and grow to her full potential. Katharine and Paul were wonderful, loving grandparents, but their overprotectiveness, while understandable, would not be good for Janie in the long run. Eliza and Janie had to get their own rhythm going again, as a family, small though their family was. And maybe, if things continued as well as they had been going, Mack would join their family, too.

Eliza thought about Mack as she watched her daughter smiling triumphantly from the tree-house platform. Mack McBride, a keenly intelligent, no-nonsense news correspondent, was gentle and loving with Janie, and with her. Their relationship was relatively new, but the emotional bond had grown quickly in the turmoil of the last few months. Mack had been a rock of stability and it felt right to have him beside her after all the years she had been alone. Eliza marveled at the notion that she was being given another chance to love.

CHAPTER

8

At the Manhattan Ocean Club on West Fifty-eighth Street, KEY News president Yelena Gregory sat across the table from Mack McBride. As the waiter brought their cocktails, Yelena raised her glass.

"To you, Mack, and the wonderful work you've been doing for us."

Mack nodded at his boss and took a swallow of scotch. "That's a relief," he exhaled. "I was wondering if you were taking me out to give me some bad news."

Yelena didn't smile in response as he had expected her to. Something was up and he wasn't sure he was going to like it. He waited for her to speak.

"Well, as a matter fact, I do have some news. News that I hope you will be happy about, Mack."

He raised his eyebrows.

"As I'm sure you are fully aware, Mack," Yelena continued carefully, "there are some correspondent positions that are considered more important than others."

Mack nodded. "Go on."

"We've got you earmarked for one of those slots."

Mack's mind raced. It was a move from New York, he was sure of it. But where? He waited.

Yelena took a sip of her drink, resentful because she knew that the gift she was about to bestow was not going to be all that appreciated.

"We want to make you chief European correspondent, stationed, of course, in London."

Just a few months ago, Mack would have had everything he could do to keep himself from kissing the older, heavyset woman on the mouth. All the way back to the old Edward R. Murrow days, at the dawn of broadcast journalism, being the London correspondent was one of the most coveted assignments a newsman could dream of. He had often fantasized about being good enough professionally to win the spot.

But now the accomplishment staring him in the face was bittersweet. London. An ocean and five times zones away from Eliza.

Yelena was looking at him keenly for reaction. He was careful not to betray with his facial expression the turmoil tossing inside.

"When would I start?"

"Almost immediately," Yelena answered firmly.

The steamed lobster the waiter placed before him sat almost untouched as Yelena prattled on about the importance of the position and how KEY News wanted new blood to revitalize what she considered a complacent London bureau. To that end, a new bureau chief had been appointed. Marcy McGinnis was stirring things up over there.

"We'll have two micks in London, now," Yelena joked, heedless of political correctness.

Mack McBride managed a smile. He knew full well that the president of the news division was aware that he and Eliza Blake were romantically involved, but Yelena did not bring up the subject. What was also left unsaid was something else they both knew. If Mack turned down the assignment, his career would never recover.

CHAPTER

9

It was after eleven o'clock when Eliza finally tucked Janie into bed for the night. The child's eyes closed immediately as her head hit the pillow. Smoothing Janie's wispy brown hair back from her forehead, Eliza kissed the soft skin over her brow.

"Sleep tight, my sweet angel," she whispered.

Unbuttoning the jacket of her suit as she walked toward her own bedroom, Eliza reflected on what she had just done. She had signed a contract for a house more expensive than she had ever dreamed of buying.

It wasn't that she couldn't afford it. She could. Her new contract took care of that. But she hadn't grown up with money. Though Eliza had offered to buy them something larger, her parents still lived in her small childhood house in Newport, Rhode Island. She had gone to public schools and attended the in-state, affordable University of Rhode Island, double-majoring in journalism and political science. When people heard or read that she grew up in Newport, they assumed she had led a privileged life. They didn't realize that Newport was packed with a lot of folks who struggled just to get by.

Talent, hard work and some good professional luck had gotten her to this point.

Eliza felt her stomach rumble as she hung her suit in the bedroom closet and remembered that she hadn't eaten dinner. Pulling a nightgown over her head, she ignored the flashing red light of the answering machine on her bedside table, and headed down the hall to the kitchen.

It was too late to eat a big meal, nor did she have the energy to fix one. She poured a bowl full of Janie's Rice Krispies, sliced a banana and covered it all with milk. Taking her supper with her, Eliza walked back down the hall and gratefully sank onto her bed. After concentrating on three or four mouthfuls, she reached over and hit the button on the answering machine.

"It's me. Call me when you get in. It doesn't matter what time."

Mack's voice sounded tense. Had the dinner with Yelena turned out to be a disaster? Mack's contract was up for renewal. KEY News couldn't be stupid enough not to re-sign him. But you never knew, they had been known to make some extremely dumb decisions in the past. Eliza punched in the number she knew by heart and braced herself.

CHAPTER

10

When she arrived at the office each morning, the first thing Paige did was play back the telephone messages that had come in since close-of-business the night before. This morning, she felt sorry for the somewhat pathetic caller who confessed such deep admiration for Eliza Blake. The answering system, which time-stamped each call, indicated the message had come in just after midnight.

"People's lives," Paige sighed as she erased the call.

For the most part Paige Tintle enjoyed the next task of the morning, sifting through Eliza's mail. There were all sorts of letters and invitations from interesting people doing important things. As Eliza's personal assistant, Paige's job was to sort though the incoming documents, cull the things that Eliza had to see to herself, and deal with answering the dozens of requests for Eliza to speak or to attend various functions.

Paige also handled the mail from viewers. Much of it was routine. Viewers complimenting Eliza on a story she had done, or the clothes she had worn, or the way her hair had been styled. Some of it was critical, accusing Eliza of having a liberal or conservative agenda which, according to the particular writer's viewpoint, she was unfairly advancing through her stories as the anchor of a major television network's evening news broadcast.

But the letters Paige dreaded reading were the ones from the nuts. Some were mildly troubling. Some were downright scary.

This morning's mail had brought another really sick one from the guy who had written before, and Paige reread this new one nervously, fingering the small diamond cross that hung from the silver chain around her neck.

> Dear Miss Arrogant Defiant Eliza Blake,
>
> How many times do I have to tell you?
>
> In spite of my persistent warnings, you continue to wear those tight, short skirts that show too much. You look like a whore.
>
> You are really asking for it. And I am going to be the one to give it to you.
>
> Keep it up, news girl, and I swear to God, you'll be red and raw and bloody when I'm finished with you.

Paige shivered as she read the scrawled signature. MEAT.

Carefully she held the letter by its corner as she had been told to do, and slipped it and its envelope into a larger paper wrapper. She was relieved to send it on to security.

She didn't want it anywhere near her.

CHAPTER

11

Eliza hadn't slept well and it showed when she arrived at work. Paige immediately noticed the puffiness under her boss's eyes.

"Don't say a word," Eliza warned. "I tossed and turned all night. Thank God I have Doris to work her magic."

"How did it go with the house?" Paige asked hopefully. She had been the one who had made the phone calls arranging for the driver to pick up Janie and her grandmother for the ride out to New Jersey.

"Loved it. Bought it."

"Wow! That was quick. Congratulations."

For someone who had just found her perfect home, Eliza didn't seem too happy. But Paige didn't think it was her place to pursue it further. Twenty-two years old, she still couldn't believe she was working at KEY News for Eliza Blake. She held her boss in awe, though she tried hard not to show it.

"Any important messages?" Eliza asked briskly.

"Range would like to see you when it's convenient, and Abigail Snow wants to know when you'll be available to tape the new promos."

"Mail?"

The letter from Meat passed unsettlingly through Paige's mind but she did not mention it.

"FRAXA, the Fragile X Research Foundation, would like you to be their keynote speaker at a fundraising dinner at Tavern on the Green next May."

"Fine. Check my calendar. If I'm open, accept for me. If I have something else booked, move it around."

Eliza had never even heard of Fragile X syndrome, the most common form of inherited mental retardation, until she had gotten to know Bill Kendall, her predecessor, the legendary KEY News anchorman who had committed suicide last spring. Bill's son, William, had Fragile X. Bill had always been so kind to Eliza, especially when she was going through the worst of it after John had died and Janie was born. Louise Kendall, William's mother, had found the house she was about to buy. And William was the sweetest young man. There was no way she was going to refuse FRAXA.

Eliza turned to go into her office but stopped as Paige remembered something else.

"There was another letter from Sarah Morton."

"Oh? Let me see it." There was a tone of concern and sadness in Eliza's voice. She took the envelope from Paige's outstretched hand and began to read it as she walked to her desk.

Sarah was a twelve-year-old from Sarasota, Florida, and had been writing to Eliza for months. Eliza was her idol; the young girl had first written her when Eliza was still anchoring the morning show. The letter probably never would have reached Eliza's desk, as most fan letters failed to do. But Sarah's case was special.

After just a dozen years on this earth, Sarah Morton was undergoing cancer treatments. An A student who loved to play soccer and softball, Sarah explained that she watched *KEY to America* each morning and dreamed of becoming a television newswoman one day. Of all the women on TV, Sarah declared, Eliza was her favorite.

Eliza had answered Sarah's letter personally, thanking her, encouraging her to keep up with the news and wishing her good luck. The following week Sarah sent another letter, thrilled that Eliza had responded to her letter and asking for an autographed picture.

And so it started. Eliza made it a point to take a few minutes each week to answer Sarah's sweet, handwritten letters. The girl was so grateful for her revered pen pal, Eliza hadn't had the heart to stop their correspondence. As Sarah described the torturous route of chemotherapy she was undergoing, and talked about losing her hair and how embarrassed she was about it, Eliza found herself weeping for the child and, of course, she knew she was crying for John as well. Many nights she thought of Sarah as she tucked her own Janie into bed and said a silent prayer of thanksgiving that her own little girl was healthy.

Now, as Eliza scanned the latest note, Sarah said she was coming to New York next week to see the doctors at Sloan–Kettering. Eliza instinctively felt fear as she saw the leading cancer hospital's name on the white sheet before her. Sloan was where John had died.

Things must really be bad.

There was a second, typed letter in the envelope, on the letterhead of Samuel Morton, Attorney-at-Law.

Dear Ms. Blake,

Thank you from the bottom of my heart for the correspondence you have so generously and faithfully kept up with Sarah. It has meant the world to her.

On her worst days, she rereads your letters to take her mind off the pain she is in. For all the hellish treatments she has been through, we've seen no real improvement. In fact, she is getting worse. The trip to New York is really a last-ditch attempt to see if there is anything else that can be done.

Sarah doesn't know that I am writing you, and I know that it is terribly presumptuous of me to ask what I am about to request. Is there any chance that we could set up some time for Sarah to meet you personally while we are in New York? It would mean the world to her, and to me, to see my daughter happy.

Before she dies, was the great unspoken.

CHAPTER

1 2

Louise Kendall presented the signed, full-price offer to Larson Richards, the executor of his parents' estate. She could tell he was trying to seem unimpressed when she told him who the buyer of his childhood home was.

"I don't care who buys the house, Mrs. Kendall, as long as at the end of the day the deal goes through and I have my money in the bank."

Louise could play that game. "I understand that, Mr. Richards. And you can have your money in the bank by the end of next week. My client is anxious to have her child start the school year here."

Even the pompous Larson Richards had to be impressed with a buyer who could get a couple million dollars together in a few days.

But Louise should have predicted his next words.

"Maybe your agency underpriced the house. I'm wondering if I should have asked for more." He sat back smugly in his office chair.

Louise put on her best poker face. She refused to let him rile her. "That's your option, of course, Mr. Richards. But if I were you, I'd take the money and run. And, of course, whether you accept the contract of sale or not, you will be liable for the complete real-estate commission to my office. We've brought you a full-price offer, with no contingencies. We've fulfilled our obligation under the listing agreement."

The Realtor had him and he knew it. Larson could fight it in court and he would inevitably lose. The last thing he needed right now was a legal battle. He had bigger fish to fry.

CHAPTER

13

Abigail Snow was engrossed in her task of screening videotapes, searching for just the right shots of Eliza to use for the new promos for *KEY Evening Headlines*. Though ratings had stayed basically stable from the time Eliza took over as anchor, executive producer Range Bullock was hell-bent on boosting them in his constant battle to gain audience market share. With CBS, NBC, ABC, FOX and CNN all competing for the same viewers as KEY, Range was constantly fiddling with ideas designed to entice news watchers to tune in to KEY News. Bullock's ego, along with his job security, rode on the *Evening Headlines* ratings.

Market research showed that while Eliza had a high likability factor, some viewers thought she was too young to bring the gravitas necessary to anchor a network news broadcast. The anchormen at the Big Three networks were all sixty-plus, with decades of broadcast journalism experience behind them. At thirty-four, Eliza had been working in her field for only twelve years. While those years had been packed with plenty of reporting experience, she didn't have anywhere near the track record that Rather, Brokaw and Jennings did.

She was, though, much prettier.

Abigail studied the video clip on the monitor before her. Eliza's cornflower-blue eyes nearly popped from the screen. The eyes were crowned with perfectly arched brows, the exact rich-brown shade of her lustrous shoulder-length hair. Nature had blessed Eliza with alabaster skin, a small, straight nose and a full-lipped mouth, a perfect combination for television and, for that matter, life as well.

Range had talked to Abigail several times now about his vision for the latest promotional spots. He wanted to play to what some would think was Eliza's weakness, her youth. The slogan for the new promos:

"A Fresh Look at Your World.
"Eliza Blake.
"KEY News."

Abigail continued to look through tape after tape, loading into the computerized editing system the various shots of Eliza that best showed off her beautiful blue eyes. For Abigail Snow, it was a labor of love.

CHAPTER

14

Eliza's mind raced ahead as she hung up the telephone after Louise Kendall's call informing her that the contracts were all signed and she had bought herself a house. They would close just before Labor Day.

Though Louise had assured her that she was arranging for the home inspection and would take care of all the calls to the real-estate attorneys and the jockeying of papers back and forth that inevitably came with buying a house, especially so quickly, Eliza felt overwhelmed. The thought of the actual move itself was nerve-wracking. All the packing up. The new house, while wonderful, did need some cosmetic changes to make it more to Eliza's liking, and she would have preferred to have all the painting and wallpapering done before they moved in. But she wanted Janie to start at the new school on the first day, so they would move in and then have the redecorating done around them. *Great.*

Stay calm, she told herself. *You have the money now. It can all be arranged. Paige can call the movers and they'll do all the packing up at the apartment. You don't have to do it.*

She did, however, have to make sure that Janie had the birthday party on Saturday that she had been promising her all summer. Fifteen four- and five-year-olds, her preschool buddies, were coming on Saturday afternoon. Eliza had been looking forward to it too. But she hadn't realized that she would be in the midst of this house purchase and heartsick about the fact that Mack was going to London.

As if on cue, she heard a tap on her opened office door.

Wordlessly they looked at each other and Eliza did everything she could to keep from bursting into tears. In the five years since John had died, she hadn't been ready to open her heart to anyone else. Now, when she finally had, Mack, too, was going away.

Mack walked over to her desk and stood before it.

"I've made up my mind. I'm not going."

Eliza wanted to leap with joy, so much did she want him to stay here, with her, with Janie. She wanted them to let things take their course and see if they found that they wanted to spend the rest of their lives together. But she knew deep down he couldn't stay. Mack had to take this job.

"Nice try, Mack. You have to go and we both know it." She bit her lower lip.

"No. We both *don't* know it. The job isn't all that important to me." Mack was trying hard to be determined.

Eliza laughed in spite of herself. "Yeah, right. 'Chief European Correspondent' isn't all that important to you. Who are you kidding? If you turn this down—a chance to do a job you've dreamed about—you'll wonder about it for the rest of your life, Mack. And you will, eventually and inevitably, begin to resent me because I kept you here. You'll watch me anchoring the broadcast each night, getting all the acclaim and awards that go with it, and you'll resent the fact that you held yourself back, that you didn't go for the whole enchilada. Not to mention that the Front Row would write you off."

"I don't give a damn about the Front Row! What the executives think or don't think about me doesn't matter. I'm in love with you, Eliza. And I don't want to leave you."

That did it. The tears welled in Eliza's eyes and she felt sorry for poor Doris, who would really have her work cut out for her tonight. She began to sob, and as Mack took her in his arms and held her, it took all of her strength to say what came next.

"Well, I'm not sure I'm in love with you. You shouldn't stay in New York on my account."

She was lying and they both knew it.

CHAPTER

15

Susan Feeney loved her garden. Each clear morning, before her children woke, she would pour herself a cup of coffee, go outside and walk slowly around her well-tended yard, checking on the progress of all the flowers she had lovingly planted. In the three years they had lived in this, their second and much bigger house, she had managed to plant hundreds of seedlings and bulbs selected so that from late winter through autumn, a large number of plants bloomed gaily.

Around Valentine's Day, the tiny white snowdrops and yellow and purple crocuses bravely poked their heads up first through the drab winter soil. Then the showy daffodils trumpeted the real arrival of spring as they swayed in the March and early April breezes. Bright red tulips planted where they would get warm sun and blue phlox planted in the shady spots weren't far behind. Susan's spring garden too quickly transformed into beds of happy Oriental poppies in May and bushes of pink-and-white peonies in June.

The Shasta daisies she had planted ensured that she had cut flowers from June until the first frost. Black-eyed Susans and orange daylilies, totally self-sufficient, had multiplied on their own. Yellow yarrow planted in the dry parts of the yard bloomed all summer as well.

Now, in late August, Susan watched for the chrysanthemums. The year they moved in, she had planted pots and pots of yellow and deep-orange mums. Each year they had bloomed again, better than the year before. The buds were on them now, almost ready to burst open.

She was glad they had moved to HoHoKus. *HoHoKus*—such a funny name for a town. There were so many Native American names in the northern New Jersey area. Pascack Valley, Mahwah, Kinderkamack Road, Musquapsink Brook. The area's original inhabitants were long gone, but their legacy remained.

Susan was cutting some of her beloved flowers to bring into the house when James popped his sleepy-eyed, five-year-old head out from the side door that led from the kitchen to the garden.

"Hi, sweetheart, did you have a good sleep?" Her heart burst at the sight of her firstborn. He was such a dear little boy and the thought that he would be starting kindergarten soon astounded her. She could remember so clearly the day he was born, the nurse rolling him into her hospital room in his Lucite bassinet, the wonder of holding her perfectly formed miracle in her arms. The time had gone by so quickly. First James, named for his father; then, two years later, Kimberly; and a year after that, Kelly.

As she walked toward her son, she thought about how good God had been to the Feeney family. They were all healthy. And James's cable business had skyrocketed. It was hard sometimes, his traveling so much, but the couple had agreed that it was something they could endure now, knowing it wouldn't be this way forever.

James was looking inquisitively at the bunch of flowers gathered in his mother's hand. "What are those flowers named, Mommy?"

"Black–eyed Susans, honey."

The little boy's green eyes widened. "Just like you?"

Susan laughed with delight at the observation. "You're right, James. But my eyes are really just a very deep brown."

"And mine are green," he stated solemnly.

"Mm–hmm."

"And so are Kelly's."

"Right. And what about Kimberly? What color are her eyes?"

"Blue," he declared proudly.

Susan got a kick out of the fact that none of her children had inherited her dark eyes. She knew it was genetically improbable, but the surprise of it stared her clearly in the face each day.

"How about some French toast?" she suggested to her son, knowing in advance what his response would be. "Let me just get these flowers in some water and I'll make your favorite right away."

As Susan went to the kitchen sink to fill a vase with water, her feeling of well-being suddenly evaporated as her eyes trained out the window toward the Richardses' empty house. Those dear, sweet people who had welcomed her so warmly into the neighborhood had died such a sad and senseless death.

CHAPTER

16

At the Home and Hearth real-estate office, the physical inspection report on the house that would soon be Eliza's sat on Louise's desk. The house inspector had concluded in his twenty-page summary that the forty-year-old colonial was in sound condition, though there were two slight cracks in a retaining wall at the rear of the property and many of the slates on the roof needed to be replaced. The bathroom fixtures were those originally installed and all of the appliances in the kitchen were older. There was one "plus," however: the hot-water heater was brand-new.

Louise was sure that nothing in the report would deter Eliza from buying the house. Eliza had seen for herself that the house was tired and ached for the vitality and energy of a new owner. Four decades ago, when the Richardses had moved into their brand-new HoHoKus home, Bergen County had been a much simpler place. The house had been expensive even then by the standards of the time, but people did not expect the bells and whistles demanded by buyers of premium real estate today. The Richardses had done virtually nothing to update the interior of their home. But they had done a top-of-the-line job when they added their swimming pool, hot tub and cabana. Louise found that a bit strange, but quickly shrugged it off. Selling real estate provided a window on some of the most intimate parts of people's lives. She had seen plenty of bizarre behavior and lifestyles. The disparity between the inside and the outside of the Richardses' home was nothing.

Loading the report into the fax machine, Louise was punching the numbers to Eliza's office on the keypad when Vivienne Dusart, the listing agent, walked by.

"Everything holding together?" she asked.

Louise nodded with certainty. "Yes. The physical report came back basically clean. I'm faxing it to Eliza now. We're lucky, Viv. Eliza isn't going to nickel-and-dime over the state of things in the house. Those bathrooms and the kitchen are ancient. We both know that most buyers in this price category want a lot more glitz."

"Hey, she's buying the location," Vivienne shrugged matter-of-factly. "It's a shame, but she's got to pay." She started to walk away.

Vivienne was right.

"At least it's nice that she'll have a new hot-water heater."

The agent stopped and turned to stare at her. "That's not funny, Louise."

Puzzled by her friend's response, Louise looked at her alertly.

"What do you mean?"

"You're kidding, right? You know what happened there. It was in the newspaper."

"Obviously I don't know what you're talking about, Viv. Cut to the chase."

"There was a faulty gas valve on the old hot-water heater. Mr. and Mrs. Richards died of carbon-monoxide poisoning. You better tell your buyer right away, Louise. You don't want her suing you for lack of disclosure later." Vivienne patted Louise on the shoulder. "If she wants out, let me know. I have someone else interested in the house."

CHAPTER

17

Purple helium-filled balloons hugged the ceiling above the chattering five-year-olds in the happy bedlam of Eliza's apartment's living room. The young guests gleefully took turns having their faces painted, unaware that their tender skin was being designed and brushed by one of the best makeup artists in New York City.

When, in one of their conversations before going on air, Eliza had mentioned to Doris that Janie was having a birthday party and wondered aloud what she was going to do with the kids for two hours, Doris had volunteered to come over and do some face-painting. While Doris had no children of her own, she was youthful in her sense of wonder and fun.

Like the children at the party, Doris herself looked forward all year to Halloween, spending months in the planning of her annual costume. It was well known at KEY News that the makeup woman spent Halloween disguised in her creative gear and entering every costume contest she could find in New York. She would start the day by going over to the ABC studios and try her luck on *LIVE with Regis and Kelly*, and then, after work, she would pick her way through carefully selected spots she had found while poring through the pages of *New York* magazine. The city was full of masquerade parties and contests at clubs and hotels. She called ahead, ascertaining times and locations and carefully charting out her itinerary.

Doris took pains to make her costumes abstract enough so that on the spot she could, with some quick thinking, name her costume to coincide with the sometimes "surprise" themes of the Halloween contests. The first time she had been on what was then *LIVE with Regis and Kathie Lee*, Doris came decked out in a costume of crystals, sparkles and shimmering Christmas balls. When she learned while waiting outside the studio that the contest theme would be "The Seventies," she quickly dubbed her costume "Lucy in the Sky with Diamonds." But the other show-goers waiting in line with her told her she looked like a disco ball. So when her turn came, that's what Doris told Regis she was. Her "Disco Ball" costume won the $500 first prize and a lava-lamp trophy. That night she went to a benefit ball, christened the same costume "Champagne Bubbles" and won again—this time, bleacher seats for the Macy's Thanksgiving Day Parade and $250. Over the years she had won cash, golf trips, theater tickets and seaside vacations. But for Doris it was not so much about the prizes as the fun and satisfaction of being recognized for her creativity.

Doris was flamboyant, talented and had an extremely good heart. Eliza smiled as she watched her, dressed in a form-fitting purple leotard in honor of Janie's favorite color, her long, dark hair flowing freely as she airbrushed green water-based makeup all over Gregory Leslie's serious little face. The boy shifted impatiently from one foot to the other as Doris carefully drew the brown-and-black scales on his cheeks, above his eyebrows and around his mouth that would make him into the dinosaur he had requested to be. For good measure, she painted on some silver sprinkles across his forehead. The payoff for Doris was the wide grin on the child's face as he looked at himself in the large hand mirror she held up for him.

"Wow! That's cool!"

Doris grinned in return. "Want a dinosaur tattoo?" she offered.

But Gregory, thrilled though he was with his new reptile visage, had had enough. He scampered off to show his new face to the other dinosaurs, butterflies and fairy princesses in the room.

As Doris turned to the next child on line and began her new work of art, Eliza felt the strength of Mack's arm wrap around her waist and the warmth of his lips near her ear.

"Looks like the party's a success. Janie is clearly loving it," he said softly.

The smile faded from Eliza's face as she turned to look up at him. Mack was leaving at the end of the week, going to London to look at the flats that a real-estate agent there had lined up for him to see. Next weekend, she and Janie were moving into their new home in HoHoKus, on this side of the Atlantic Ocean.

Too much was happening at once. Mack going. The move. Getting Janie settled in a new school. Eliza didn't even want to think about finding a new housekeeper. Just to add a little something extra to the list, she had to buy a car, too. Living in Manhattan, she hadn't owned one in years. There was no need for it. She took taxis, had the KEY News driver pick her up and bring her home from work, rented a car when she wanted to get out of the city. But living in suburbia, a car was a must.

As she looked wistfully into Mack's handsome face and reached up to touch the familiar laugh lines that crinkled so appealingly at the corners of his eyes as he smiled down at her, Eliza knew in her heart she would get through the things on her list with the determination and organization that had served her so well in her life and her career. All the things she had to take care of were doable.

But not losing Mack. Not Mack. She didn't want him to leave.

"Mommy, when are we going to have the birthday cake?" Janie's question roused Eliza from her reflections. She glanced at her watch.

"Now, my little butterfly," she answered, picking up her daughter's hand and kissing it. "We'll have it now. Your friends' moms and dads will be coming to pick them up soon."

Eliza was in the kitchen, putting the violet candles into the ice-cream cake when she heard the buzzer sound from the downstairs lobby. Probably one of the parents arriving a bit early. She called out for Mack to answer it.

As Eliza carried the flickering cake into the dining room to the din of childish singing, she saw, from the corner of her eye, Louise Kendall standing in the doorway with a large, brightly wrapped present in her arms. Louise had called yesterday and asked if she could come into the city to talk to Eliza about the house. When told that Janie was having a birthday party, Louise insisted she bring a gift for the child. But as much as Eliza truly liked Louise, she sensed that Janie's birthday wasn't all that high on Louise's agenda. If she was driving all the way into the city on a Saturday, her prime real-estate selling day, Eliza knew Louise had to have something important on her mind.

When the children were contentedly spooning the vanilla and chocolate ice cream through their painted lips, Eliza made her way over to Louise, giving her a welcoming kiss on the cheek.

"The kids should be gone in about fifteen minutes. Can you wait, and then we can talk in relative quiet?"

"Of course," she answered amiably. "What can I do to help here?"

Eliza laughed, brushing back a strand of hair that had fallen across her brow. "Believe it or not, I think we have everything pretty well under control."

God, I hope we do, thought Louise.

CHAPTER

18

There were three nights of videotapes sitting on top of the VCR. That meant there was an hour and a half of pleasure ahead.

The VCR was programmed to record the KEY Television Network every weekday night at six-thirty. Even when someone was home to watch the show, the recorder still clicked on to tape *KEY Evening Headlines* with Eliza Blake.

It worked well this way. Sometimes the live broadcast moved too fast and it was necessary to replay it to catch every detail, every mannerism, every nuance in Eliza's speech. After the broadcast tapes were looked at, they were rewound to be used again. The newspaper stories reported that the recently appointed evening–news anchorwoman was garnering solid ratings. The network was heavily invested in her. Eliza was going to be around for a while.

Though you could never tell. It had looked like Linda Anderson was going to be around for a while, too. Five years ago, the VCR had been set to record the Garden State News Network every night at ten o'clock.

What had happened to Linda was still a source of the deepest pain. Loving Linda had been wonderful beyond belief. But Linda had spurned a perfect love.

It had taken five years to be ready to love again.

Eliza Blake was worth the wait.

CHAPTER

19

"Carbon–monoxide poisoning? Oh, how terrible!" Eliza winced.

Eliza and Louise sat together in the kitchen while, in the living room, Mack helped Janie assemble the skeleton of the plastic playhouse she had received as a birthday gift. The two women made certain to keep their voices low.

"I'm so sorry, Eliza," whispered the distressed Realtor. "I should have known about this and told you before you bought the house. But I was away at the beach with William for a few days in July when the Richardses died, and I missed the gossip about it in the office and didn't read about it in the local papers. By the time I got back I guess it was old news and no one was even talking about it anymore. When the listing came out, I jumped on it, knowing it would be the perfect house for you. I still think it is. But I just found out what happened from the listing agent yesterday and, of course, I wanted to tell you myself."

Eliza's mind raced. She had done a story on carbon-monoxide poisoning. Hundreds of people died in their homes each year from the poisonous gas that had no smell, no taste and no color. But she also knew that carbon-monoxide poisoning was easily preventable by making sure appliances were properly installed, checking vents and chimneys regularly for improper connections, and making sure that heating systems were inspected and serviced on a regular basis. If everything checked out and had been corrected, as the building inspector guaranteed, Eliza wasn't unduly concerned about the safety of the house she was about to buy. She would be vigilant in having inspections done and make sure to have carbon-monoxide detectors installed.

It bothered her far more that two people had died so tragically in the house she and Janie were going to move into. She didn't think of herself as a superstitious person, but knowing that a husband and wife had died so senselessly within the walls of the home where she planned to live with her child gave Eliza pause. She felt the fine hairs on her bare arms rise.

CHAPTER

2 0

In the warm-weather months, Sunday night at dusk was Meat's favorite hour of the week. He didn't have to work at the bar, didn't have to get aggravated watching Eliza Blake flaunt herself on the news, and he could clear his mind by concentrating on his other passion.

Bats.

Since childhood, Meat had been fascinated with the world's only flying mammals. He remembered his mother's hysterics when she discovered that bats were nesting in the attic of their modest home. She had made Meat's father go up there during the day and hammer the tiny creatures while they slept. Meat had been only seven years old, but he could still recall the brutality of it.

Young Cornelius identified with the maligned, misunderstood night creatures. Yes, they were scary at first, menacing-looking with their webbed wings, flying with their mouths wide open. But as he learned from the library books he checked out after the hammering episode, their open mouths were the way they "saw" the insects they ate. Echolocation, it was called. A flying bat sent out a stream of clicks through its open mouth. By listening to the echoes that came back, the bat could tell where another object was, how big it was, how fast it was moving.

Meat had tried to explain to his mother that the bats were good for them. They lived near the marshy, New Jersey meadowlands where mosquitoes and other insects thrived. The bats were a natural pesticide.

His mother had stared at him, as if he were strange. But she was always doing that. The nuns yelled at him when he chose bats for the subject of his book reports. The other kids said his bat fixation was weird.

So Cornelius stopped talking about bats, but he kept learning about them. And as soon as he moved out of his parents' home, he bought a bat house, erecting it on a fifteen-foot pole in a clearing in the woods behind his apartment building, making sure the wooden house would be able to get at least the six hours of direct sunlight it needed during the day. First he bought a common single-chambered house that could hold fifty bats. After that was filled, he ordered a larger, multichambered design that could contain a nursery colony of two hundred.

The bats gave birth just once a year, one pup at a time. The babies fed on their mother's milk for about six weeks before they were weaned. In the springtime, Meat could wait in the clearing until the adult bats flew out at night in search of food, and then approach the house, seeing the tiny, bald pups clustered together helplessly inside.

Meat felt sad as he lounged at the edge of the clearing on this late-summer evening, anticipating the emergence of the bats as they flew out to feed in the night sky. Soon the cold weather would set in and the bats would leave for the winter. They would fly to caves and mines up to a hundred miles away and go into hibernation, hanging in their characteristic upside-down position, their body temperatures dropping and their breathing and heart rates slowing down. In their sleeping state they would use very little energy and could live through the winter months when food was scarce.

He would miss his winged mysteries, but he consoled himself with the knowledge that they would be back next year. An average bat could live fifteen years, some as long as thirty-four.

If someone didn't hammer them.

CHAPTER

21

Monday morning Eliza was in her office even before Paige showed up for work. When her young assistant arrived, Eliza handed her a list of the personal things she needed Paige to take care of for her.

"I'm sorry, Paige. I really don't like asking you to do all this stuff for me," Eliza apologized. "I know it's not really KEY News–related. But I guess we could stretch the validity of it by rationalizing that the anchorwoman will go out of her mind if she doesn't get her personal life in order."

Paige glanced at the handwritten list. "It's not a problem at all, Ms. Blake. Really. I'm happy to do it."

"Thank you, Paige. You're a doll and I promise that I'll keep this sort of thing to a minimum. You've just come aboard at a particularly chaotic time. But could you start calling around and find the best employment agencies that handle housekeepers in northern New Jersey and have them send over some prospective candidates? Schedule the interviews around the other things in my book."

Paige nodded her curl–covered head and started back toward her desk.

"And, Paige?"

"Yes?" she answered eagerly, turning to face her boss again.

"Please. Call me Eliza. You make me feel so old when you call me Ms. Blake."

The younger woman smiled and Eliza noticed her cheeks blush a bit. It was not the first time they had had this exchange. Paige was so respectful and Eliza liked her for it. But Eliza wanted Paige to know that, young as her assistant was, Eliza considered her to be a colleague. They would be working very closely together over the months to come and Eliza felt it was important to both of them that they be on a first-name basis. Besides, there was only a twelve-year age difference between them. She could be Paige's older sister.

Eliza watched Paige as she walked out of the office and tried to remember what being twenty-two had been like. Fresh out of the journalism and political-science departments at the University of Rhode Island, Eliza had graduated with high hopes and some trepidations. She wasn't naive enough to think that following her dream to work in broadcast journalism was going to be a walk in the park. Though glamorous and romantic to outsiders, it was an extremely competitive field. But, since she was twelve years old, that was all she had ever really wanted to do. The dozen years since college graduation had consistently rewarded her professionally, first working in local television, then going on to the network. It was the private part of her life that had had its share of ups and downs.

Sarah Morton's last letter crossed Eliza's mind. Another twelve-year-old bitten with the television-news bug, fighting a courageous fight against a brutal disease. Eliza reached for the phone and called Paige on the intercom.

"When is Sarah Morton scheduled to come in, Paige?"

"Tomorrow morning at eleven-thirty, Eliza." The last word did not come out easily, and Eliza could sense it. But she was glad that Paige was trying.

"Do I have a lunch engagement?"

"No. You are actually free for lunch tomorrow."

"Great. Would you make a reservation for three at Jekyll and Hyde's? I'd like to take Sarah and her father out for lunch after the tour."

Of all the theme restaurants around Fifty-seventh Street, the Jekyll and Hyde Club was probably the most amusing. Kids loved the suspenseful atmosphere. And at least the hamburgers were pretty good. Eliza hoped Sarah would be up to eating one.

CHAPTER

2 2

Down the long hallway from Eliza's office, Keith Chapel sat behind his desk and doodled on a yellow legal pad. At the top he had written A FRESHER LOOK, and beneath it he was listing the story ideas he had lined up for production over the next two months.

The new series was scheduled to begin right after Labor Day. Weekly packages would air each Wednesday during the *Evening Headlines*, with Eliza Blake reporting on a story that was of particular interest to her. It was being sponsored by a Wall Street investment firm which was paying to get a special mention at the beginning and end of each report. So there was big money to be made for KEY News and the pressure was on to make sure the series was a success and thereby renewed.

Keith pulled a stick of Doublemint gum from one of the packs he kept in constant supply in his desk drawer. As he unwrapped the silver paper, he noticed his fingernails with disgust. They were bitten down to the quick. *Pathetic.*

But there was no way he was going to quit biting his nails anytime soon, he reasoned with himself. Not with this FRESHER LOOK project and Cindy seven months pregnant and growing more miserable every day.

He popped the chewing gum into his mouth and groaned inwardly as he remembered the scene at home last night. Cindy had been complaining again about how fat she was, crying that she couldn't see her feet anymore when she tried to look past her protruding stomach as she stood in the shower. And then, when she sat down on the toilet seat to dry her legs and feet off, she thought her toes looked like little sausages ready to pop if pricked by a fork, they were so full of retained water. August was no time to be in the late stages of pregnancy. Cindy vowed that she would never, ever do this again. This would be their only child.

Keith had tried to console her. She still looked beautiful to him and there were just two months to go, he reassured her.

"Easy for you to say," Cindy ranted. "Your life hasn't changed one bit. You still slide into your clothes every day, you still eat everything you want, you can sleep at night, you aren't having nosebleeds and you have no idea what sciatica feels like. No one is kicking at you from the inside and you don't have to run to the bathroom every twenty minutes. I don't see any stretch marks growing across *your* stomach!"

At first she pulled away as he tried to put his arms around her, but then she had dissolved into tears as she buried her blond head in his shoulder. She sobbed and apologized for being such a shrew. She wasn't herself, she promised. Of course she was happy about the baby, but she just hated being pregnant.

"I wish I could make it easier for you, sweetheart," Keith whispered, as he kissed her wet cheeks. "I love you so much and I know we are going to get through this together."

It was true. He did love her. Had loved her from the first time he saw her. He had never been so attracted to a woman as he was to Cindy, and he still was, pregnant or not. He lifted her chin and kissed her on the mouth. At first she had responded, so he was encouraged to continue, hoping that it would be different from the last few times he had tried to make love to her. There was absolutely no reason why they shouldn't, the doctor had told them. But Cindy, always so willing pre-pregnancy, had lost all desire. Keith was going out of his mind.

He tried to the force the issue, hating himself for it. If she didn't want to, she didn't want to. Wasn't she going through enough already? What kind of animal was he that he couldn't control himself?

He could see by the fearful look in her wide brown eyes that it was not going to go well. He should have stopped. But he didn't. And then, instead of falling peacefully asleep in each other's arms, they had spent the night on extreme opposite sides of their queen-sized bed, their backs turned coldly to each another.

This morning they hadn't spoken. He knew Cindy was awake when he had left for the office, but, wanting to avoid him, she had stayed in bed until he was out of the apartment.

Keith was reaching for the telephone to call his wife when Range Bullock appeared at the office doorway.

"How's it going?" asked the executive producer. "You're looking awfully glum. Anything going on I should know about?"

Keith was tempted to spill his guts about the stress at home, but his instincts told him Range wouldn't want to hear it, might even think less of Keith for it. Range wasn't interested in his producers' personal lives unless he felt they were getting in the way of job performance. Keith sat up straighter in his chair and tried to look more upbeat.

"No. Nothing's wrong. That's just my look of extreme concentration." He forced a joke. "I'm actually working on the FRESHER LOOKS. I want them to be great."

Range walked into the office and took a seat on the couch against the wall, staring at Keith intensely.

"How are they coming?"

"Well, I think you'll be pleased with the first one. Eliza has tracked it already and the editing is just about finished." Keith prayed that the executive producer would be satisfied. Bullock had a high standard for all the pieces that appeared on his broadcast.

But with so much advertising money on the line for these FRESHER LOOK pieces, Keith knew that Range was going to be extraordinarily critical.

Range nodded as he ran his fingers through his salt-and-pepper hair. "That's the one about the child-care nightmares, right?"

"Uh-huh. We've got some really powerful, and bizarre, hidden-camera video of kids being abused by their caretakers, and great sound from overwrought parents. We're also getting into what parents can do to try to make sure it doesn't happen to them."

"Love it," declared Range, slapping his hand on his leg. "That's what we want to achieve whenever possible in these pieces. They can't all be 'feel-good' stories. I want our viewers coming away with a feeling that they want to tune in to us again because we've given them news they haven't gotten before, news that makes them think and reflect. And always," Range continued adamantly, "I want these pieces to showcase Eliza. We want lots of her on-camera involvement in these stories."

"Gotcha."

Range rose from the sofa and put his hand on Keith's shoulder. "You're the right man for this job, Keith. I have confidence in you."

As he watched Bullock leave, Keith wished he had more confidence in himself. Lately he wasn't feeling like much of a man at all.

CHAPTER

23

"Sinisi's," answered the man dressed in navy-blue mechanic's overalls. He balanced the phone on his shoulder and grabbed a pencil as he scanned the pages of the oversized appointment ledger that lay on the paper-strewn metal desk.

"Sure, Mrs. Palumbo, we can fit you in tomorrow. Just bring in the car in the morning and I'll have one of the guys drive you back home or, if you want, I can have someone come over and pick up the car."

Augie squeezed his eyes shut, hoping she would choose the latter.

"Fine." He pumped his beefy fist into the air. "No, it's no problem at all. We'll be there in the morning. Give me your address again."

Augie Sinisi had quite a clientele at his service station. Specializing in foreign cars, he had a roster of steady customers who brought in their Mercedes, BMWs and Jaguars when it was time for their oil changes and tuneups. He had built his business by having highly skilled mechanics and treating his customers right. Going the extra mile for them, making things as easy as possible for them, ensured they would come back, give him more business and recommend him to their friends. Friends who also drove expensive cars. Wealthy friends who lived in big houses filled with lots of grown-up toys.

Though Augie pretended otherwise, he knew damn well where the Palumbos lived. Mr. Palumbo usually dropped their Lexus off at the station, taking the car key from his key ring and leaving it in the ignition. After the work was done, Augie had returned the vehicle himself, having one of the boys follow behind to drive him back to the garage.

The Palumbos had a seriously nice spread.

Now, if only Mrs. Palumbo would leave her entire key ring in the car.

It was surprising how many people did that.

CHAPTER

24

Paige recognized the caller's last name immediately.

"This is Samuel Morton. My daughter Sarah has been corresponding with Ms. Blake."

"Yes, Mr. Morton, of course. This is Paige Tintle, Ms. Blake's assistant. How can I help you?" Paige asked, picking up her pencil to jot down the message.

"Well, Sarah and I were supposed to come into the news studio tomorrow and meet Ms. Blake." Paige thought the man's voice sounded stressed and it crossed her mind that he might just be nervous about calling the prestigious news organization's anchorwoman. She knew she would have been, had she been making the call as an outsider.

"Yes. We're all set up for eleven-thirty tomorrow," she answered brightly, trying to put him at ease. "And Ms. Blake has made lunch reservations for after your tour if you and Sarah are available."

A loud sob burst through the receiver Paige held to her ear. As the man wept, Paige took down his message.

Sarah had died at Sloan-Kettering the night before.

CHAPTER

25

Larson Richards pulled his big black late-model Mercedes sedan into the driveway of the home where he had grown up. As he opened the car door, a blast of hot, sticky air met him. He pulled off his soft beige, elegantly cut suit jacket and hung it on the hook in the back seat.

Rolling back the sleeves of his crisp white shirt, he loosened his Hermès tie and wished he had realized that he would be coming to do this today when he dressed this morning. But after the meeting with his investors in his office this afternoon, it was clear that, if he wanted to go through the house one more time before the closing on Friday, today was going to be his last opportunity.

Richards took a handkerchief from his pocket and wiped away the film of perspiration that covered his brow. Things were not going well with this deal. He had organized a syndicate of investors contributing millions of dollars to back him as he attempted to buy and consolidate the individual, small, mom-and-pop owned pizzerias that operated in just about every town in the northern half of New Jersey. Richards had seen an opportunity. If he could buy up all the little pizza parlors and consolidate them under one umbrella, he could turn around and sell the whole package to a national company, trading as "Jersey Pizza," making a huge profit for his investors and himself in the process.

Approximately three billion pizzas were sold in the United States each year, but the tomato and cheese pies sold in New Jersey were in a class of their own. Residents who moved away from the Garden State claimed that pizza made in other parts of the country was not nearly as good. Since *The Sopranos*, with its northern New Jersey locale, had become such a cultural phenomenon, Larson was even more convinced his "Jersey Pizza" idea would work. But he had to find a buyer with deep pockets and he needed money to keep his business afloat until he could get to that finish line.

The investors, confident because of their fantastically good luck in the booming stock market, piled on board happily at first. The double-digit profits on Wall Street had made them very wealthy in a relatively short period of time. What Larson Richards outlined for them promised to double or even triple their investments. Who could say no to a business opportunity like that?

But as Wall Street corrected and the pizza deal suffered one set-back after another, the investors had become less cocky and more worried. Richards was struggling from week to week to make his pay-roll. The expensive cars he had leased so that his offices could impress the prospective business sellers sat unused in his company parking lot, as he had had to let some of his people go. But the Mercedes and BMW dealerships didn't give a rat's ass about Richards's economic hard times. The costly leases still had to be paid each month. So did the mortgage on his office building.

He had so much invested now, there was no turning back. He had long ago divested himself of his stock portfolio, taken a second mort-gage on his house, and emptied his sizable IRA account, plowing all the money back into the pizza deal. He was convinced that if he could just keep things afloat a few more months, ultimately it would be all right. And he had just spent most of his afternoon trying to convince his skeptical and angry investors the same thing.

Thank God this house is closing on Friday, he thought as he let himself in through the front door. *There will be another two million dollars in the bank next week.*

He walked slowly from room to deserted room, wondering why he didn't feel sadder or more nostalgic. He had spent his boyhood and teenage years in this house and his parents had tried hard to provide a life for him that was full of happy memories.

But he was angry with them nonetheless. They hadn't been there for him when he really needed them.

He climbed the large, center hall staircase, feeling tired, his feet shuffling heavily on the polished wooden steps. In the upstairs hall-way, he walked right past his old bedroom without stopping, heading directly to his parents' room.

It was empty now, the furniture all carted away by the bargain-hunting antiques dealer who had purchased the contents of the gra-cious home for a fraction of its true worth. But what else could he have done? He didn't have the time to do the calling around and researching necessary to find out how he could get the best prices for his mother's carefully acquired antique furniture collection. His time was better spent trying to hold his business deal together, and the quicker the house was empty and sold, the sooner he would have the big cash infusion he so desperately needed.

The walls of the master bedroom were marked with smudged outlines where the triple dresser and massive four-poster bed once stood. Images of jumping up and down on that big bed as a kid flashed through Richards's mind, but he pushed the memories aside. He didn't want to remember the good times. Those were history. The recent past had not been so kind.

He opened the heavy paneled door and stepped into his mother's walk-in closet. It, too, was empty now. All her dresses and suits were gone, but the smell of her perfume still lingered. He exhaled deeply to clear his mind as he reached for the dial on the wall at the back of the closet.

He knew the combination by heart and methodically he turned the safe's dial back and forth, listening for the sound of the tumblers clicking softly into place. The square panel opened quietly, revealing, just as he expected, nothing inside.

Larson had known the safe would be empty because he had checked it right after his parents' death, removing everything in it at the time. His mother's jewelry, the promissory notes his parents had asked him to sign. This last trip today was a final attempt to make sure that he hadn't missed anything.

CHAPTER

26

Eliza's eyes were red-rimmed and her cheeks were blotchy when she showed up in the makeup room a half hour before airtime.

"Honey!" cried Doris, rushing over and putting her arms around Eliza. "What's wrong? What happened?"

"Oh, Doris," Eliza whimpered. "Remember that girl I told you was writing me? The one with cancer? Well, she died." The tears began to flow again.

As she held on to Eliza, Doris, ever professional, glanced up at the wall clock. There was a lot of work to do in a relatively short time if Eliza was going to look decent on television tonight.

"Here, sweetie, sit down." Doris calmly guided the anchorwoman to the chair. As she listened to Eliza's story about Sarah Morton's father's call canceling the meeting, Doris went to the mini-refrigerator under the counter and pulled out an ice pack. It was imperative they get that eye swelling down.

Eliza leaned her skull back against the headrest and Doris squeezed drops of Visine into the anchorwoman's troubled eyes. Closing her heavy lids, Eliza felt the soothing cold of the frozen blue ice mask. She sat quietly for a few moments while Doris clucked over her and massaged her neck and shoulders, wondering why she was taking this so hard. Eliza hadn't even met Sarah Morton.

"You've got a lot on your plate right now, Eliza," said Doris gently. "Everything will work out. You'll see."

Eliza reached back to pat Doris's arm, knowing full well that

Sarah's death wasn't the only thing that had put her into such a state. Hearing about the tragedy had just pushed her over the top. It brought up all the old memories of John's death and struck the most terror-filled chord of all. The fear of losing her own Janie. With everything going on in Eliza's life right now, she was vulnerable and she knew it.

Tonight they wouldn't be able to get away with merely airbrushing Eliza's beautiful skin. More corrective measures would be necessary. Doris expertly dabbed at each dark pink blotch that scattered across Eliza's face and then smoothed a creamy foundation to even things out. Blush and powder followed. With the eyes she took even more special care. The ice pack and Visine had only been able to do so much.

Doris brushed taupey eyeshadow over Eliza's lids and outlined them with a fine aubergine eyeliner. The plum color made the blue of Eliza's eyes pop out, taking attention away from the bloodshot white parts. She applied a darker brown powder along the orbs, to give the eyes depth and drama. On the middle of the eyelids, Doris defied the general rule among makeup artists not to use sparkle on television, ever so lightly brushing on a bit of shiny light peach glitter and thereby adding warmth and life to Eliza's tired eyes.

"God, Doris, you deserve an Emmy for the job you did tonight," Eliza said in wonderment as she looked at the final result of Doris's labors in the brightly lit mirror that covered the wall in front of them.

Eliza rose tiredly from the chair and air-kissed Doris on the cheek, careful not to smudge the lipstick Doris had so painstakingly painted. Eliza squared back her shoulders and stood erect.

In a half hour, she could go home and gather Janie in her arms.

As she walked across the studio, Eliza wore a marine-blue dress that covered her knees. Good. Finally she was listening to him.

But the dress was sleeveless. He didn't like that.

"Hey, Meat! How 'bout another beer here?"

He grudgingly turned away from the television set and grabbed the empty mug from the gleaming bar top. He pulled the lever to fill the glass from the Budweiser tap and he tried to block out the loud conversation that filled the crowded bar. Yeah, he cared about how the Giants were doing in preseason, but from six-thirty to seven, all he wanted to hear was Eliza's voice.

Now an annoying newcomer to the bar was asking him how he had come to be called Meat.

"It's a nickname I got in junior high," he grumbled.

"Because of your size, I guess," the unknowing customer supposed, eyeing the beefy arms protruding from the striped polo shirt.

"Yeah, that, and because my last name's Bacon." Meat turned back to the television set. He wasn't going to be telling the clown that he had been relieved when he was christened "Meat" by the guys on the JV football team. He hated his real first name, couldn't stand it all through grammar school when the nuns insisted on calling him Cornelius even though he had repeatedly asked them to call him Neil. In a classroom filled with Johns, Josephs, Kevins and Tommys, the kids teased him mercilessly about his weird, old-fashioned name, but his mother and father, always the cowards, weren't about to go into school and chastise the sisters.

Meat chuckled to himself. Cornelius Bacon Sr. was dead now and his son hadn't shed a tear. He had despised his father for his timidity with the outside world. Always playing by those pathetic rules of his that never got him anywhere. Back and forth, back and forth every day to that job at the post office, always insisting that while a government job may not make a man a millionaire, he would have a good retirement and medical insurance for the rest of his life. But the joke was on the poor slob: he dropped dead of a heart attack two months before he was set to retire.

The good thing about it was that his mother didn't have to worry about money now, and that meant she wasn't looking to him to kick in to support her. She got enough from the government each month to cover her needs and go to bingo at the church twice a week. She was satisfied with that.

She wasn't satisfied, though, with the way her son made his living. Tending bar was not respectable as far as she was concerned. She nagged him about it whenever she called him. He should get a solid, dependable job with benefits.

"Not for me, Ma," he droned time after time. "I don't want any suits bossing me around."

A man should be a man, and set down his own set of rules.

Eliza looked beautiful as always, but Abigail Snow detected something different about her eyes tonight. There was a sadness to them and Abigail ached to reach out to her.

Leaning back in her chair in the promotion office, she told herself again that she had to get over this obsession with Eliza. It wasn't healthy. Abigail had stopped talking to her therapist about it, sensing that Dr. Flock was beginning to think she was really going over the deep end in her wishful relationship with Eliza. But with no other woman in her life, Abigail's fascination with Eliza grew and grew.

It wasn't that Abigail wasn't trying to meet someone else. But it was difficult. She had posted her picture and biography on PlanetOut.com, one of the Web sites featuring gay "personals," and she had received many responses. But when she actually took the step of meeting the women for dinner or drinks, she was always disappointed.

A soul mate was hard to find.

Abigail thought about her last girlfriend, Cosima. The year they had been together had started out wonderfully. They shared the same love of the outdoors, spending weekend afternoons hiking out in New Jersey or cycling and Rollerblading in Central Park. In the winter, they had driven out to the Poconos to ski or stayed in the city, catching a movie or just staying in together, Abigail reading while Cosima cooked delicious Greek meals. Abigail had reveled in those long, leisurely, companionable Sunday afternoons.

Abigail had cared about Cosima, but Cosima had found someone new.

The lesbian community was a small world. Everyone seemed to know who was with whom. Abigail had heard from her friend Shannon, who spent July and August in Sag Harbor, that Cosima was totally in love with the woman for whom she had left Abigail. Shannon had seen them, hand in hand and inseparable, at several parties during the summer. It was clear they were mad for each other.

Abigail's sadness only deepened when Shannon well-meaningly suggested they go together to the Chubby Hole some Friday night. It would be a kick, Shannon said, to go to a lesbian strip joint. Fun to have a few drinks and watch the G-string-clad women dance. According to Shannon, Abigail needed to get out and have some laughs.

Abigail doubted that erotic dancers would make her feel better. She wanted someone to love, someone with whom she could have an emotional connection.

Someone like Eliza.

Each time their work put them together, Eliza never disappointed Abigail.

Eliza was her dream woman. Intelligent, witty, beautiful and so feminine. Abigail, who had long ago come to grips with the fact that she was butch and preferred taking the more aggressive role, fantasized nightly about making love to Eliza.

She had to get over it! Accept the fact that Eliza Blake was not gay. She had been married and had a daughter. Everyone around KEY News was aware that she and Mack McBride were romantically involved.

But Abigail still held out hope. After all, she had been married once herself. Many lesbians she knew had been in heterosexual relationships before they realized and accepted that they were gay. Maybe that could be the case with Eliza.

CHAPTER

27

Paige found an excellent agency that sent in a half dozen potential housekeepers for Eliza to interview. Three of them seemed like
they would be the type of people Eliza might be able to trust her
child with and feel comfortable having in her home. But one of them
stood out and Eliza, after checking her references, hired her.

The one hitch was that Carmen Garcia couldn't start until the
middle of September. She insisted that she had to give notice at her
current job. The family she had been employed by for eight years
was relocating to the West Coast and Carmen had promised she
would help them get ready for their move.

"How do you think you'll be able to deal with helping me get
settled in my new home, coming right off of packing up another?"
Eliza asked with some concern as she interviewed the Guatemalan
woman in her office.

"It is fine, señora. I like to get things in order," Carmen answered,
clasping her hands across her ample lap. "The Howards are very good
to me. They help me get my green card. But their children are big
now. They have no toys to pick up, only laundry now. The family
goes out to dinner all the time. I like to cook and I miss having *una
niña* to take care of."

This was too good to be true.

"Do you have your driver's license, Mrs. Garcia? There will be lots
of chauffeuring my daughter to do."

"Yes. I know how to drive, but I do not have my own car." Carmen looked worried.

"No, you don't have to have your own car. I will have a car for you to use. But you must have your own way to get to work in the morning and someone to pick you up at the end of the day. I can drive you in a pinch but, as a general rule, I don't want to have to build time into my schedule to do that."

"Of course not, señora. I know you are very busy. I will have my daughter or a friend drive me."

"You have to know that sometimes I get home late, Mrs. Garcia. If there is a breaking news story or if I have a professional obligation at night, I have to know that it will be no problem for you to stay."

"It is no problem, señora. I live with my grown-up daughter and her family in Westwood, just ten minutes away from HoHoKus. My other children are back in Guatemala, so there is no need of me to take care of them. If you can't come right home after work, that is okay, because no one is waiting for me."

The woman had come dressed for her interview in a flowered shirtwaist dress and wore a double strand of costume pearls at her neck, and round pearl button earrings. Her low-heeled, black patent-leather pumps, while undoubtedly purchased at a discount store, looked like they were brand-new. Eliza sensed that Mrs. Garcia had made a special effort to make a good first impression.

"Do you mind my asking how old you are, Mrs. Garcia?" Eliza knew that at KEY she could be sued for asking a prospective employee that question.

"Fifty."

"You look much younger."

Carmen Garcia may have been a little older than Eliza would have preferred, but Eliza liked everything else about her. There was a certain loveliness and modesty and formality to her. She expected that Janie would like her too. A bonus would be the chance for Janie to pick up some Spanish.

As Mrs. Garcia left the office, Eliza heaved a deep sigh of relief. This was the job she had been dreading, finding someone she could trust enough, feel confident enough about, to leave her daughter in her care. Her instincts told her that this woman was the right one to watch out for her little girl.

Thank God, one huge thing off the list.

Now she had to get through saying good-bye to Mack.

CHAPTER

28

"Once I get the lay of the land over there, I'll be able to tell when I'll be able to come back for a long weekend. It shouldn't be too long."

Mack was trying hard to sound positive as they sat, arms wrapped around each other, in Eliza's moving-crate-strewn living room. This would be their last night together. The transatlantic flight schedule meant that Mack would be in the air tomorrow as Eliza was anchoring the news. It was just as well, Eliza rationalized, to say their good-byes here tonight, privately, rather than bid farewell at the crowded British Airways terminal at Kennedy Airport.

Eliza stared silently into her wineglass as she swirled the deep red Merlot inside. They both knew it was going to be extremely difficult for either one of them to get away for a long weekend anytime soon. She had been anchoring *Evening Headlines* for less than two months, there was a presidential election coming up, and she didn't feel comfortable taking time off yet. She was certain Range wouldn't appreciate it.

Mack was even less likely to be able to get away. As the chief London correspondent, his beat was all of Europe. Any news event, election, war or disaster, natural or man-made, was his to cover. He had to be available, ready to go anywhere at anytime.

They would be lucky if they saw each other at Christmas, Eliza thought glumly.

Snap out of it! Was she going to spend their last hours together drowning in sadness, whining and worrying about what was to become of their relationship? She didn't want Mack to remember her like that. She wanted him flying away tomorrow with peace of mind yet aching to be together again. She wanted to feel that way herself.

Be brave. Have some style. She tried to rally.

"More wine?" she offered, too brightly, eyeing his empty glass. She emptied the rest of the bottle into both their glasses and took a long swallow. A droplet escaped from the corner of her mouth and Mack leaned over and tenderly kissed it away.

She responded to his lips hungrily, inhaling the familiar, wonderful smell of his aftershave and feeling overwhelmed with desperation. She wanted to wrap herself around him and never let go. She wanted Mack to be with her now and, she hoped, always. They needed more time together.

Why was it that every man she loved was taken from her?

CHAPTER

29

Before pulling the cream-colored Lexus onto the hydraulic lift, Augie sorted through the keys on the silver ring. He slipped off the three that looked like house keys and put them in the top pocket of his overalls.

At lunchtime he told the mechanics he was going to the bank. And he did, but first he drove out to the Home Depot on Route 17. There, he had copies of the keys made. Augie rarely got the same guy twice at the giant supply center. If he routinely brought in keys to be copied at the small local hardware store, the owner would surely become suspicious.

The Lexus was back in the Palumbos' long driveway by four o'clock. Augie rang the doorbell and handed the complete key ring to Mrs. Palumbo.

"Thank you so much for squeezing me in on such short notice, Augie. We're leaving for Point Pleasant tomorrow and I really wanted to have the car gone over before we go."

"No problem, Mrs. P. Happy to do it. Mr. Palumbo can settle with me next time he stops in for gas."

He smiled and shook his head as he walked down the driveway to the truck that had followed him over so that he would have a ride back to the station.

God, people were stupid. Trusting, but stupid.

CHAPTER

30

Joe Connelly remained in his small office adjoining the main security room at the Broadcast Center later than usual that evening, entering the newest data into his ABERRANT BEHAVIOR computer program. He currently had sixty cases in his computer culled from mail and telephone threats coming into KEY News headquarters and KEY affiliates around the United States. Some of the cases were simple. Some were extremely complex.

Eliza Blake received lots of odd correspondence, but not all that many threats. Most of the letters that came addressed to her were more persistent nuisances than anything truly alarming. After years of experience, Joe had learned what to dismiss and what to take notice of.

The ordinary letters, those commenting on stories or asking for a signed photo of Eliza, went to KEY Audience Services. The scary stuff was sent to security. As Joe typed in a fresh entry about this clown Meat's latest letter, he marveled that Eliza's new assistant had such a knack for separating the wheat from the chaff.

In Connelly's experience, on-air women got more letters than on-air men. Female correspondents, especially at local stations, bore the brunt of the nut mail. Joe thought it was because the women gave off a more approachable aura on the screen. It wasn't a function of how cutesy they were. It was because they looked open and welcoming.

For Eliza Blake, the same qualities that made her popular with the sane viewing audience made her vulnerable to wackos.

The trick was to tell how bad the threat really was. And to decide when to intervene and with what. If he intervened prematurely or inappropriately it could exacerbate the situation.

Joe scanned the letter again, looking for common verbiage used in the preceding letters. "Blood" was Meat's word of choice.

Dear Miss Arrogant Defiant Eliza Blake,
    You think you know so much.
    But you don't.
    Vampire bats suck blood, but did you also know that they adopt orphans and risk their lives to share food with less fortunate roost-mates?
    That's what you should do. Learn from the bats. Stay home and take care of that little girl of yours like a good mother

would. Instead you choose to parade around each night, strutting your stuff out in the open for the whole country to see.

I've told you before and I'm getting sick of repeating myself. Clean up your act. Cover yourself up and stop showing skin.

I'd like nothing more than to suck *your* crimson blood. Keep it up, white Eliza, and I will. I promise you I will.

Meat.

Evaluating a letter was always a judgment call based on experience and intuition. Joe Connelly's gut told him that Meat was trouble.

CHAPTER

31

KayKay and Poppie were lifesavers, insisting that Eliza take their car until she found the time to buy one.

"It just sits in that garage for days on end, dear. We rarely use it," offered Katharine. "You'd be doing us a *favor* by driving it for a while. A car should be driven, you know. Poppie says that it's not good for it to sit idle all the time."

Eliza had just gotten home from work and she was acutely aware that at this moment Mack was now somewhere over the Atlantic. She was too tired and upset to protest, and truth be known, she was very thankful for the offer.

"That's so generous of you, Katharine. If you really don't mind, I will take you up on it. The closing is tomorrow, we move in on Saturday and I just haven't had a minute to even think about getting a car. I promise it won't be for too long."

Katharine stared at Eliza with a look of concern in her knowing eyes. She knew all about her daughter–in–law's relationship with Mack McBride and she approved of it wholeheartedly. It had been five years now since John had died. Much as Katharine struggled every day with the loss of her son, she wanted his widow to have a happy life and find love again. In the short time Eliza had been with Mack, Katharine had seen the difference in Eliza's demeanor, the way she laughed more easily than she had in years. Mack had been there for Eliza to lean on during the past difficult summer and Katharine had observed his obvious devotion. Janie adored Mack as well and Katharine wanted her grandchild to have a father figure.

She was worried about both mother and child. Just too much was happening at once.

"You keep it as long as you need it, dear," she said, gathering up her pocketbook, and kissing Eliza on the cheek. "Janie, sweetheart," she called down the hall toward the child's bedroom, "KayKay's leaving now."

Both women smiled at each other as they heard the rapid little steps approaching from the hallway.

"'Bye, KayKay. Love you." The small arms held tight around her grandmother's waist as Katharine leaned down and kissed the top of the sweet–smelling brown head. "Thank you for taking me for my haircut today." The child beamed, proud of her freshly cut bangs and the purple nail polish that her grandmother had let her have applied on the tiny nailbeds.

"My pleasure, my darling. You'll be the prettiest girl in kindergarten next week."

Janie's face clouded and Eliza stepped in, kneeling down to speak face–to–face with her child.

"Janie, I know you're a little worried about starting at your new school. All kids are a little worried when they start school. I remember I was. Weren't you, KayKay?"

Janie looked up at her grandmother skeptically. KayKay didn't seem like she had ever been afraid of anything.

"I was, Janie," Katharine nodded solemnly, "but once I got there, I loved it. Kindergarten will be so much fun." What was the point in telling the child that she used to be so nervous before going to school every morning that she could barely swallow a glass of milk, much less eat the full breakfast her mother set out for her?

Janie's face told them she wasn't really buying it. Katharine decided to try to divert the child's attention.

"Hey, run down to your room and get the new shoes we bought today to show Mommy!" she urged.

The child scampered away obediently and Katharine headed for the door. As she reached for the knob to let herself out, Katharine turned to her daughter-in-law and spoke in a low voice.

"You know, Eliza, I think it's just as well that the new housekeeper can't start right away. I think it will be good for Poppie and me to be there when Janie comes home from school in the beginning. I think she'll feel more secure that way."

As Janie came trotting back with her small cardboard shoebox, Eliza answered:

"I'll feel more secure that way, too."

CHAPTER

32

As the saying among real-estate brokers went, when it came to the closings, you went to the money. So Louise Kendall, Larson Richards and two lawyers showed up at the KEY News Broadcast Center at nine-thirty Friday morning to complete the final paperwork to transfer ownership of the house on Saddle Ridge Road. The lawyers were members of the bar in both New Jersey and New York, so there was no problem conducting the closing of a Garden State house in the Empire State office.

Louise had risen especially early, walking through the house one last time before driving into the city. Eliza had entrusted Louise with the task most homebuyers insisted on doing themselves: inspecting the home, room by room, one last time, before the final checks were handed over to the seller. The house was broom–clean and everything looked in order. The Realtor prayed that there would be no surprises once Eliza moved in.

Paige escorted the group from the lobby up the elevator to Eliza's office. Ms. Blake was running just a few minutes behind, her assistant explained, but would be there soon.

While the others took seats, Larson Richards walked around the office, browsing at the books and inspecting the four Emmy statuettes that sat on the shelves. He looked at the picture of the little girl in the silver frame on Eliza's desk. He noted the hand–knotted Turkish rug, in tones of blues and reds, that lay atop the standard–issue office wall-to-wall, lending an air of elegance to the room. The tufted leather sofa was strewn with attractive kilim pillows. Framed awards dotted the walls. But the best part of the office was the view through the windowed wall looking out at the news studio below.

The floor beneath buzzed with energy as dozens of men and women sat at their modern desks, typing busily on their computer keyboards, reading the wires and talking on the phones.

The anchor desk Richards had seen so often on television was located in the middle of the large studio, lit with dozens of bright lights suspended from the ceiling. Large television cameras were trained on the anchor chair. There was a glass office at the side of room where four men and one woman sat around an oblong table. He could see television screens in front of all of them, along with an additional half dozen television sets affixed to the walls.

"What goes on in there?" asked Richards, gesturing out the window to the glass office as Paige approached him with one of the cups of coffee that she was offering to everyone in the room.

Paige held out a paper napkin to Richards. "We call that 'the Fishbowl.' All the senior producers sit in there. It's the command post for all the planning and coordinating of the *Evening Headlines*."

Richards nodded nonchalantly, determined not to show any enthusiasm. He was impressed, all right, but he wasn't about to act it. He was thrilled Eliza Blake was buying his parents' house. He had been certain the deal would go through. There would be no problem with her coming up with the money. And maybe, if he played his cards right, he might be able to interest her in doing some investing with him.

Right now he just wanted Eliza to show up. He wanted to get this house closed and get the check in the bank before it shut its doors this afternoon. With the long Labor Day weekend ahead, he didn't want to have to wait until Tuesday to make the deposit. He had to start drawing against the house money immediately.

"I'm so sorry I'm late. Please, excuse me." Dressed in a stunning magenta suit, Eliza entered briskly, shaking her attorney's hand and kissing Louise on the cheek. Eliza was sensitive to the fact that this once had been Louise's husband's office, and she guessed it might be somewhat difficult for her to be here.

But if it bothered Louise, she was courageous enough not to show it. The Realtor graciously introduced Eliza to the seller and his lawyer.

"It's so nice to meet you, Mr. Richards. Your parents had a beautiful home and I'm so glad to be able to buy it."

"I hope you'll be very happy there, Ms. Blake," said Richards, with his most charming smile. "We had great times in that house."

He's smooth, Eliza found herself thinking. *Too smooth.*

"Should we get to it?" suggested Eliza's attorney. "I know Ms. Blake is very busy."

One by one, the papers were signed. The homeowners' insurance, the title insurance, the RESPA form so Uncle Sam would know who paid what to whom, and the Realtor's commission statement. When Louise was handed her commission check, always paid by the seller, Eliza saw Larson Richards wince.

Finally the title was transferred, the deed was presented to the new owner of the home and the seller had his money. Richards rose quickly and extended his hand to Eliza.

"Well, good luck, Eliza, if I may call you that, seeing as I'm sure we'll be seeing each other around."

Eliza didn't look forward to it.

As Richards and his lawyer headed toward the door, Louise called out.

"Oh, Mr. Richards, we need to get the combination for the safe in the master bedroom. Eliza may want to change it, of course, but in the meantime, with all the workmen in the house, she might have some things she wants to lock up."

A look of annoyance crossed Richards' face.

Too bad if he's bugged, thought Louise. With two million dollars in his pocket, it was little enough to cough up the combination. *Larson damned well better come up with it.*

Before leaving the Broadcast Center, Louise took the back stair-case from the hallway outside Eliza's office down to the Fishbowl on the floor below. Knowing that she would be in the building for Eliza's closing, Range had told her to stop by and say hello.

Louise had known Range Bullock for years, in his role as her for-mer husband's producer. But it was only after Bill had died last spring that Louise and Range had become close.

"Died" is the nice way of saying it, Louise thought as she approached the Fishbowl doorway. Bill Kendall, world-renowned anchor of *KEY Evening Headlines,* had committed suicide. And devastated though she was that Bill had felt desperate enough to do the unthinkable, part of her

still couldn't forgive him for it, and for what he had done to their son, William. She would never understand how Bill could have left their child behind. She had had many dark days herself since the time they had found out that William had Fragile X syndrome, yet any thoughts she had had of checking out—and there had been a few of them—she had resolutely pushed out of her mind. William needed her. He needed both his parents.

In fairness to Bill, for nineteen years he had been a great father. He loved their boy. And William adored his dad. It had been almost six months since his father had died, but William still looked into the car expectantly when she came to pick him up at his group home. It broke her heart every time she saw the puzzlement in his face when she explained to him again that Daddy was gone now and wasn't coming back.

"Daddy's in heaven, right, Mom?"

"Yes, sweetheart, Dad's in heaven, watching over you and still loving you every single day."

Damn Bill.

Range, a telephone cradled against his shoulder, was busily tapping at his computer keyboard. Sensing the presence of someone watching him, he looked up and smiled when he saw her. *Come in,* he mouthed.

The Fishbowl was empty save for the two of them, but Louise knew that the office wouldn't remain that way for long. The digital clock on the wall read 11:06. Nine minutes until Range would preside over the morning meeting in which the senior producers and writers would take their seats in the glass office and report on the dozens of stories developing around the world. By the end of the day only seven or eight would make the final lineup as pieces on the broadcast.

"All right, we'll talk later. Let me know what you hear from the Hurricane Center."

Range hung up the phone and groaned. "Each year it's the same damned thing. From August to October we have to gear up with every freakin' hurricane alert. Most of 'em peter out to be no big deal, but there's always the chance that the whopper will hit."

"Tell me about it," said Louise, "I remember Bill going off to cover those nightmares and worrying myself sick over him." She walked behind Range's chair and reached out to massage the muscles at the base of his neck. "A little tight today, are we?"

"Yeah, and I don't want this hurricane to interrupt our plans for the long weekend."

After twenty years of being involved with men who worked in the news business, Louise had never really gotten used to the fact that breaking stories that had nothing to do with her life could very often force her to cancel her long-anticipated plans. But she had learned to be philosophical. There was nothing she could do about it if she was to be involved with the two men who had excited her the most.

"Look. If it turns out we can't drive up to the Cape, it's not the end of the world. The traffic will be horrendous anyway. The weather up here is supposed to be glorious. We'll spend the weekend out at my place and relax out there. We'll barbecue and swim and do what-ever our little hearts desire. Then, if you have to come into the office, you can."

Range reached behind and pulled her hand from his neck and kissed the inside of her palm. "God, what a relief you understand this lunacy."

For the tingle that ran through her at the touch of his lips, Louise was willing to be understanding.

CHAPTER

33

Though Eliza was going to be in on Labor Day to anchor the evening broadcast, she had told Paige she wanted her to take the holiday off. It would be a quiet day, Eliza assured her assistant, and Eliza herself planned to come in late.

"Really, Paige, there's no need for you to come in. Nothing is going to happen on Monday that can't wait to be dealt with until Tuesday. Go and have a good weekend."

Paige was psyched to hit the end-of-season department-store sales and she was hoping to find some fall bargains at her favorite, T. J. Maxx. She needed some new clothes to wear to the office in this, her first autumn in the working world. She had her eye on a Calvin Klein knee-length camel pea coat and she had the feeling it could be marked down this weekend.

Eliza left after the broadcast Friday night and Paige planned to be minutes behind her. She straightened up her own desk and went into Eliza's office to make sure all was in order there. Grabbing a coffee mug Eliza had left on her desk, Paige took it to the small kitchen next door off the hallway and washed it out in the sink. She opened up the tiny refrigerator and restocked it with the Diet Snapple iced tea that Eliza liked. Switching off the light, she went back to the office to gather up her things to leave.

Conscientiously Paige checked her voice mail once more before she left. There was one new message, left just minutes earlier, in the time she must have been in the kitchen.

She recognized the voice. It was the guy who had been calling every day for almost two weeks now, professing his admiration for Eliza, telling her how beautiful she was. Paige hadn't been paying much attention to the calls. The man sounded harmless enough— sad, really. She had deleted the calls from the machine without a second thought.

But it was different this time. He had always called late at night. This was the earliest the man had ever phoned, as if he really thought he might reach Eliza. Up until now, the calls had merely expressed admiration for the anchorwoman. What the caller said this time was different, too.

"I love you, Eliza. And I can't live without you."

SEPTEMBER

CHAPTER

34

Eliza knew exactly how Paige was able to manage to get movers to work on the Saturday of Labor Day weekend. The jumbo check Eliza had already written out solved that mystery.

As the muscle men made their trips back and forth to the moving van, Eliza was thankful the day wasn't too hot. The sky was blue and cloudless and the sun was strong, but the air was clear and a cooling breeze blew intermittently.

Standing in her elegant front hallway, Eliza directed the movers on which room to go to with which pieces of furniture. Her mahogany table and Chinese Chippendale–style chairs, which had fit so well in her apartment, looked lost in the cavernous dining room. The large living room could easily accommodate two sofas rather than the one she had brought from New York. And the walls. They were expansive. What was she going to hang on them?

She shrugged. At this point she really did not care how long it took to get the house together. As long as Janie's bedroom was in order, the guest room made comfortable for Katharine and Paul, the clothes organized in Eliza's closets, and as long as they got things set up and put away in the kitchen, the rest could wait.

In fact, it would be fun to shop for antiques and choose wallpapers on the weekends. It might fill the time and keep her from thinking about Mack. Janie wouldn't like it much, though.

Eliza wandered into the sunny kitchen and looked out the picture window into the backyard. Her daughter was happily splashing away in the pool with Katharine and Paul standing at the side, praising their granddaughter's every jellyfish float while watching her like hawks. Eliza made a mental note that she would have to get some pool furniture, too. Meanwhile she carried two of the dining-room chairs outside so that her in-laws would have someplace to sit.

Katharine and Paul weren't kids and she could only imagine how much strain they had been under, but never once did Eliza get even the tiniest hint they resented the fact that taking care of Janie had taken over their lives. She and Janie were so blessed to have them.

"How's it going in there?" Paul asked, wisps of his pure white hair blowing gently in the breeze.

"They're just about finished bringing everything in," Eliza answered, sinking tiredly onto the deck and stretching out her long, capri-clad legs on the warm Tennessee crabstones. "Anybody have any suggestions about what we should do for dinner tonight? We could go out somewhere or we could order-in Chinese," she offered.

"Chinese, Chinese," cheered Janie from the pool. "I want wonton soup and sesame chicken." Eliza was a little embarrassed at how often her daughter had eaten takeout food delivered by the Chinese restaurant around the corner from their apartment. Usually on Sundays, when they crammed in a dayful of activities because Eliza felt guilty about how much she was gone the rest of the week, it was just easier to pick up the phone and place an order. Eliza recalled the Sunday dinners she had when she was growing up in Rhode Island, her mother roasting a chicken or leg of lamb, baking potatoes, snapping fresh green beans. Janie wouldn't have those memories. But Eliza consoled herself with the fact that Janie had been exposed to more cultural opportunities in her first five years of life than Eliza had in her first twenty.

They would have a quieter life out here on the weekends, Eliza reflected, closing her eyes and turning her face upward toward the late-afternoon sun. She resolved to ask Mrs. Garcia to make sure the refrigerator was well stocked when she left on Friday evenings, and Eliza vowed to start cooking Sunday dinners.

But the big meals would be prepared just for her and Janie.

She bit the inside of her mouth as she wondered what Mack was doing right now, calculating the time difference between them and realizing that he would be going to bed soon.

"Hello!"

The four at the pool turned toward the voice and watched as a trim, attractive brunette carrying a tray and a little dark-haired boy carrying a big bunch of black-eyed Susans walked in their direction from the side of the house. Eliza rose to her feet and smiled as mother and son approached.

"Hi, I'm Susan Feeney and this is my son, James. We live across the street and we wanted to welcome you to the neighborhood and invite you to a barbecue we're having tomorrow. I thought it might be a good way for you to meet some of the neighbors." Susan balanced the tray in one hand as she reached out to shake Eliza's with the other.

"That's so sweet of you!" exclaimed Eliza, holding on to Susan's warm, firm grip. So many women Eliza knew gave the limpest handshake, lacking any confidence whatever. Score one for Susan.

After introducing Katharine and Paul to her new neighbors, Eliza pointed to the pool. "And this is Janie, my five-year-old."

James's green eyes widened. "I'm five too!"

"Are you starting kindergarten this week?" Eliza asked, knowing the answer as Susan winked at her.

The boy nodded emphatically.

"At the HoHoKus Public School?"

"Yup."

"Wow! That's great! Janie is starting there too. You'll be in the same class."

James thrust his bouquet into Eliza's hand and headed toward the swimming pool as Eliza called out her thanks after him. Laughing, she turned to Susan and asked if James would like to go for a swim.

"Gee, thanks," Susan responded, "but James, my husband, is home with our other two kids. Kimberly is three and Kelly is two, so he has his hands full over there. I've got to get back, but I just wanted to introduce myself and drop this over."

Eliza put the flowers down on the lawn in order to take the golden cake Susan presented.

"I hope you like pineapple."

"We do. It looks scrumptious. Thank you so much!"

"You're so welcome. And if there is anything at all I can do, just let me know. I can show you the lay of the land around here and I'll be driving James to and from school every day. If you'd like me to pick up Janie, I'd be glad to."

There is a God, thought Eliza. If nothing else, it was reassuring to know she would have a backup if for some reason Janie's grandparents, or later, Mrs. Garcia, couldn't pick her up after school. Eliza planned to drop Janie off herself in the mornings before she headed into Manhattan. She was tempted to ask Susan if she was interested in forming a carpool, but she thought better of it for the moment. She wanted to get Janie quietly settled in the new house and the new school before she made any commitments.

At the water's edge, James was pulling off his green–and–white–striped T–shirt, ready to jump.

"If you have to get back, James can stay and take a swim," Eliza offered. "It would be great for Janie to make a first new friend."

"Gosh, you've got so much to do," Susan cocked her head to the side skeptically. "You don't need another child to watch."

Eliza looked at Katharine and Paul. "No problem at all," chimed Paul.

"All right, if you're sure about this. James can swim in his sport shorts and I'll be back in half an hour to pick him up."

Eliza escorted Susan across the grass toward the front of the house. "I'd invite you in for a tour, but there isn't much to see yet."

Susan's smiling mouth fell at the corners. "I know the house very well already," she sighed. "The Richardses were such wonderful people. I miss them so. We moved into our house three years ago on Good Friday, of all days. The house was a mess, boxes all over the place, I was pregnant with Kimberly and I had promised James we would dye Easter eggs. Even though he was only two, he was so excited about it. But when I went to turn on the stove for the first time, it didn't work so I couldn't boil the eggs. James cried and cried."

The two women stopped in the driveway as Susan finished her story.

"But the funniest, dearest thing happened. On Easter morning, the doorbell rang. It was Mrs. Richards, welcoming us and carrying a basket of colored eggs she had dyed and decorated. Of course she had no idea that the stove was on the fritz, it was just a coincidence that she brought those eggs over. But I always felt it was some kind of good sign or something, you know? Like we were getting off to a good start in our new home."

Eliza nodded. "You coming over here with James makes me feel the same way. Thank you."

Susan smiled and started down the driveway. Why bring up what had happened to the Richardses? If Eliza ever wanted to ask her about it, Susan would tell her what she knew. But today was her first day in her new home. It should be a happy day.

CHAPTER

35

After they finished eating their Chinese dinners, with plastic forks, straight out of the partitioned foil containers they'd been delivered in, Eliza and KayKay set about making up beds and unpacking towels and toiletries upstairs. Poppie hooked up the VCR to the television for Janie's VHS tapes and plugged in the beta cassette playback deck Eliza had for screening professional tapes. It was nine o'clock when Eliza came downstairs to summon Janie for bedtime. She found her daughter sitting on her grandfather's lap, both of them sound asleep in the den while *Free Willy* played away on the TV screen.

Paul, his mouth slightly open, snored lightly and did not stir as Eliza gingerly lifted the child from him. As she slowly mounted the stairs, carrying Janie in her arms, she passed Katharine coming down. They smiled and winked at each other and Katharine reached out to softly pat her granddaughter's cheek.

Choosing not to wake the child by undressing her, Eliza laid Janie in her twin bed in her T-shirt and shorts and covered her with the *101 Dalmatians* comforter they had brought from the apartment. As always, the sight of her sleeping little girl tucked in snug beneath the covers made Eliza inhale with the emotions she felt. Love—profound love and gratitude that she had been blessed with this perfect little girl. If Janie was all right, nothing else really mattered.

She thought of Samuel Morton and wondered how he was bearing the loss of his Sarah.

Zippy. Where was Zippy? Eliza glanced around the room. If Janie woke up in her new room during the night, she would be reaching out for her worn, comforting, stuffed monkey. Where had she seen it last?

Out by the pool this afternoon.

She pulled down the window shades that had been left behind with the house and tiptoed out of the bedroom, leaving the door ajar so light from the hallway would ensure that Janie's room was not completely dark. Walking down the hall, she approached the room Katharine and Paul would be sleeping in and, hearing their voices, poked her head through the opened door to say good night.

Paul, sleepy-eyed, beckoned her to enter. Eliza went over to each of them and hugged them tight.

"I don't know how much I can ever thank you both, for every-thing."

"Don't thank us, honey," said Paul. "We want to be here. You and Janie are everything to us. Don't you know that by now?"

"Of course I know it, but not every set of grandparents or in-laws are like the two of you. I just want to make sure you know how much I appreciate you...how much I love you." Eliza's eyes welled with the start of tears, but she blinked them back. The last thing she wanted was for Katharine and Paul to be any more worried about her than they were.

"The worst is over now, dear," said Katharine soothingly. "You're in your new house now. And this will be a wonderful place for Janie to grow up. Tomorrow we'll unpack and get everything stowed away in the kitchen. We'll put out your pictures and arrange your books in the cases in the den. Before you know it, we'll have this place feeling like home."

Eliza nodded and closed the door behind her as she left them, envying them for a moment that they would soon be climbing into bed, together. She wished she wasn't going to be sleeping alone again tonight and, tiredly, she thought of Mack. She considered calling him, but it was the middle of the night in England. He knew she was moving. Why hadn't he called to give a little moral support?

Don't be angry, she reasoned with herself as she headed toward the master bedroom, eager to shed her clothes and step into a hot shower. *You don't know. He might have been sent out on a story and had no chance to call.*

Eliza was pulling her shirt over her head when she remembered. *Zippy.*

Back on went the shirt, and she hurried barefoot downstairs and out the kitchen door to the backyard. It took her just a few minutes to find the stuffed chimpanzee in the grass behind the pool.

The kitchen door was left open the entire time.

CHAPTER

36

Oh, God! What had he done?

Mack listened to the soft breathing of the sleeping blonde lying beside him in room 509 of the newly refurbished Mandarin Oriental Hotel, his home until his KEY News service flat was ready.

He hated himself.

There was no excuse for it. Too bad if he was heartsick about leaving Eliza. Too bad if he was lonely. Too bad if he had downed one vodka martini after another at dinner with Marcy McGinnis and her pretty young assistant. The assistant whom Mack would now be seeing day after day at work. The assistant who had just turned over on her side and pulled the covers closer around her.

How could he have been so stupid?

Mack groggily remembered the resigned expression on his bureau chief's face as she excused herself and said her good-byes for the evening, leaving Mack and the blonde at the table at Harvey Nick's. This was certainly not the first time that dinner in the posh "see and be seen" department-store restaurant had been the prelude to an indiscreet dalliance.

As his head throbbed, the old warning about dipping your pen in the company ink passed through Mack's mind. He had always made it a policy not to get involved with anyone where he worked. Eliza had been the notable and totally worthwhile exception.

He didn't even know this young woman. Was she trustworthy or would she be sharing the news of their encounter with her friends in the London office? Even if she only told one person, word would get around. It always did. And what if it got back to Eliza?

Mack slipped from the bed and felt his way in the dark to the bathroom. He closed the door behind him, switched on the light, turned on the faucet and doused his face with cold water. His blood-shot eyes stared back at him in the mirror. He loathed himself.

How could he have betrayed Eliza so easily and so quickly?

CHAPTER

37

Eliza awoke in the semidarkness, a thin ray of white light peering through from the hallway beyond her bedroom door. She had left the door slightly open so she could hear Janie.

"Janie?"

No reply.

What she heard instead was a rhythmic tapping noise and a rus-tling sound. She lay still in her bed, actually feeling the beating of her heart as instinctive-danger adrenaline coursed through her. Some-thing or someone was in her room.

The soft knocking sound continued as Eliza tried to get a fix on its source. It seemed to be coming from the left side of the room.

She lay there a few minutes more, listening to the sound, trying to figure out what she should do. She considered running down the hall to wake Paul. No, she should face whatever it was herself. Know-ing that Janie was asleep nearby galvanized her to reach over and turn on the lamp on the table next to the bed.

Her eyes adjusted quickly to the full light as they strained in the direction of the noise. She saw no one. But the sound continued and as she stared she noticed that the shade on the window was moving almost imperceptibly. It wasn't a breeze that was making the shade flutter. There was a small lump beneath the fabric.

Summoning up her courage, Eliza slowly rose from her bed, grabbed a shoe from the floor and walked deliberately toward the window. She took a deep breath as she lifted the shade and looked underneath.

For a split second she wasn't sure what she was seeing. The dark, furry pulsating animal stared at her with beady dark eyes. It had pointy ears and a snout that looked a little bit like a fox.

She dropped the shade and ran from the bedroom, closing the door firmly behind her.

It was a bat.

On the first night in her new home, there was a brown, furry bat in her bedroom.

CHAPTER

38

Keith Chapel awoke early, relieved he had an excuse to get out of the apartment on Sunday morning. Cindy had been upset last night when he had gotten up the nerve to tell her he had to go to the Broad-cast Center and get some work done on the holiday weekend.

"Look, honey, it won't be for the entire day," he promised. "Range wasn't happy with the first FRESHER LOOK when I played it for him late Friday afternoon. I just need some time to rework the script a little so Eliza can track it again when she comes in tomorrow."

"Eliza, Eliza, Eliza! I'm so sick and tired of hearing about Eliza Blake," Cindy cried shrilly. "What about *me*?"

You're driving me crazy and I need to get away from you.

Keith didn't say what he thought. Instead he hugged her increasing girth, kissed her wet cheeks and suggested that when he got home they go to that movie she had been talking about wanting to see. Cindy had been mollified, for the moment. Until, inevitably, the next outburst.

He prayed things would be different between them once the baby came. And he wished to God he would stop dreaming about Eliza. Last night's dream was so explicit that he had awakened in a cold sweat. The things he was doing with Eliza were things he would never dare suggest doing with his wife.

CHAPTER

39

"Mommy, why are you sleeping in the living room?"

Eliza sleepily opened her eyes to find Janie's inquisitive blue ones staring intensely into hers. She bolted upright on the sofa, remembering the bat upstairs.

"Janie, did you go into Mommy's room to look for me?" she asked fearfully.

"Yup. But you weren't there."

"Stay right here, Janie. I mean it," Eliza said firmly as she sprang from the couch and ran upstairs to her room, slamming the door Janie had left ajar.

Katharine came out of her bedroom, tying the sash of the bathrobe around her waist.

"What's going on?"

"I found a bat in my room last night."

"Dear Lord!" Katharine looked at the closed door behind Eliza. "It's in there now?"

"God, I hope so. I hope it didn't fly out and hide somewhere else in the house."

"What should we do?"

"I called the police in the middle of the night and they had a woman from Wildlife Control call me back. She said she would come right away if I really wanted her to, but if I could wait until morning she would really appreciate it. So I slept on the couch and the woman promised she would get here first thing today."

"Mommy," Janie's voice called from downstairs. "There's a lady coming to the door."

"Thank God," Eliza whispered as she hurried down the staircase.

The middle-aged woman was dressed in farmer's overalls and a long-sleeved flannel workshirt. She carried a heavy plastic pail. Eliza saw a pair of thick leather gloves resting on top of the paraphernalia in the bucket.

Matter-of-factly the woman followed as Eliza led the way to the master bedroom.

"There really isn't too much to be worried about, miss," said the woman. "Bats are actually very useful. A single bat can eat thousands of bugs each night, including those mosquitoes everyone around here is so riled up about."

"What about rabies?" Eliza asked, unready to love bats.

"That's pretty much a non-issue. You are more likely to get bitten by a rabid dog than a rabid bat. Bat rabies cause about one human death a year in this country."

The woman pulled on her work gloves and opened the bedroom door. "Now, you wait outside here while I go in and take a look around."

Eliza stood in the hallway, listening. She heard the shade rolling up inside.

"He's not in the shade anymore," the woman called through the door.

Oh, God. Eliza's heart sank.

But a few minutes later, the women opened the bedroom door, a satisfied expression upon her face.

"You got it?"

"Yes, ma'am."

"Where was it?"

"In the bottom of your wastepaper basket in the bathroom. As the daylight comes, they try to get as far away from the sunlight as they can."

"So it's in there?" Eliza eyed the bucket.

"Yes, ma'am."

"What are you going to do with it?"

The woman looked over Eliza's shoulder where the little girl was standing listening at the top of the staircase.

"I'm gonna take it for a nice long ride," she answered.

Eliza escorted the woman out to her truck.

"How did it get in? I don't want it to happen again."

"Well, you should probably have your attic checked to see if there are any bats roosting up there."

"I just bought this house. We moved in yesterday. I had the house inspected just over a week ago."

The woman shrugged. "Well, it could have flown in yesterday if you had your doors open for a while with all the moving."

Or last night when I was out looking for Zippy, Eliza thought, with a shiver.

"Are you really just going to let it free someplace?" Eliza asked as the woman climbed into her truck.

"Nah. I just didn't want your little kid to hear. I'm going to take it out later and stomp on it and break its neck."

CHAPTER

40

Abigail got to the gym early so she wouldn't have to wait for the equipment. She started out with the free weights, then did a circuit of Nautilus machines and finished up on the treadmill. She had showered and was dressing in front of her locker when she heard a voice call her name.

"Abigail? It that you?"

She turned toward the voice and saw a woman Abigail guessed to be in her late twenties.

"It's Monica," the woman smiled. "Monica Anderson."

Abigail tried to mask the confusion and guilt she immediately felt.

"Of course. Monica! It's so good to see you again. How have you been?"

"Great. I finally moved into the city. I'd been wanting to do it for so long but, you know, with everything that happened, I felt I should stay with my parents for a while."

Abigail nodded. "How are your parents?"

Monica's face clouded. "Well, Dad died last spring. He was never really the same after everything happened. Heart attack, the doctors said. But his heart really broke five years ago."

"I'm so sorry, Monica. If I had known, I would have come out to pay my respects."

There was an awkward silence and Abigail folded her workout

clothes and placed them in her gym bag, buying herself time. She felt she should say something about Linda.

"You know," Abigail began haltingly, "I'm sorry I didn't keep in touch, Monica. But after Linda disappeared, I felt I had to get away. I couldn't work at Garden State Network anymore, with all the memories there."

Monica nodded. "Don't worry about it, Abigail. I think everyone understood. I was away at college most of the time when you and Linda worked together, but I remember you coming to our house for Easter that last year. Linda told me what a good friend you were, how much fun you had starting out in the business together. She treasured you."

"And I her," Abigail said softly. "For the first year or two, I'd call the news director every month to see if there were any leads in the case. After a while I just stopped calling."

"It's better that way, Abigail. They're never going to find out what happened to Linda. I'm convinced of it. It's one of those horrible things in life that has to be accepted. Of course, my mother still calls the police all the time. She can't let it go."

CHAPTER

41

Around four o'clock, Eliza took Janie by the hand and headed across the street to the Feeneys' house. After a day spent unpacking, Katharine and Paul begged off going to the barbecue. They wanted to relax and take naps.

As mother and daughter tentatively entered the fenced backyard through the gate, Susan saw them and hurried over with two little girls toddling behind her.

"We're so glad you came! Let me introduce you around to everyone."

Eliza met at least twenty people, trying to remember names and knowing that she wouldn't, while Janie and James ran away to frolic with Buddy, the Feeneys' black-and-white Brittany spaniel.

Chicken and steaks were cooking aromatically on the grill alongside aluminum foil–wrapped loaves of garlic bread. A long buffet table was covered with a red, white and blue–striped tablecloth and a huge centerpiece of flowers Eliza recognized as cut from the gardens that edged the yard.

James Feeney offered her a drink. "What will it be?"

"Iced tea?"

"How about a little vodka in that?" offered her host.

"Even better." Eliza smiled.

She took a seat in one of the chairs, and took a quick count of the guests. An even number of men and women. She assumed she was the only single woman at the party.

"Eliza, if I may call you that," said one of the women, whose name she couldn't remember, "I can't tell you how everyone has been buzzing about you moving into our neighborhood."

"Please. Of course you should call me Eliza. And I can't tell you how happy I am to be here. Janie and I were really looking forward to moving out of the city. I'm hoping we can have a more normal, quieter life here."

"Yes," clucked the woman. "I read in the paper about the nastiness you went through. I hope you'll be very happy out here."

One of the men chimed in. "Well, I hate to burst anyone's bubble, but everything's not perfect in suburbia. Did you hear that there was another robbery? The Palumbos got back from vacation and found their house totally stripped."

"How many is that now?" someone asked.

"Six this summer, that I know of," answered another. "And there hasn't been a sign of forced entry in any of them. Either people aren't being careful enough about locking up when they leave or someone has a key."

"What about alarm systems?"

"You know how it is around here. Some of these people have lived in their houses for thirty years. They moved out when it was real country and no one even thought of having security systems installed."

Eliza had been surprised to learn that the Richardses hadn't had an alarm system. Louise had arranged for one to be installed for her, but the company was so backed up with orders that they weren't going to be able to come out for a few weeks.

"Come on, everyone. Come and eat," Susan called, placing a huge glass bowl full of spinach salad laced with raisins and onions and drizzled with sweet-and-sour dressing on the buffet table. People began to rise from their seats. Susan scanned the yard to make sure everything was in order for her guests. As she looked toward the fence gate, her pleasant expression changed.

Eliza looked over her shoulder to see Larson Richards approaching.

"Larson," Susan said coolly. "How have you been?"

"I'm fine, just fine, Susan. I don't mean to crash your party, but I stopped over to welcome Eliza to the neighborhood and was told she was over here."

How rude of him to come by uninvited. Eliza disliked him even more now than she had at the closing.

CHAPTER

42

Eliza stayed in bed for a while after she woke up Labor Day morning, listening to the quiet and wishing she didn't have to go to work. She resolved to tell Range she would work Columbus Day, but, once the election was over, she was definitely taking Thanksgiving off. Feeling the soft sheets against her bare legs as she shifted position, Eliza thought about a long weekend in London. After that slug Larson had attached himself to her for the rest of the barbecue, she had missed Mack even more.

She glanced at the clock and calculated it was lunchtime in England. She reached for the phone but thought better of it. It might be hard for Mack to talk at the office. She could call him when she got into the Broadcast Center, and, hopefully, he would be back at his hotel.

Better yet, he could call her. That was what she was really waiting for.

Staring at the bedroom wall she noted the marks left by the Richardses' triple dresser peeking out from the side of her own smaller chest. She had to get cracking on getting this place together.

The neighbors had been friendly last night, giving her names of local workmen and a good painting and wallpaper man. The general consensus was that Bruno Taveroni did the best work around. He was meticulous and always booked.

It might take longer than she had planned to get her new house in order.

Eliza heard the soft murmur of voices coming from downstairs. She should get up and fix Janie's breakfast. But the aroma of fresh-brewed coffee and frying bacon was already wafting from below. Katharine had things well in hand.

She prayed that Carmen Garcia would be as capable and helpful when she started her job. Eliza got up and pulled on her robe, suddenly remembering that Keith would have the FRESHER LOOK piece on child care ready for her to retrack when she got to the office.

The piece had to be good. The pressure was on.

CHAPTER

43

Larson listened to the soft clicking sound of the cleats on his golf shoes as he walked across the thin strip of pavement that led from the clubhouse to the first tee. Dressed in a black-and-beige Greg Norman shirt and crisply creased golf slacks, he looked every bit the prosperous country-club member. If these three guys getting ready to tee off with him in the late-summer sunshine only knew the financial trouble he was in...

Playing a round of golf was a great way to do business. The camaraderie grew as the foursome traversed the lush green fairways. There were plenty of opportunities to back-slap after the great shots and commiserate after the duds. Today Larson planned to lose and he would graciously and effortlessly peel off the bills from his sterling money clip to pay off his bet.

But after the eighteenth hole, when they sauntered into the Members' Grill for drinks, Larson desperately hoped he would be able to accomplish what he must do. The oncologist, periodontist and divorce attorney had deep pockets and they were always looking for ways to make them deeper. With just the right approach, careful not to push too hard, Larson's goal was to get them to commit to investing in his business.

Of course, he wasn't going to tell them the business was hemorrhaging.

He carefully positioned the round white Pinnacle on the wooden tee and lined up to take his first shot. As his club made contact he knew the shot would be good and he watched as the ball flew a respectable two hundred yards straight down the fairway. A positive sign of things to come today.

While he waited for the others to take their opening swings, his mind wandered from his business worries to a much more pleasurable subject: Eliza Blake.

God, she was beautiful. And wealthy. He had read in the *Wall Street Journal* about her new KEY contract. Big bucks.

While Eliza hadn't shown him the interest he had hoped for at the Feeneys' barbecue last night, Larson felt confident he could bring her around. There was always some way to get what you wanted. You just had to figure out how.

Larson handed his club to the caddy and climbed into the golf cart. How to reach Eliza?

As his foot pressed the pedal, he smiled at the answer to his question.

The kid.

CHAPTER

44

The black-rimmed ivory stationery sat blank upon his desk. Samuel Morton was having a very hard time deciding exactly what to write. Such a special person deserved a carefully worded acknow-ledgment of her kindness.

He pulled out a yellow legal pad to make a first draft of his letter. With a fine-tipped black pen he wrote.

Dear Ms. Blake,

First of all, I want to thank you from the depths of my heart for the kindness that you showed to my Sarah. Every time she received a letter from you, her spirits soared. There was so little for Sarah to be happy about in these last difficult months and the memories of those smiles on my daughter's sweet face as she read and reread your notes are ones that I will always trea-sure. I am so grateful that you provided her with some relief from the agony she was forced to endure.

I try to comfort myself with the hope that Sarah is at peace now, is not suffering anymore. But I am selfish. I wish that I still had her with me, sick or not. I try not to think of what life will be like without her. I cannot fathom it.

The flowers you sent to our home were beautiful. I am press-ing them, keeping them with your letters that Sarah saved. I fear that I will be holding on to everything that was Sarah's for far too long. I cannot give her up.

That was enough, he thought as he reread what he had written. Eliza Blake would think he was a nut if he poured out any more of his aching feelings.

Samuel carefully copied his words onto the heavy bonded paper.

CHAPTER

45

As Eliza drove over the upper level of the George Washington Bridge, she noticed with concern that the dashboard oil light popped up bright yellow. By the time she got to the Seventy-second Street exit of the Henry Hudson Parkway, she was sure she heard a knocking noise coming from somewhere under the hood of Poppie's car. *Oh, brother, now this has to be fixed. Please, just let it get me back home tonight.*

The halls of the Broadcast Center were deserted as they always were on holidays, a skeletal staff manning the broadcasting ship. Eliza walked through the *Evening Headlines* studio, stopping at the Fishbowl and checking in before going up to her office. With Range taking Labor Day off, David Carter, one of the senior producers, had been bumped up to executive for the day.

"It's fairly quiet. Thank God that hurricane turned and swerved out to sea."

"What are we leading with?" asked Eliza, peering over Carter's shoulder to look at the rundown on his gray computer screen.

"Travel nightmares. Big delays at airports and backed-up highways as Americans return from their last summer weekend."

"See? I knew there was a bright side to working this weekend. We could be stuck out in all that," Eliza said with a wry smile. "I'll be upstairs if you need me."

The telephone was ringing as she switched the light on in her office. She picked up the receiver in time to hear the click of the caller hanging up. Was it Mack?

He might be back in his hotel by now. She dialed the hotel, got the front desk, and asked for Mr. McBride's room. The shrill buzzer rang a dozen times until Eliza heard a very English voice say that the party she was calling was not answering. Did she care to leave a message?

For some reason she didn't.

Instead she dialed her new telephone number. Paul answered on the third ring.

"Everything okay out there, Paul?"

"Yes. We're all fine. Janie is out in the pool with that new friend of hers."

"James?"

"Yeah. They're really getting along well. He seems like a nice little kid."

"Great, but if it gets to be too much for you and Katharine, tell Janie that playtime is over."

"It's no problem, honey. Besides, that Mrs. Feeney said she was only going to let James stay for an hour. She'll be back to pick him up in a few minutes."

"Okay, then, Paul. I'll see you later." She remembered the oil light and the funny sound. "Oh, and when Susan gets there, would you get her phone number and ask who she uses as a mechanic for her car?"

"What's wrong with the car?" Paul asked suspiciously.

"Nothing," she lied. Why give him something to worry about? "I'm just trying to get my list of suppliers together."

She looked up to see Keith Chapel standing in the doorway.

"I've got to record a track now, Paul. I'll be home right after the show."

CHAPTER

46

Bats.

Now she wanted him to look into bats.

Keith sighed deeply as he sat beside Joe Leiding in the editing booth.

"What's the matter? You don't like the way the shot looks?" asked the editor. "I'll change it."

"No, no. It's fine just the way it is," said Keith, glancing at the image on the television monitor stationed on top of the editing bay. "I was thinking of something else."

Leiding looked at his producer skeptically. They had been teamed to put these FRESHER LOOKS together and would, over the months to come, be spending hours and hours side by side in the cramped editing booth. He wasn't in the mood for Keith to be thinking of anything other than the piece they were working on right now.

Sure, the guy had a lot on his mind with his first baby coming and the pressures of this new series. But he better suck it up and stay focused.

The editor cued up the new section of narration Eliza had just recorded and inserted it into the middle of the child-care piece. Joe was pleased with the way the story was turning out, but it would be great to feel a little energy coming from Keith.

Instead the producer was doodling on the lined paper on his clipboard.

"Eliza wants to do a story on bats," Keith murmured glumly.

Joe shrugged. After two decades in this business nothing fazed him and he had long since stopped trying to figure out why some stories were produced and others weren't. He did know one thing, though. If the anchor of the broadcast wanted a story done, the story was done.

"She found one in the bedroom of her new house the other night," Keith continued.

"Nice housewarming."

"Yeah. Lucky for me the wildlife controller had to inform Eliza that bats are helpful little creatures. Eliza thinks people would be interested in knowing the real skinny on bats and that we should dispel some of the gruesome myths about them."

"What are you gonna do?" asked Joe as he loaded another beta tape into the editing deck.

"I'll be damned if I know. I guess I'll start by calling the Bronx Zoo tomorrow and asking for their bat expert. They must have one." Keith groaned tiredly, slouched down in his chair and closed his eyes. He tried to imagine Eliza in her bedroom in the middle of the night, confronting the beady-eyed bat.

He wondered what she had been wearing.

CHAPTER

47

The Friday-evening phone message had been bothering her all weekend and the first thing Paige did when she arrived at work Tuesday morning was call the security office.

"Just transfer the message down here to me, Paige. I'll take care of it," Joe Connelly instructed.

"I'm sorry I didn't save those other calls, Mr. Connelly," Paige apologized. "They always sounded harmless before this one."

"Don't worry about it. If this guy is really dangerous, he'll call again. When he does, let me know and transfer the messages to me. And, Paige, make sure you mark down what time the calls come in. Be as exact as possible. There could be dozens of other calls coming into the Broadcast Center at any time. It helps a lot to have a precise time."

Connelly had saved hundreds of calls over the years, but he girded himself to begin the painstaking procedure to determine who this latest caller was. Executing a successful phone trap was not as easy as it looked on *Law and Order*.

It was simple enough to order the trap but increasingly more difficult to pull it off. There were very few "hard wire" telephone lines anymore. Satellites, prepaid phone cards, cellular accounts, unlisted and blocked numbers, had made tracing much more complicated. The phone companies had outsmarted themselves.

The security chief gave Eliza's assistant a few minutes to transfer the call and then he played it back to hear for himself.

"I love you, Eliza. And I can't live without you."

If this had been the first call, Connelly would have waited awhile to see what developed. But Paige said she recognized the voice as a man who had been calling every day for two weeks.

Aberrant behavior escalates. The dictum was etched in Connelly's mind.

He dialed the police department and made a complaint on behalf of Eliza Blake.

The wheels were set in motion. A complaint number and detective were assigned and the Unlawful Calls Bureau, located in Boston, gave Eliza's call a case number.

The phone company would install the "equipment" on the line, setting up an enormously complicated computer program to intercept data pertaining to the calls. To do this sort of thing in a private home was relatively simple. In a place such as the KEY Broadcast Center, with its Centrex system...wow!

The Broadcast Center's central number didn't really exist. It was in limbo until the call was transferred somewhere. The operators sat at six consoles with six trunk lines each, thirty-six lines in all, spreading out to various trees throughout the company. Once a call was transferred by the operator to a specific extension, the call was not on the operator's line anymore, making it a nightmare to track.

Connelly swiveled around to his computer to start a new file on this latest threat. As he entered the information, he wished that Paige Tintle had saved those first calls, the ones that had come in during the late-night hours. Not as many calls came into the building late at night, making tracking easier.

If this guy was going to start calling during the busiest hours at the Broadcast Center, he could take months to track down.

CHAPTER

48

There was no time to put on her makeup this morning.

Eliza hugged Janie and hurried out to the chauffeured Town Car which had been waiting at the curb out front for twenty minutes already. As she strode down the driveway, two men in a red tow truck pulled up. A heavyset man with a florid face lowered himself from the high passenger's seat.

"Ms. Blake? I'm Augie Sinisi."

"Oh, Mr. Sinisi, I didn't expect you to be coming so soon. I just left the message on your answering machine last night." Eliza reached out to shake the man's hand, but he pulled back.

"My hands are kinda dirty, ma'am, excuse me. What seems to be the trouble?"

"I'm not sure, really. But the oil light is on and I heard a knocking sound when I was driving it yesterday."

Augie eyed the blue Mercedes sedan parked up near the garage. It wasn't new, he could tell that for certain. It had to be eight or nine years old at least. It was hard to be sure with Mercedes until you got up close. Their classic design didn't change much from year to year.

He had expected Eliza Blake to have a newer, snappier car.

"Not to worry, Miz B. We'll take it in and have a look. With a little luck, we'll have it back by the time you get home tonight."

"Really? That's great," said Eliza, relieved and surprised by how easy this was. If this was a sample of service in the suburbs, she was definitely going to like it here. In Manhattan, getting anything fixed was a major hassle. "Hold on a minute, Augie. I'll run in and get the keys."

Because she was already late, and had to take the time to explain to Katharine and Paul why they would be without transportation for the day, Eliza didn't bother taking the car key off her ring when she came outside again. She just handed the whole thing over to the mechanic.

CHAPTER

49

"We could have a problem here."

The message summoning Eliza to Yelena Gregory's office at eleven forty–five was waiting for her when she arrived at work. Now Eliza, along with Range and Joe Connelly sat in the news–division president's large office. Joe Connelly, with his jacket off and shirtsleeves rolled up, was doing all the talking.

"Actually two problems."

The three listened as Connelly described the series of letters and now the phone calls that he thought should be taken seriously.

"Could they be from the same person?" asked Range.

"Possibly, but I don't think so. The letters are vicious and the phone calls, well, we'll have to see what develops with the phone calls. So far, I only have a recording of one of them, but from what Eliza's assistant tells me, this man's tone has been almost reverential when he's called before. The tone of this latest call was more intense than the others. I think we are dealing with two separate characters."

"What's being done about this?" Yelena asked brusquely.

"A phone trap is being set up."

"How long will that take?"

"It's hard to say. The more the guy calls, the better the chances are for catching him." Connelly paused and looked at Eliza. "Of course, we hope he doesn't call again."

"And what about the letters?" Yelena snapped.

"I'm sending them to the FBI, to their stylistics department at

Quantico. But it may take a long time to get something back. I sent some letters to them six weeks ago that someone in the entertainment division was getting and I still haven't heard anything on them."

"They check for fingerprints, of course," said Range.

Connelly nodded. "But don't bet the bank on prints. The guy could be wearing gloves when he writes and the envelope gets handled many times before it gets to us."

There was silence in the room. The three newspeople took it for granted that they could get pictures from the moon or from the top of Mount Everest. They were unabashed picking up their telephones and being put through to the White House. The idea that they had to sit and wait for others to do their jobs, that they had no power over this situation, didn't sit well with them.

"What should I be doing?" asked Eliza quietly, trying to keep the fear out of her voice. She knew the others were watching for her reaction. She wouldn't whimper or cry. Weakness didn't become an anchorwoman. *Take a deep breath and get a grip.* Joe Connelly had a solid reputation. She had no choice but to let him do his job. She just prayed he would do it quickly.

Over the years Eliza had reported many stories about fans—both male and female—who were obsessed with celebrities. In fact, stalking seemed to come with the territory of being a public figure. Most celebrity-stalkers believed there was a special love relationship between themselves and the celebrities they hounded. Many cases ended with the stalkers being caught and tried and sent off to prison or psychiatric hospitals. At this moment Eliza resolutely pushed from her mind the other, more tragic, violent outcomes. It wouldn't serve her well to go there now. She had to keep her wits about her.

"The key word here is 'control,' Eliza," she heard Joe saying. "It's the common element in all these types of cases. These guys lack self-esteem. They can't control other things, but they think they can control you. They want to freak you out."

"They're doing a pretty good job." Eliza managed a weak smile.

"Look, I don't want to scare you"—Connelly kept his voice even—"but I don't want to lessen the impact of what I'm telling you. Trust your instincts. If you feel something is wrong, it probably is. You've got to watch yourself. Be aware of everything around you."

CHAPTER

50

Abigail finished screening the approved first FRESHER LOOK piece, which Keith Chapel had delivered to her office. Now she sat down to the task of coming up with the twenty-second script for the promotion that would air after the broadcast this evening, teasing the audience to watch tomorrow's show.

> Millions of Americans leave their children in the care of others as they go out to make a living each day. But how do you choose the people you entrust with those you hold most precious? How can you be sure that your child is safe? Eliza Blake will share with you what she's learned on A FRESHER LOOK. Tomorrow on the *KEY Evening Headlines.*

Abigail read what she had written. Anyone who had heard or read about Eliza's experience this summer surely would want to tune in. Abigail hoped that her copy was catchy enough to pull in the others. Even more, she hoped that Eliza would be pleased.

CHAPTER

5 1

"Uh-oh. What's wrong?"

Doris stood with her back to the lighted mirrored wall as Eliza took a seat in the makeup chair and peeled back the orange wrapper of a jumbo Butterfinger.

"What could be wrong?" Eliza shrugged. "There are at least two maniacs out there obsessed with me and the one person in the world I really *want* to be obsessed with me is three thousand miles away and hasn't called me. I'm the luckiest woman in the world." She bit off a big chunk of the chocolate candy bar. "I thought I'd just really make the perfect picture complete by downing a couple hundred extra calories."

"Whoa, girl. Back up. What do you mean there are two maniacs out there?"

Eliza recounted the morning meeting as Doris nervously lit up a Marlboro Ultra Light.

"You're not supposed to smoke in here," Eliza said automatically, though she couldn't have cared less. The fact was she wanted a cigarette herself.

Doris ignored her.

"Well, what are you supposed to do?"

"I'm supposed to be careful."

"That's it?"

"Mm–hmm. Watch myself and trust my instincts. If I feel something is wrong, it probably is."

"Oh, baby." Doris threw her leopard-print long-sleeved T-shirted arms around her friend. "And Mack hasn't called either? I can't believe it. Maybe he's out on some story."

"He's not. I checked the foreign insights. He's listed as being in the London bureau today."

Doris wanted to spit out, *Bastard,* but she didn't. She also decided not to tell Eliza that Abigail Snow had come into the makeup room today, sniffing around and bringing up the subject of Eliza. She had heard Eliza had moved out of the city. Did Doris know where she was living? Was Eliza still involved with Mack McBride? She even asked exactly what Doris used to make Eliza's eyes look the way they did on air. Doris had thought it strange, since she had never seen Abigail wear any makeup.

She had heard through the grapevine that Abigail was gay. And if Doris was to trust *her* instincts, she would say that Abigail had a thing for Eliza.

But that was the last thing that Eliza needed to hear or worry about now.

CHAPTER

52

Uncharacteristically for an English hotel, the room was too hot. Mack threw off the covers and lay on the bed, eyes wide open, staring up in the darkness. It was just after midnight and, exhausted by the last several nights of fitful sleep, he was desperate to get some rest.

His conscience wouldn't allow it.

He knew that the *Evening Headlines* had just finished airing in New

York, but he couldn't bring himself to call Eliza. Yet when he imagined how puzzled and hurt she must feel at his withdrawal, he felt guiltier still. She hadn't done anything wrong. She didn't deserve such treatment.

Mack turned over and pushed his face deep into his pillow. He still couldn't believe he had done it. How could he be so stupid? More importantly, how could he have so quickly betrayed the woman he professed to love?

He did love Eliza. Of that he was certain. He had such hopes for their future together. His working in London while she was in New York wasn't going to be the end of things between them. While it was difficult to manage, many couples were able to sustain a commuter relationship.

If both were true to each another.

Now the question was, Should he tell her that he had been unfaithful?

He imagined what that would be like and groaned into his pillow. Angrily pushing himself up from the bed, he walked to the window and pulled back the blackout curtain. Hyde Park was spread out tranquilly beneath him, illuminated by soft lamplight.

It was a beautiful park—the largest, though probably the least formal of London's royal parks. A picturesque place to stroll along country paths, hold hands while sitting on a cast-iron bench, picnic on the lawn, rent a boat on the Serpentine. A place Eliza would love.

You fool!

That fact was established. Now, what was he going to do about it?

He could tell her, he supposed, as he dropped the curtain and returned to the bed. That would be honest, but he knew full well that nothing would ever be the same again. And who did the confession really serve? He might feel better for unburdening himself; Eliza, on the other hand, would be terribly wounded.

Of course, there was a good chance that Eliza would find out on her own. In this business, sooner or later, everyone seemed to know who had slept with whom. He didn't want her to hear about it through the grapevine. It would crush her and she had already been through too much.

But there was no way he was going to tell her on the phone. This was something that had to be talked about face-to-face. Maybe he could explain that he had been drunk, that he had been feeling miserable about the prospect of living every day without her near him for what would probably be at least the next two or three years— that he was despondent about the real chances of their relationship making it in this situation.

A shrill ring blared from the phone on the bedside table. For once in his journalistic life, he wished it would be the night desk editor calling to tell him to get out of bed, take a car out to Heathrow and fly to some godforsaken corner of the world, somewhere he would be out of pocket for a while. Work was the great way to avoid personal problems.

"Hello?"

"Hi."

"Eliza! How are you, honey? I was just lying here thinking about you."

"I bet you were."

He could sense the distance in her voice. Why shouldn't she be skeptical?

"How's Janie?"

"She's doing pretty well, actually. She starts at her new school tomorrow and she's already made friends with a little boy who lives across the street."

"She's a great kid. I miss her. And I miss her mommy."

"You do, huh? The phone hasn't exactly been ringing off the hook, Mack. What's going on?"

"Come on, Eliza. You know how it is. Starting at a new place, looking for somewhere to live...."

"Sure, I know how it is, Mack. All the more reason I'd think you'd want to touch base with the person you love for comfort or to bounce things off of. That's how I would feel, anyway."

Mack wanted to tell her that he had had to force himself to keep from calling her at least a hundred times in the past days. But he hadn't wanted to prattle about what was going on in London, acting as if his one–night stand hadn't happened. It was easier to avoid the situation by not picking up the phone.

"I'm sorry, Eliza."

There was silence on the overseas line.

"Eliza? Are you all right, sweetheart?"

"No. I'm not all right." Her voice cracked. "I don't understand what's going on with us and on top of that, security here is concerned that there are a couple of nuts out there who are obsessed with me. And, of course, after the nightmare with Mrs. Twomey, I automatically worry that someone will try to get to Janie."

"What do you mean, 'a couple of nuts'?" he asked sharply.

Eliza described the meeting with Joe Connelly in Yelena's office that morning.

Mack tried to sound calm. "Try not to worry too much, honey. I'm sure security is on top of it. They're used to dealing with situations like these."

Eliza had wanted a different reaction. She had been hoping that Mack would say he'd be on the next plane to New York. She wouldn't have accepted the suggestion, of course. She was a big girl and nothing bad had really happened. But she had wanted him to offer.

So much for her knight in shining armor.

CHAPTER

53

After snapping off the television with his remote control, Jerry Walinski reached for the phone on his bedside table and pushed in the numbers he knew by heart.

"Good evening—KEY."

"Eliza Blake's office, please."

"They've left for the day, sir. But I can connect you and you may leave a message."

"Fine. Thank you."

All through his massage tonight he had been thinking of making this call. He knew Eliza wouldn't be there this late and the fact was he really didn't want to get her on the phone. The thought of speaking with her directly made him tense. What had he been thinking when he had called right after the show on Friday? Lori's leaving for a long weekend had left him without his usual rubdown and he hadn't been able to control himself.

What if he had actually reached Eliza? He wasn't ready to speak to her yet. Better to leave his message and let her think about it. Let her long for him, as he longed for her.

While Jerry listened to the phone ringing to Eliza's office, he reached out and stroked the top of Drake's black snout as the German shepherd laid his head upon his master's bed. The dog's ears curled back as he listened to his owner's voice.

"I'll be coming to New York as soon as I can, Eliza," Jerry said, in the huskiest voice he could manage. "I want you and I know you'll want me. I've dreamed about you long enough. Soon it will be time for the real thing. I promise, darling, we'll be together for always. Because if I can't have you, no one will."

Drake barked in agitation as Jerry hung up the phone and wiped away the saliva that dripped from the corner of his mouth.

CHAPTER

54

The first day of school dawned clear and sunny. The three adults in the brick colonial on Saddle Ridge Road were up well before their young student. KayKay busied herself in the kitchen, packing the plastic Curious George lunchbox with pretzels and a juice box for snack time. Eliza showered, dressed quickly and searched around for the camera to record Janie's kindergarten debut. Poppie went out to get bagels, announcing when he returned that the newly tuned-up car was running like a top.

Eliza went in to wake Janie. Leaning down, she kissed her daughter's soft brow. The big blue eyes opened slowly and looked up sleepily.

"Time to get up, sweetheart. We have to get ready for school."

Janie said nothing, but she bolted upright, throwing her arms around her mother's neck and holding on tight.

"What's wrong, angel?"

"I'm scared, Mommy."

"It's natural to be a little worried, Janie," Eliza said softly, stroking Janie's sweet-smelling hair. "Starting something new is exciting, but it can also be a little scary. But I know you are going to like school.

The teacher is going to be very nice and you already have a friend. James will be there with you."

"How do you know the teacher is nice?"

"Because that's what kindergarten teachers are supposed to be. That's their job. And if they don't do their jobs, they get fired," she said, trying to reassure her child.

Janie pulled back and looked with wide eyes at her mother. "They get burned up?"

"No, sweetheart," Eliza tried not to laugh. "That's just an expression. To 'get fired' means that the boss tells you that you can't work there anymore. Come on now, get up. KayKay has breakfast all ready."

But Janie barely touched her scrambled eggs and took only a bite or two of her buttered bagel as she sat at the kitchen table. Her grandmother sliced up another bagel and stashed it into the lunchbox, too, as Eliza took Janie upstairs again to dress. Fifteen minutes later, face washed, teeth brushed, hair combed and wearing a pressed denim jumper and her new school shoes, Janie stood patiently on the front stoop to have her picture taken, alone, then with her mother, then with her grandparents.

As she squinted into the viewfinder, Eliza thought of John and wished he were here to see their child go off to school, wished he were able to put his arm around Janie and pose with her on her big day. How much he would have loved this child! He had been so terribly cheated by never knowing her. And Janie, the child who had her father's smile, lived on, without ever experiencing the love her daddy would have showered on her.

It had been over five years now since John's death and Eliza was proud that she had survived losing him, bearing their baby without him, raising their daughter by herself. The tearing anguish had ever so slowly subsided over the years, but it was at times like this, life-event moments that cried out to be shared, that the pain resurfaced.

She had gradually allowed herself to believe in love again with Mack, thought perhaps they would have a life together. Maybe it wasn't over yet, but something was definitely wrong.

"Mommy?"

Janie's worried face responded to the expression on her mother's. *Snap out of it!*

"Come on, kiddo." Eliza smiled brightly. "We've got to get you to school and Mommy's got to get to work."

On the drive into the city, Eliza called Rhode Island.

"Hi, Mom. It's me."

"Hello, dear. How's everything?"

"I just dropped Janie off for her first day of school."

"How is she?"

"Scared, but brave."

"That's my girl. I can't believe she's starting school already. It seems like she was just born."

"I know."

"Everything coming along with the house?"

"We're getting settled. It'll take awhile to get things the way I want them, though."

"How's work?"

"Okay." Eliza considered mentioning the calls and letters but decided not to tell her mother about them. She knew her mother's solution would be for her to quit the job. Anytime Eliza was forced to work late hours or cover potentially dangerous stories, her mother always lectured her and suggested that she consider getting out of the business. Yet she thoroughly enjoyed it when her friends talked about seeing her daughter on TV. If her mother knew Eliza was being threatened, she would be apoplectic.

"Have you heard from Mack? How's he doing?"

"He's doing fine, Mom. He's doing fine," she lied.

"I liked it when you came up with him this summer, Eliza. He's such a nice boy."

"Mom, he's not a boy. He's a man." Eliza wanted to get off the phone now. "I'll send the pictures I took of Janie this morning as soon as I get them developed."

"That would be great, dear."

"Is Dad there?"

"No, he's out golfing. He loves those clubs you gave him."

"Good. Tell him I said hello."

"I will, honey."

" 'Bye, Mom."

Eliza realized she had called looking for a little maternal comfort. She never learned. It was better to comfort yourself.

Her relationship with her parents was complicated and Eliza had spent many hours trying to unravel it in therapy with Dr. Karas. The bottom line: her parents had done the best they could as they raised her while, at the same time, they were struggling with their own problems. In fact, Eliza realized that, in some ways, she had benefited from the chaos of her early years. Her mother's bouts of mental illness and her father's anger and frustration over the situation had spurred Eliza to do well in school and, generally, to try and give them nothing more to worry about, a pattern that continued to this day.

She had become an achiever. An achiever who now sat in the back of her chauffeured car on the way to her powerful job. An achiever whose face was known to millions.

CHAPTER

55

The morning dragged on slowly in the Bowater Building on London's Knightsbridge Road. Mack waited for the afternoon so he could reach Joe Connelly in New York. He wanted to hear for himself what the security director was doing to ensure Eliza's safety.

As Mack was about to leave the bureau for lunch, Marcy McGinnis summoned the correspondent to her office.

"Things are heating up in the Middle East again, Mack. We want you to go to Tel Aviv."

"When?"

"Right away. Go back to the hotel and pack."

Mack knew better than to ask his bureau chief how long he would be away. Who knew how things would develop in that chaotic part of the world? He might be gone for only a few days if things seemed to settle down and the news could be covered by the regular staff stationed there. But if it really blew up, he could be gone for weeks or more.

He turned to leave McGinnis's office, wondering what she thought of his fling with her assistant. She undoubtedly didn't approve, but Marcy had been with KEY for many years and had seen this sort of thing before. And as he heard her answering a call from Yelena Gregory in New York, he was certain his indiscretion was the last thing on Marcy's mind right now. The Middle East situation was the nightmare that never ended and Marcy had to move the news troops into positions where their lives could be in danger.

Mack briefly thought about being caught in a Palestinian–Israeli skirmish. That might be a relief. When you started thinking like that, you knew things were bad.

He went to his room at the Mandarin Oriental and pulled clothes from the dresser drawers, packed his dob kit and folded the bullet-proof safari-style vest he had grabbed at the bureau. He glanced at the clock and made a final call before he left for the airport.

CHAPTER

56

The good news was they had another call to trace.

The bad news was there was another call.

Connelly listened again to last night's message, which Paige had transferred down to his office.

"...If I can't have you, no one will."

He recorded the message and made an entry on his computer's ABERRANT BEHAVIOR file.

Who was this guy, and where was he? Those were the questions Mack McBride had just asked him, the same questions Connelly was asking himself.

Connelly tried to imagine what the caller might do next. He hoped it would just be another phone call. He dreaded the thought of this nut coming to the Broadcast Center in person.

Despite the scanned electronic ID cards necessary to enter, and security guards blocking the way, the truth was that someone could get into the Broadcast Center if he was really determined to—by a simple act of subterfuge where the system was weak. A Chinese-food deliveryman, a contractor with a temporary identification card, someone mingling with a large group... There were so many ways you could just slip in with the others.

It was Connelly's worst nightmare because, once inside, anyone could freely roam the halls, concealing whatever weapon they might be carrying.

CHAPTER

57

She didn't want to tell Eliza before she went on air, especially with the first FRESHER LOOK piece airing tonight. In fact, she didn't want to tell her at all.

As she applied eyeliner and mascara, Doris listened to Eliza recount dropping Janie off at kindergarten that morning, cooing at appropriate junctures in the story. It wasn't hard, since Doris was so fond of the child.

"You talked to her when she got home, of course."

Closing her eyes, Eliza smiled as Doris shadowed her lids.

"Mmm. You'd never know it was the same child who had been clinging to me a few hours before. She was excited and happy and said that Mrs. Prescott, her teacher, was so nice."

"Thank God."

"You said it. What a relief! That's a huge load off my mind."

One load off, another to come, thought Doris. But she didn't have the heart then to tell Eliza what she had heard this afternoon when the medical correspondent had come in to be made up for the standup for her piece.

Gossip spread like a raging virus.

Eliza looked radiant when Doris was through with her paint and brushes. She followed Eliza down the hallway to the studio and watched as the anchor took her seat. Doris positioned herself in her customary spot on the side of the set, ready to jump in at commercial breaks to lightly powder Eliza's nose or forehead if they became shiny in the bright lights.

The broadcast went smoothly, leading with the breaking developments in the Middle East, moving to stories on the Republican and Democratic Presidential candidates, and closing with Eliza's FRESHER LOOK. As she watched the child-care story on the monitor, Doris was glad, for once, that she didn't have kids. She would be a nervous wreck with so many sickos out there.

When the show was over, Doris waited outside the Fishbowl while Eliza went in to conduct the postmortem with Range and the other producers. She could tell by the cheerful expressions behind the glass wall that everyone was pleased and she wished more than anything that she didn't have to be the one to throw ice water on Eliza's great day. But it would be better for Eliza to hear about Mack from her friend than from someone else who would feign concern and sympathy while inwardly enjoying Eliza's reaction.

Ten minutes later, in the privacy of the anchorwoman's office, Doris broke the sordid news while she gently removed the heavy television makeup from Eliza's stunned face.

CHAPTER

58

On her way home from work, Abigail stopped at Victoria's Secret, heading directly to the back of the store. She knew exactly what she wanted. She picked up five of the plain black cotton underpants she always bought there.

Then it was fantasy time.

She strolled around the store, stopping to caress a violet lace teddy with a low décolletage. Appreciatively she rubbed her fingers across zebra-print satin boxer pajamas. Abigail held up a sexy slip with slim straps that crossed in the back and imagined. Imagined what Eliza would look like wearing the lingerie.

A girl could dream, couldn't she?

But making the dream a reality, that was the tricky part.

On impulse Abigail took the silk slip up to the cash register and placed it carefully on the counter along with the underpants. The saleswoman wrapped the pants in pink tissue paper and began to do the same with the slip.

"Could you put that in a box, please?" asked Abigail. "It's a gift."

Back home in her apartment, Abigail carefully took the mauve silk slip from the box. It was the sort of thing Eliza would wear, Abigail was certain of it. She thought back to her shopping expeditions with Linda Anderson. Linda had loved this sort of feminine lingerie, while Abigail had always gone for basic undergarments and flannel pajamas.

Eliza reminded Abigail so much of Linda Anderson.

CHAPTER

59

Paige almost wept as she read the letter from Samuel Morton that had arrived in the morning mail and she hesitated before giving it to Eliza. Her boss's eyes had been red-rimmed when she came in and she had—unusual for her—closed the door behind her when she went into her office an hour ago.

Something had happened and Paige knew it wasn't good.

Tentatively she knocked on Eliza's door.

"Come in, Paige."

Eliza sat with her back to the door, staring down at the busy newsroom.

"I thought you'd want to see this letter from Sarah's father." Paige offered the note to Eliza.

"Sarah?" There was a look of puzzlement on Eliza's face.

"Sarah Morton."

"Oh, of course. I'm sorry, Paige. I'm just not with it today."

She took the paper from her assistant and began to read it as Paige left the room. Slowly she digested Samuel Morton's anguished words—words written from the deepest grief imaginable. Here was a man who felt even worse than she did today.

Because after it was all said and done, no matter what happened in her career, no matter how disappointing her love life was, no matter how deeply she was betrayed, Eliza had Janie.

Samuel Morton had lost his child.

How would he go on?

As long as she had Janie, Eliza knew she could. She had to.

CHAPTER

60

"Gee, Ms. Blake, I'd really like to accommodate you, I really would. But the soonest we can get out there to install the system will be the week after next."

Eliza was trying in vain to get the security-alarm company to get to her house sooner, but there was a backlog of orders that waited in front of hers. Eliza would just have to get in line.

She had known the house didn't have a security system when she bought it and it hadn't much concerned her. It was one of those things she would get around to doing, without particular urgency. That, and getting the locks on the doors changed.

But the threatening letters and phone calls at work had left her usual confidence shaken. Mack's betrayal had left her hurt and vulnerable. And Samuel Morton's loss highlighted in the extreme the imperative of ensuring that her own child was safe and secure.

"Fine. A week from Monday, then," she agreed grudgingly, marking the date in her daybook.

CHAPTER

61

Eliza was relieved when the weekend finally came. Saturday morning she slept later than usual, waking to the soft kiss that Janie planted on her cheek.

"Hi, my sweetheart," she smiled, holding open the covers to invite the child inside.

Janie climbed into the bed and mother and daughter snuggled together.

"What are we going to do today, Mommy?"

"Well, I thought we should go and pick out a new car. KayKay and Poppie will be going back to their apartment and we need to have our own car. Plus Mrs. Garcia is coming and she'll be needing the car, too."

Janie played with a strand of Eliza's hair, twisting it in her small fingers. "I don't want Mrs. Garcia. I want KayKay and Poppie."

"You'll still have KayKay and Poppie, honey. We'll see them all the time. They just won't be here every single day. Mrs. Garcia will take care of you. She's very nice and I know you are going to like her."

"I liked Mrs. Twomey."

Eliza made a concerted effort not to change the expression on her face as the child peered into it.

"I liked Mrs. Twomey, too, Janie. But Mrs. Twomey is sick and she can't take care of you anymore."

"But I thought Mrs. Twomey loved me."

"She did, honey."

"But she never calls me and she didn't send me a birthday card." There was puzzlement and hurt on Janie's face.

Eliza pushed the soft hair back from the child's brow and stroked the top of her head. "She can't, Janie. Mrs. Twomey has problems that she has to work out and she has to concentrate all her efforts on those."

"Will I ever see her again?"

"I don't know, Janie."

Please, God, I certainly hope not. That would be all they needed.

"Come on. Let's get up and get dressed," she said, trying to divert her daughter. "Want to go out for breakfast?"

"Pancakes?" Janie's eyes widened.

"Great idea. Go see if KayKay and Poppie want to come with us."

Janie hopped from the bed and scurried down the hallway while Eliza rose and went to the bathroom to shower. Twenty minutes later, wearing no makeup and dressed in jeans, a red T-shirt and soft moccasins, Eliza was putting her wallet and checkbook into a casual shoulder bag when the doorbell rang.

Larson Richards was standing at the front door, a tiny, golden puppy cradled in his arms. The moment Eliza saw him, she instantly resented him for what she anticipated he was about to do. *How dare he?*

And how could she say no to the little girl who jumped up and down in excitement as she took the soft little yellow Lab into her arms?

CHAPTER

62

Early Sunday morning, a shiny white Volvo station wagon stood parked in Eliza's driveway and Janie giggled with delight as she romped with her new puppy on the front lawn's dewy grass. Eliza had been up three times during the night to comfort the whimpering puppy, the last time at five A.M. Janie was up at six, ready to play. For the next several hours Eliza had to repeatedly rein in the child from running over to the Feeneys' to show James the cuddly pet she had christened Daisy.

At ten o'clock James appeared outside with his mother.

"Thank goodness," called Eliza as she beckoned to them to cross the street. "We've been waiting for you. I don't know how much longer I could have held Janie back."

"My, you're ambitious, aren't you?" Susan whispered as they stood watching the kids encouraging the dog.

Eliza sighed tiredly. "I could kill that Larson Richards. He just showed up with the dog for Janie."

"You're kidding."

"No. This was the last thing I was planning on. Our new house-keeper is starting tomorrow. Won't she be absolutely thrilled! Now Mrs. Garcia can add paper-training a puppy to her duties."

Susan shook her head. "Larson had some nerve, bringing a dog over without checking with you first."

Not knowing how Susan felt about Larson, Eliza hesitated before revealing her feelings about the man.

"Maybe he was just trying to be nice."

Susan's mouth turned down at the corner. "Larson doesn't do anything just to be nice. He always has an ulterior motive. In this case, I'd bet he wanted to get close to you."

"Well, he failed, miserably."

Janie had picked up the puppy and was walking with James toward the backyard. "We're going to take Daisy up into the treehouse, Mommy," she called over her shoulder.

"Okay, but be careful and watch out for Daisy. Don't let her fall out." Eliza turned back to Susan. "What do you mean, Larson always has an ulterior motive?"

Susan looked a bit uncomfortable. "Maybe I shouldn't be saying this, but when we moved in here and the Richardses were so kind to us, Larson approached my husband with a so-called terrific investment opportunity. He was buying up all the local pizza parlors and uniting them under one umbrella which he planned on selling to a national company. He promised we would at least double our money within a year. Well, it's three years later, and Larson has come back to us a dozen times for more. We were dumb enough to throw in additional money the first few times. After that, even though we loved the Richardses, we weren't going to throw in another dime with their son."

"I wonder if he'll be hitting me up to invest," Eliza said.

"You can count on it. But take my advice, no matter how persuasive Larson is, *don't*. At the end, even his parents wouldn't give him any more money for his cockamamie company."

CHAPTER

63

Eliza was arranging silver-framed family pictures on the round Henredon table in the living room when the telephone rang. A week ago she would have been delighted to hear Mack's voice coming from overseas on a leisurely Sunday afternoon. Today her tone was icy as she answered his call.

"How's it going over there?" she asked perfunctorily.

"It's quiet now. But you always have the feeling that things could blow at any time."

"Be careful."

To Mack, her voice sounded detached, uninterested. She was holding back. She knew.

"Anything new on the threats?"

"Security is on top of it," she answered shortly.

"I don't want anything to happen to you, Eliza. You mean too much to me."

"Sure, Mack. I mean so much to you. Don't bother with the charade. I heard all about your little tryst."

What should he say? This was the conversation he had been dreading. Girding himself, he plunged ahead.

"I wanted to tell you, Eliza. I wanted to tell you myself. I didn't want you to hear from someone else."

"Well, I did. It really felt great, too. I especially like the fact that so many of the people I have to work with every day know about it as well. Thanks so much."

"I'm sorry, Eliza. I really am. I never wanted to hurt you."

"That's nice. That makes me feel a lot better."

There was a pause on the line that had nothing to do with the long–distance transmission delay.

"I guess it would sound pretty lame if I said that it didn't mean anything. I was drunk and down and it just happened."

"Spare me the pretty details, Mack. Please."

"Look, honey, this isn't something that we can work out over the telephone. I have to see you. We have to talk in person. We have too much going for us to let my stupid screwup ruin everything."

"Number one, don't call me 'honey.' Number two, this is a bit more than a 'stupid screwup.' And number three, it doesn't look like we're going to get the chance anytime soon to talk face-to-face. And to tell you the truth, Mack, that's just fine with me."

With that, she hung up on him and forced herself not to cry.

CHAPTER

64

Augie was at the service station by six A.M. He had made a clean getaway this morning, rising well before Helene. That wasn't hard to do. His wife would sleep late and then get started with her busy day of going to the health club, lunching with friends, shopping and getting her nails done. When he got home tonight, she would complain about how tired she was, too tired to cook. They would have to go out for dinner or order something in.

Why had he hooked up with Helene? He knew the answer as he thought about her flowing blonde hair, the tight–fitting, cleavage-revealing sweaters she wore, the way her perfect backside filled out her designer jeans. It was sex, pure and simple. That was the reason he had married her.

A double bell rang as a car ran over the black rubber tubing in front of the gas pumps. Augie zipped up his tight overalls against the cool September morning as he went out to fill the customer's tank. He stood with his hand on the gas pump nozzle and admitted to himself that he knew the reason Helene had married him.

Money.

He was no Adonis, that was for sure. He wasn't good–looking and he was overweight. His career wasn't glamorous and he wasn't a great intellect. Although with Helene that certainly didn't matter. She wasn't exactly the sharpest knife in the drawer.

Augie swiped the credit card through the scanner and handed it back through the opened window to the customer.

Okay, he thought. They had made their deal. Many couples did. He had been keeping up his side of things. They had a damned big house filled with all the gaudy crap Helene had picked out. He hadn't realized how trashy the stuff was until he started robbing other houses. In a funny way, stealing had educated him, as he noticed the antiques and tasteful furnishings and art that decorated the homes in the exclusive neighborhoods in which his customers lived.

Augie was willing to live with things as they were with Helene as long as she kept her side of their bargain. He'd be damned if she was going to withhold from him. Yet that's what she had been doing over the last few months.

She always had an excuse. She had a headache or she was too tired. He was never home and she was feeling lonely and neglected. Of course there was always something new she wanted. Another pair of earrings, a new leather jacket, or a trip to a spa with her girlfriends. If Augie came through with the goodies, Helene would come through with hers.

But things were tight right now. He couldn't afford to pay for everything she wanted. He didn't dare give her any of the jewelry he stole. Someone might recognize it as Helene paraded around town. And even as he fenced the loot he got from his raids, he knew where the money had to go.

He was in up to his eyeballs in that damned Larson Richards's cheesy pizza deal. Augie had so much money invested now, that every time Richards came back with his promises that they were "almost there," or that they just needed "a little more" to get to the closing, Augie felt he had to keep kicking in. If the pizza deal failed, Augie would lose everything.

Why had he ever let that guy talk him into it in the first place?

Augie knew the answer to that one, too. He was greedy. Greedy and insecure. When Larson Richards had tooled into the station in his big black $80,000 Mercedes, wearing his expensive suit and Italian shoes, Augie had been flattered that Richards had thought enough of him to let him in on the deal. When people saw you in mechanic's workclothes with grease under your fingernails, they didn't exactly fawn all over you.

Larson had buttered him up, all right, treated Augie like an equal. And Augie had fallen for it.

CHAPTER

65

If Mrs. Garcia was upset by the puppy and the newspaper spread across the kitchen floor, she had the good grace not to show it when she showed up for her first day of work. She knelt right down to pet the little dog as Janie, still in her pajamas, hung back in the doorway and watched. KayKay and Paul had gone back to Manhattan last night amid clinging and tears from their granddaughter.

"I'm sorry, Mrs. Garcia. I didn't know we were going to have Daisy when I hired you," Eliza apologized.

"Oh no, señora. I like dogs. This is a sweet little one." She held her finger out and Daisy licked it with her tiny, warm pink tongue.

"Thanks for being such a good sport," Eliza said. "Let's hope it doesn't take too much time to get Daisy trained."

"I think Daisy will be very fast. What do you think, Janie *preciosa?*"

Janie didn't answer, hugging her stuffed monkey to her chest.

Both adults tried to ignore the child's silence. Eliza showed Mrs. Garcia where the car keys were kept on a hook over the small, built-in desk in the corner of the kitchen. "A driver takes me to and from work every day. So the car is all yours for driving Janie and doing whatever errands you have to do." She opened the door to the garage and Mrs. Garcia gazed at the station wagon.

"It looks brand-new."

"It is. We bought if off the lot this weekend." Seeing the expression on Mrs. Garcia's face, Eliza added, "Don't be concerned about that. It's just a car that happens to be new. I'm not worried about you driving it at all. The only thing I care about is your and Janie's safety."

"Of course, señora." But the housekeeper didn't look convinced.

Eliza turned to her daughter who had quietly followed behind them. "Janie, why don't you show Mrs. Garcia where your room is?" Eliza suggested brightly.

The child didn't look too enthusiastic about the idea, but she nodded solemnly and led the way upstairs. Eliza made the conscious decision to remain behind. The two of them had to work it out.

Brainstorming with Keith about possibilities for FRESHER LOOK pieces, Eliza had proposed that they do one on "commuter relationships." Statistics showed that they were on the rise, as more and more dual-career couples followed professional advancement opportunities in different cities.

Eliza had suggested that Keith try to find a couple that was doing a United States-to-Great Britain commute, hoping that shooting it would entail her making a trip to London and provide a chance to see Mack. Unfortunately, her producer had found exactly what she had asked for.

Keith held a manila folder open on his lap as he sat in a chair across the desk from Eliza, enthusiastically explaining the elements he had lined up.

"She'd just been promoted to a vice president's slot at a Madison Avenue advertising firm, when his investment bank offered him the chance to head up their London office. They are alternating flying back and forth between cities every other weekend. They're willing to be interviewed and let us shoot them at their workplaces and homes. We could even go along for the plane ride and shoot her the next time she flies to London."

Keith looked at Eliza with an expectant smile upon his face. This was just what she had asked for and he wanted Eliza to be enthusiastic.

Her dull expression told him otherwise.

"What's wrong?"

Eliza shifted uncomfortably in her chair. "I'm sorry, Keith. I don't want to do this story anymore. Not a London-to-New York version anyway."

He felt like asking Eliza why the change of heart, but he didn't dare. If the *Evening Headlines* anchor didn't want to do a piece a certain way, the piece wasn't done that way. End of story.

Keith tried to keep any trace of anger or disappointment from his face. He had spent hours and hours trying to get this story lined up and now she didn't want to do it. He felt he was owed an explanation, but Eliza would have to offer it; he couldn't demand it.

"I see," he said. "Well, should I look for another couple?"

Eliza shrugged. "Yeah, I suppose so. See if you can find a couple who are commuting within the United States. I'd still be up for that. I want to avoid going out of town as much as possible right now. See if you can find a pair who are commuting along the Eastern seaboard, will you?"

Keith nodded as he made a notation in his folder.

"Are we all set with *this* week's FRESHER LOOK?" Eliza asked.

He handed her a piece of paper across the desk. "Here's the script. Range has already looked at it and likes it. See what you think. If you're satisfied, we can track it this morning and start cutting right away."

Keith rose to leave. As he got to the door, Eliza called out.

"Thanks, Keith. I appreciate all the work you must have done setting up that story. I'm sorry I nixed it."

"You're welcome, and don't worry about it. It's no big deal."

It was only later, at lunchtime, as he sat with two other producers who told him the latest gossip, that Keith understood why the story he had worked so hard on had been killed.

Mack McBride was a fool.

How appropriate that this week's FRESHER LOOK was on depression. Eliza carefully read the script Keith had written. He had done a good job on it and there was nothing of substance that needed to be changed. Eliza amended only a few words here and there to reflect her speaking style.

She laid her head back in her chair and her hand absentmindedly played with the antique charm that dangled from the gold bracelet on her left wrist. She thought about finding another psychiatrist. She so wished that Dr. Karas was still alive. He had seen her through her depression after John died and Janie was born. He had accompanied her through the worst of it when she needed to be hospitalized.

Eliza had learned from that painful experience and she was determined not to let herself slide again. If she felt she really needed to go for help, she would. But she dreaded having to find another doctor she could trust—and with whom she would feel comfortable. It wasn't an easy combination to come by.

It was normal to be sad over the death of a relationship, she rationalized to herself. The end of things with Mack hurt, deeply. But she wanted to see if she could tough it out herself. Her life was very full, and she would have no problem keeping busy. Throwing herself into work and Janie would get her through.

The intercom buzzer rang.

"Yes, Paige?"

"Mr. Connelly is on line two."

"Okay. Thanks."

She took a deep breath before pushing in the button on the phone panel.

"Hi, Joe. Why do I have the feeling you're not calling with good news?"

"I wish I were, Eliza."

"What is it this time?"

"Another letter."

Eliza felt her chest tighten.

"From the same guy?"

"Yeah. It's our friend Meat."

"Great. And what's he selling now?"

"Want me to read it to you?"

Protect yourself, the inner voice warned.

"No thanks, Joe. Just give me the highlights."

"He wants you to get him a job at KEY News so he can be near you and give you some pointers on how a lady should conduct herself."

Eliza laughed in spite of herself.

"Did he send in a résumé?"

Connelly didn't answer.

"Okay, Joe. I know this is no joke," Eliza said, turning serious.

"It really isn't, Eliza. I don't like the fact that he is suggesting that he come to KEY. I don't like it at all."

When her driver dropped her off at the curb in front of her house that evening, Eliza braced herself for what she would find inside. Eliza dreaded a scene of Janie running up to her and throwing her arms around her, crying that she didn't like Mrs. Garcia.

She slid her house key into the lock and opened the front door as quietly as she could. The delicious aroma of roasting chicken greeted her in the empty hallway and she could hear voices singing happily from upstairs.

Thank God.

She dropped her tote bag on the hall table, kicked off her shoes and tiptoed up the staircase. As she passed by the bathroom, she heard water draining from the tub. The strains of "Cielito Lindo" came sweetly from Janie's bedroom.

"Mommy!" screeched Janie as her mother entered. The child's scrubbed face beamed. Dressed in her pink nightgown, and smelling of Mr. Bubble, she ran to Eliza and hugged her.

"Hey, my pumpkin pie. It looks like you had a good day!"

Janie nodded emphatically. "I did, Mommy. Mrs. Garcia is teaching me Spanish."

"I heard."

"And we walked Daisy around the pond and we made chocolate-chip cookies together."

"I hope you saved me some."

"We did. We made lots."

"And how was school today?"

"Good. James came over to play after lunch."

Eliza looked over her daughter's head to Mrs. Garcia. The housekeeper was gathering up Janie's clothes to carry down to the washing machine.

"Janie, you take your clothes from Mrs. Garcia and go put them in the hamper in the closet in the bathroom, please."

As the child complied with her mother's request, Eliza sank onto the corner of her daughter's bed and smiled. "Looks like you two got off to a good start."

"Janie is a good girl. I think we get along fine."

"I'm so glad, Mrs. Garcia," Eliza said with relief.

The housekeeper started to leave the room. "I make your dinner before I go."

"That would be great. Thank you."

Mrs. Garcia turned as she reached the doorway. "There was one thing I didn't like today, Señora Blake."

Eliza's elation sank. "What?"

"This man come to the house today. He say he gave Janie the puppy and want to know if Janie likes the puppy. I have no good feeling about that man. I told him not to come here if you not home. I hope that is all right."

"You did the right thing, Mrs. Garcia. I don't like that man, either."

CHAPTER

66

Larson hadn't been returning his calls, and Augie didn't like it.

He wanted his money out of the pizza deal. He was sick and tired of waiting for the payoff that never came.

The summer was ending and so was vacation time. That meant

there would be fewer opportunities in the months ahead to score in the empty houses. The influx of cash that Augie had reaped over the last three months was over, probably until Thanksgiving or Christmastime when residents would next be going away.

He had a huge overhead and the income from the garage wasn't enough, not if he wanted to get Helene primed.

He dialed the number to Richards's office again.

"Mr. Richards is in a meeting right now, Mr. Sinisi. I'll give him the message that you called."

"He's always in a meeting and he never calls me back," Augie growled.

"I'm sorry, Mr. Sinisi. I'll tell Mr. Richards that you called," the secretary repeated.

"You tell your boss that if he doesn't call me back, I'm coming up to that big office of his to speak to him in person."

Larson had his assistant screen his calls carefully. There were very few he wanted to take these days because most of them were from disgruntled investors. But when the secretary buzzed to say that Eliza Blake was on the line, Larson picked up immediately.

"Eliza! How nice to hear from you. How is Janie liking her puppy?"

"She's crazy about her, Larson."

"Great. I thought she would be."

"I'd be more enthusiastic if you'd checked with me first."

"Oh. Well, I guess I should have, but I thought it would be all right with you."

"Larson, you don't know me well enough to assess whether it would be all right or not."

Bitch. Two hundred dollars on that damned dog ... But go easy, fella. You can't afford to alienate Eliza Blake.

"Gee, I'm sorry, Eliza. I thought I was doing a good thing. Forgive me."

She ignored his request. "Actually, I'm calling because Mrs. Garcia told me that you came to our home yesterday."

"Yeah, I wanted to see how Janie was doing with the dog. Is that a problem?"

"To tell you the truth, Larson, it is. I would prefer it if you didn't do that again. Mrs. Garcia is just starting with us and I want to keep things as controlled and peaceful as I can."

"Eliza, it was really no big deal," Larson protested. "And if you want my opinion, I think you should be glad to have someone stopping by once in a while to check on things when you are at the office. You know there is a big colony of those Guatemalans living around here and most of us think they're pretty skeevy. I see the Guats waiting on street corners for landscapers to pick them up for day work and there is a crew of them working at the car wash. Filthy. You may like your Mrs. Garcia, but you don't know what her friends are like. And you certainly wouldn't want them stopping by to visit when you're not home."

Eliza could not contain her contempt for the man. "The Guatemalans are lovely people, Larson. Their culture, maybe because it is so poor, values cleanliness, dignity and politeness. We could all learn a lot from them."

"You're saying *I* could learn a lot from them, aren't you?"

"As a matter of fact, yes, I am. Please don't stop by unannounced at my home again."

As she hung up the phone, repulsed by his bigotry, Eliza remembered the safe. Larson still hadn't gotten the combination to her.

To hell with it. There was no way she was going to call him back.

CHAPTER

67

Cornelius watched out the bus window as the soot-covered tiled walls of the Lincoln Tunnel passed by. Once he got to the Port Authority terminal, he would take a quick subway ride uptown to the KEY Broadcast Center. He could do what he had to do and get back to Moonachie in time for his shift at the bar.

Meat was tired of watching her on TV. It wasn't enough anymore. He needed to get a glimpse of Eliza in the flesh. He was prepared to come into the city every day until he got what he wanted.

He had to get a handle on her schedule. When did Eliza arrive in the morning? Did she go out to lunch? The best time to get her had to be after the *Evening Headlines,* as she left the Broadcast Center. But at seven o'clock Meat had to be at work and he wasn't ready to give up his hours at the bar. At least not yet.

Dressed in jeans and a blue New York Giants sweatshirt, Meat waited for the A train on the subway platform, looking with disdain at the other straphangers standing around him. Some of the women, dressed in tight pants and short skirts, particularly disgusted him. *Sluts.*

The train dropped him off at Columbus Circle and he trudged up the steps with the masses to the sunlight above. He bought a hot, salted pretzel and a Coke from a vendor's steel cart and wolfed it down as he headed west. He glanced at his watch. It was after eleven o'clock. He had gotten a later start than he should have. Eliza was probably already in the office by now.

But as he reached the long brick building that housed the Broadcast Center, he had hopes of spotting Eliza as she went out to lunch. He stationed himself across the street, where he had a clear view of the entrance. He watched carefully as dozens of people went in and left through the heavy revolving door. After half an hour, he walked forty feet up the block to a pizza parlor, went inside and ordered a slice with sausage and pepperoni, keeping his eyes trained out the plate-glass window while he waited for the pizza to heat. He paid for the slice and a can of cream soda and took a seat in one of the white plastic chairs at a bistro table out on the sidewalk.

More people were coming out of the Broadcast Center now.

"You are a miracle worker! I can't believe you got this organized so quickly."

Keith smiled sheepishly. "I can't take all the credit on this one, Eliza. I mentioned the story to my wife and she happens to have a girlfriend who is a literary agent and feels she has to stay in New York while her husband has an opportunity in Dallas he didn't want to pass up. He left six months ago. It's been wreaking havoc on their relationship, but they are determined to work things out."

"You've talked to them, of course."

Keith nodded. "Yeah, and they're willing for us to do their story. In fact, she's flying to Texas this weekend. We can accompany her on the plane and then shoot them together in Dallas. I was thinking it would be cool for you to interview her on the plane ride Friday night, get her feelings of anticipation and then get the letdown as she flies back on Sunday."

He watched Eliza's face for reaction.

Eliza knew Keith was right. This would be a good way to do the story. She didn't want to be away for the weekend, though. Yet after killing the New York–to–London idea, she couldn't be a prima donna now and say no to this plan. That wouldn't be fair.

Eliza glanced at her watch. "Are you hungry? Let's go out and grab some lunch and talk about it."

Meat was accustomed to waiting.

In fact, he enjoyed the anticipation—and the reward for his patience. He waited for his bats to emerge. Now he waited for Eliza.

There she was, coming through the revolving door! A man followed behind her and together they walked onto the street. The man raised his arm to hail a cab.

It took awhile for an empty taxi to come. Time for Meat to fume. Eliza still wasn't listening.

Her brown hair gleamed in the midday sunlight. Her navy business suit, if it could be called that, showed way too much thigh.

She laughed at something the man said as they got into the cab. *Whore.*

CHAPTER

68

When she got home from work, Eliza announced that she was going to have to go away for the weekend. Janie didn't seem to mind at all if her mother went out of town when presented with the option of going into the city to stay with KayKay and Poppie for two nights.

She knew that meant a trip to see the monkeys at the Central Park Zoo, a movie and, maybe, if she was good, a visit to FAO Schwarz for the toy of her choice.

"How do you feel about driving Janie into New York after school on Friday afternoon?" Eliza asked Mrs. Garcia. "Janie's grandparents live right off the Harlem River Drive."

"Whatever you want me to do is fine, señora. I know how to get into the city. I have relatives who live in Washington Heights and I see signs for Harlem River Drive. It is very easy."

"Good, then. It's settled. I'll leave for work Friday morning and after the broadcast I'll be flying to Texas. I'll be back Sunday night. Janie's grandparents will bring her home then."

The logistics of balancing her career and child care were relent-less. Yet Eliza knew she was one of the lucky ones. Most people didn't have the means of support, both financial and personal, that she did.

Knowing that Janie would be with Katharine and Paul made it easier for her to go and do her job. She hadn't even wanted to broach the subject of the housekeeper staying through this, her first weekend with them. It would be too much for Mrs. Garcia and too much for Janie. They were getting along splendidly, but Eliza didn't want to rock the boat. It would be better if they had the weekend break from one another.

And with the uneasy feeling left by the continuing threats that were coming into the Broadcast Center, Eliza did not want to leave her daughter and the housekeeper alone in the house for the weekend.

CHAPTER

69

Carmen Garcia picked Janie up from school, took her charge for a Happy Meal at McDonald's and headed toward the George Washington Bridge. The signs for the Harlem River Drive were clearly marked, and by one-thirty Janie was safely in the care of her grandparents. By two-thirty, Carmen was back in HoHoKus.

She glanced at the gas gauge and noted that there was still over half a tank. She could leave it as it was and just put the car in the garage and call her daughter to pick her up early and knock off for the day. But Carmen felt she owed Señora Eliza a full day's work. She would change the linens on the beds and finish the laundry before she went home. She wanted her boss to come home to an orderly house and a car with a full tank of gas.

She turned into the service station. The man who came out to pump the gasoline looked at her skeptically. *He doesn't think someone like me can be driving a new car like this.*

"Please, fill it up."

"What kind?" the man asked gruffly.

Carmen looked at him with a puzzled expression on her face.

"What kind of gas? Regular or high-test?"

She wasn't sure quite what to say. No one had ever asked her before when she bought gas for the old car she sometimes borrowed from her daughter. She realized that the gas-station man must have just assumed that she would want the cheaper gasoline. But Carmen caught on quickly.

"High–test."

Holding her head erect, she sat in the driver's seat and stared straight in front of her as the gas surged into the new Volvo.

"Twelve dollars."

Carmen handed the man the credit card Eliza had given her. The man looked at it suspiciously.

"You're not Eliza Blake."

"I know this, sir. I work for her and she give me this card to use."

"How do I know that you are telling me the truth? How do I know you didn't steal it from her? For that matter, how do I know you didn't steal this car?"

Carmen was speechless, a stricken look on her face.

"I know Ms. Blake," said the man. "I think I'll go right in and call her and check out your story."

"Please, sir, you cannot reach her now. She is at work." Carmen was clearly flustered.

"All right, I'll give you a pass this time," the man said, sliding the card through the scanner. "But I am going to call Ms. Blake tonight and make sure you're not ripping her off."

"She won't be home tonight. She will be gone all weekend," said the intimidated woman.

Bingo! thought the man in the tight overalls.

CHAPTER

70

Eliza, Keith and B.J. inched behind the other passengers down the portable tunnel that led to the airplane. The Friday–evening New York–to–Dallas flight was fully booked.

B.J. D'Elia was saddled with camera gear slung over his shoulder and strapped to a wheeled cart that he pulled behind him. Keith carried the camera itself because B.J. couldn't handle one more thing. By rights they should have had a soundman with them, but Keith hadn't been able to get another plane ticket on the flight on such short notice. It was just as well. Keith was always being nagged about keeping expenses down on his stories. Without the extra crew guy, he saved on travel expenses, hotel room and salary. B.J., God love him, was able to do both the camera and audio work well.

Keith and B.J. took their seats next to each other in the row in front of Eliza and Lauren Houghton, the subject of the commuter-relationships piece. The plan was for B.J. to point the camera over the back of his seat, recording Eliza's interview. The airline had been happy to accommodate the seating arrangements when told that the story was not about air–travel safety. With standing orders from their sponsors at KEY News that any scheduled airline commercial should be pulled from running in a broadcast featuring a plane crash, Keith was well aware that the air carriers were extremely sensitive to their images. A story emphasizing that air flight was integral to keeping personal relationships strong, was right up the airline's PR alley. The press-information people were eager to accommodate the news crew and very apologetic that they couldn't guarantee the fourth seat for the soundman.

Keith was glad he had been able to get this shoot together so quickly. At the very end of Cindy's pregnancy, he should limit his time away from home, so it was good to do all the out-of-town work he could now. And, truth be known, he was relieved to be getting away from his wife for the weekend.

He had turned a deaf ear to Cindy's latest round of hysterics this morning when she vented her resentment that he was leaving her alone. Keith was getting very good at appearing to be listening sympathetically while actually not letting her words affect him. He was tired of Cindy's exhausting tirades, losing patience with her endless complaints and nagging. If things didn't improve once the baby was born, he didn't know what he was going to do.

This weekend would provide a respite from the miserable situation at home, and Keith welcomed it. At least at work he knew what he had to do, and accomplished it. No one questioned his motives or whined about his coming up short in pleasing them. He didn't have to make anyone happy.

Of course, there was the care and feeding of the anchorwoman to consider. But Eliza was basically low maintenance, as on-air types went. She was a pro, expecting her producer to set up the story and coordinate the elements. She was not going to expect Keith to research the finest restaurant in town and make sure they had reservations in place, or book a spa visit for her to squeeze in a facial and massage while they were on the road. Eliza wanted to get the job done, and at the end of the day was just as happy to go back to her hotel and order room service. Any personal needs she had, she scheduled herself.

Keith pulled the seatbelt tight across his lap, laid his head against the back of his chair and closed his eyes as the plane began to taxi down the runway. He could think of a few of Eliza's personal needs he'd love to take care of for her. While the plane made its slow ascent, he fantasized about how Eliza would respond to any overtures he might make. With Mack McBride cheating on her and out of the picture, Eliza must be feeling vulnerable. This could be a good opportunity.

But Eliza knew he was married and knew Keith was awaiting his first child. Everything he knew about her suggested that she wouldn't be the kind of woman who would consider getting involved with a married man. Nor had Eliza had never shown any attraction to him.

But you could never tell. There was something about being on the road. People did things while they were traveling on assignment, things that would never happen in New York at the tension–filled Broadcast Center. Inhibitions came down in the freewheeling atmosphere. Many an internecine liaison "happened" on the road.

Afterwards, there was no honor in talking about it. The motto was, What goes on the road, stays on the road.

Road rules. No rules.

CHAPTER

71

The golden lights in the pink–and–cream–colored high-rise condominiums that dotted the edge of Sarasota Bay were starting to blink on as Samuel Morton drove homeward on Ringling Boulevard. The sky at sunset over the Gulf of Mexico was a melding of rose, purple and blue hues. If an artist were to paint a picture of it, the painting's beholder would be skeptical the depiction was accurate, so unlikely was it that such a vivid, magical spectacle could occur naturally. But many evenings in Sarasota, it did.

The southwest Florida city was an incredibly beautiful place to live, with much to enjoy besides the world's whitest sand beaches and breathtaking sunsets, and Samuel had never regretted moving down from the North. Sarasota was a cultural cornucopia. The Asolo and Florida Studio Theaters provided first-rate dramatic productions. The strains of Beethoven, Bach and Puccini filled the Opera House. The Van Wezel Performing Arts Center staged Broadway shows, touring national celebrities, musical comedy, dance companies and orchestras. Shaped like a giant lavender seashell, the locals affectionately referred to the Van Wezel as "the purple cow."

The Ringling Museum of Art, Florida's official state art museum covered a sixty-six-acre estate that included the art museum, circus galleries, a charming rose garden and Ca'd'Zan, John and Mabel Ringling's thirty-room Venetian mansion. Works by El Greco, Velasquez, Rubens and Van Dyke hung on the art museum's walls.

The city attracted artists, actors, dancers, painters, musicians, authors and Northerners like Samuel who wanted to escape. They hated the winter months in colder climates and longed to get away to warmth, wide beaches, soothing water, great shopping and excellent dining. Though the summer months were long, warm and humid, the heat was tempered by afternoon or early-evening thunderstorms. Sam infinitely preferred the tradeoff of staying inside in the air-conditioning in July and August, to dealing with the cold, ice and snow of Northern winters.

Until now.

The "big" season would be beginning again in earnest next month, and the population of the city would swell as many of the retired residents returned from summering up North. The thought of being barraged with invitations to charity fundraisers, theater and gallery openings, galas, receptions, balls, banquets and cocktail parties on the circuit overwhelmed Sam.

He wasn't up to it this year.

Sam put his foot on the brake when he reached the causeway leading to Siesta Key and his car waited in line with all the others as the hinged bridge opened to permit a high-masted schooner to sail through. In the dimming light the white sailboat skimmed peacefully through the placid bay water. Sam could see a woman and man on board. The breeze was blowing back the woman's long hair. The man had a drink in his hand. It was a serene picture.

But Sam knew things weren't always as they seemed. He wondered about the prosperous, attractive couple on that boat. Were they really happy? Samuel certainly wasn't. Yet anyone watching him, tanned, well-dressed and driving home with the convertible top down, would look at him and think he had the world by the tail. Instead he was wracked with anguish.

It was time to get away for a while. He had to.

His parents still kept their pied-à-terre in New York. He could stay there, in the city he enjoyed so much. The firm would just have to do without him. Samuel wasn't much good at the practice of contract law right now, he hadn't been for months. Always preoccupied, he had been going through the motions and Leo had been carrying things. He knew his brother was worried about him, and Samuel was certain Leo would understand when he heard that Sam wanted to take a leave of absence from the firm. In fact, Leo would probably be relieved not to see his dour puss around the office for a while.

The bridge came down and the cars drove on. As he crossed the causeway, Samuel looked out at the mesmerizing expanse of water and felt somewhat soothed. A decision had been made.

CHAPTER

7 2

The Houghtons had agreed that KEY News could spend the day with them Saturday, taping them as they tried to do the things couples who were together all week long did on the weekends. Sensitive to the fact that the Houghtons might want to sleep in on their first morning after a week apart, Keith had agreed that they wouldn't come to their apartment until eleven o'clock.

Keith was almost embarrassed by how well he had slept without Cindy by his side. She was always getting up several times during the night to go the bathroom and, when she came back to bed, she tossed and turned, sighing heavily until she fell back asleep. He pretended to be asleep, not wanting to start any conversation that might lead to unpleasantness. Nonetheless, his night's rest was constantly interrupted.

Now he rolled over happily in the king–sized bed and checked the clock, seeing that he had time to go down to the hotel gym before breakfast. What a treat! He had let his exercise routine go, too, over the last months, sensing that Cindy would be resentful of the time he spent working out while her body was going to seed. A good strong run on the treadmill, if he could manage it, would be just the thing. Maybe he could pound the improper thoughts of Eliza from his mind.

The gym walls were glass. When he approached and saw Eliza striding on the treadmill, dressed in a pair of black bike shorts and an exercise bra, it was too late to turn back. She had spotted him and waved.

Eliza wore no makeup, yet still she was beautiful.

He got on the treadmill beside hers and they began to run to–gether.

"I thought we got some good sound in the interview on the plane last night, didn't you, Keith?" Eliza said between halting breaths.

"Definitely. We'll get his side of things today."

"What else are we going for?"

"Hanging around the house, going to do some errands together. I told them to do whatever they would normally do. I think they are going out to dinner and a movie tonight."

"Lucky."

"Come again?"

"They're lucky," said Eliza, without breaking her stride. "That sounds like a great day to me."

Keith wasn't sure exactly what to say in response. Was she letting him into a tiny window on her soul? Was she telling him she yearned for an ordinary life, that the thought of just spending a day doing routine things with someone she loved was so appealing to her? Could Eliza possibly be looking for something from him?

Impulsively he switched off the machine, and went over and pulled Eliza from her treadmill and kissed her urgently on the mouth. She pushed him away. The alarmed expression on her face told Keith everything.

CHAPTER

73

Augie picked a fight with Helene just so he could storm out of the house. That was easy enough since she was pleading another one of her headaches.

Angrily he got into his van and drove the few miles to Eliza's neighborhood. He cruised around until well past midnight, watching as surrounding homes darkened one by one. Several lamps were on in Eliza's house, though he noticed no activity behind the windows. Finally, the lights inside went out as their timers clicked off, leaving only the outside front-door light glowing in the September night.

He backed his van into the driveway, pulling it all the way to the end and then turned the vehicle onto the grass behind the kitchen. No one would be able to see it from the road. He left the van running.

Augie was taking a big chance and he knew it. If Eliza had an alarm system, he would have to get out in a hurry. His plan was to let himself in and quickly check for alarm panels at the back, garage and front doors. If he found one, or if a screeching siren blared, he'd get right out and be well gone before the police could get there.

The latex gloves did not slip easily over his sweaty palms. Once he got them on, he pulled the copied key from his pocket and grabbed the flashlight from the front seat. He gingerly slid the key into the back-door lock. The knob didn't turn.

Damn! The key must be for the front door. The front door with the bright light hanging over it. The door facing the street.

He snapped off the flashlight and walked around the side of the house, careful to keep close to the building. When he reached the corner, he stood for a while, hidden behind a large evergreen, and collected his thoughts. *Easy does it.*

After ten minutes, no cars had driven by. There were no lights on at the Feeneys' across the street. With those three little kids, the parents were probably exhausted and in as deep a sleep as their children were. It paid to know your customers.

Augie came from his hiding place and hurried to the front door. This was no time for fumbling. He used all his powers of concentration to slide the key into the lock.

The brass knob twisted and the door opened. Augie stepped right in and closed the door behind him. He switched on his flashlight and scanned the walls on either side of the doorway. Nothing.

Then he hurried to the rear of the house, training the beams of yellow light on the walls around the back door and the door to the garage. The walls were bare. He was probably safe, but he had to act fast.

He headed directly upstairs and quickly found the master bedroom. The first place to check was the bureau. He opened the top drawer and hit immediate pay dirt. He grabbed the leather jewelry box, not stopping to open it, and dropped it into a pillowcase that he stripped from one of the pillows on the bed. The flashlight scanned the darkness. No television or VCR.

Eliza's walk-in closet was illuminated the moment the door opened by a light in the ceiling. He rifled through the racks of clothes. He could tell these were expensive duds, but he wasn't inclined to bother with them. There was no real money to be made by bringing them to a resale shop. And wouldn't he look like an ass doing it? An ass and suspicious as hell.

His gloved hand felt a protrusion coming from the wall. Though he had no skill at lock-picking, he gave the safe handle a try anyway. Unexpectedly, it opened. His heart raced as he anticipated the booty.

The safe was empty.

Augie retraced his steps from Eliza's bedroom to the hallway and down the staircase. In the dining room, he found a mahogany case containing sterling–silver flatware and serving pieces. He greedily emptied the silver into the pillowcase. A large silver bowl filled with flowers sat in the middle of the dining–room table. He dumped the flowers and grabbed the bowl. He hoped it was sterling.

A glare flickered on something as his light flashed in the direction of the living room. He followed the light to the round table that was decorated with at least two dozen picture frames. He swept them all into the bag. He would check if they were silver plate or the real thing later.

Enough with the pillowcase. He went to the kitchen and laid it by the back door. He tried to see if he could open the door out to the backyard from the inside. He could. Augie left it ajar, walked over to the refrigerator and opened the door. Sometimes people hid things in there. He rifled through the freezer.

Nothing.

Augie continued on to the den where he disconnected the big-screen television, a DVD player, a VCR and another tape deck of some kind. Since Eliza had a kid, a video camera had to be around some-where, too. He found it in the paneled closet.

In four trips back and forth he carried all of the loot out to the van and pulled away. He checked his watch. Nice haul for thirty–five minutes' work.

Later he carelessly discarded all the photographs, knowing he would make a pretty penny on the silver frames. They were all sterling.

CHAPTER

74

Somehow they had gotten through the rest of the shoot. Now Eliza was going to have to decide whether she could still work with her FRESHER LOOK producer.

Keith had been mortified the moment he saw the expression on her face after he had kissed her, knowing instantly that he had stepped over the line. He had apologized profusely, begging Eliza for forgiveness. Tears had welled in his eyes and his voice cracked as he explained that he was under so much pressure right now. There was friction at home with the new baby coming. The last thing he could afford was to lose his job.

Eliza had told Keith to forget about it. She understood. It was just one of those things. They hadn't brought up the subject the rest of the tension–filled time they were in Dallas.

At the airport back in New York, a car was waiting to drive her home and she didn't offer, as she might have done at other times, to drop off the producer and cameraman. She was eager to get home, she explained. That was true. She wanted to be there when Katharine and Paul arrived with Janie.

Now the limousine was pulling off onto the Saddle River Road exit on Route 17 and Eliza was trying to figure out what to do. She felt sorry for Keith and didn't want him to be irreparably harmed by a momentary lapse in judgment. But she *was* the *Evening Headlines* anchorwoman. If word ever got out that Keith had pulled that stunt and she had stood for it, her own standing would be diminished.

But how would the word get out? Keith surely wasn't going to tell anyone. Eliza decided that she would talk to him about the whole episode at work in the morning. They would clear the air and take it from there. She was willing to drop the matter as long as it never happened again.

The limo glided to a stop in front of her house and the driver unloaded her suitcase from the trunk and carried it to the front entrance. Eliza unlocked the door and the chauffeur deposited the bag in the hallway and left.

It wasn't quite dark yet, but Eliza flipped on the light anyway. She kicked off her shoes and went directly to check the mail Mrs. Garcia had left neatly stacked on the hallway table. She casually sorted through the pile as she walked into the dimly-lit living room and took a seat in the wing chair by the window. She recognized the handwriting on the thin airmail envelope. She switched on the lamp next to her chair to be able to better read Mack's letter.

It was then, as her eyes swept the room, that Eliza noticed that all of her precious pictures were gone.

CHAPTER

75

A day late and a dollar short, the crew from Advantage Alarm Systems arrived Monday morning to install the safety electronics and change the locks.

Eliza had downplayed the missing television and VCR to Janie when she arrived back home from her weekend with her grandparents. She had promised that Mrs. Garcia would go out and buy another set in the morning while Janie was at school. But after her in-laws had left and a mollified Janie was tucked into bed for the night, Eliza had made a detailed inventory of all that had been taken. It made her weep.

All the sterling flatware, eighteen place settings, given as wedding presents to her and John. Her jewelry, including her diamond solitaire engagement ring and the simple gold wedding band her husband had lovingly slipped on her finger. The diamond studs that had been John's first-anniversary gift. An emerald bracelet that had been in the Blake family for three generations, which Katharine and Paul had given her when Janie was born. Her University of Rhode Island class ring. The watch her parents had given her as a graduation present. Things that had been lovingly bestowed upon her, representing the milestones of her life.

If she could have just one thing back, it would be the sapphire-and-diamond pin John had bought before he died, to be given to his wife after the birth of their child. He had known he wouldn't see the expression on her face as she opened the velvet jewelry box. Eliza treasured that pin. It linked them between this world and, she hoped, the next.

As far as Eliza was concerned, the sentimental value of the stolen items far exceeded their monetary worth. She would gladly write a check out to the thief if she could buy back the things he had taken from her. She could easily replace a camcorder or a DVD player. She could order another beta-tape playback machine. She couldn't replace pieces of her life.

And the pictures. To take all the personal pictures for their ridiculous frames! It was cruel and Eliza felt raped.

Someone had come into her home and callously taken what was hers. He shouldn't get away with that. But so far he was. The police had taken their report and mumbled something about being on the case. They had seen it all before.

No sign of forced entry. Someone with a key had just come in and helped himself.

Eliza didn't want to allow herself to suspect that Mrs. Garcia could be involved in this, but Larson's virulent warning sprang to her mind. She dismissed it. Carmen Garcia had worked for her previous family for years and they had had nothing but glowing reports about her. If they had had doubts about her honesty, they surely wouldn't have kept her on.

But, come to think of it, with the locks unchanged until today, Larson Richards himself could still have a key to the house. Had he never given her the combination for the safe so that her jewelry wouldn't be locked up?

CHAPTER

76

Once Eliza got to the Broadcast Center Monday morning, she had little time to dwell on the burglary. Her schedule was packed, starting with an eleven–thirty interview booked with a Nobel Prize winner up at Columbia University who was doing research on Fragile X syndrome. Keith asked Eliza if she would mind if Farrell Slater, another *Evening Headlines* producer, accompanied her. The "Bowl" wanted to move up the commuter–relationships piece to air this week, and with only two days to get it together, Keith wanted to screen the tapes they had shot over the weekend and get working on a script.

"Sure, Keith. That's fine."

The producer was chewing a cuticle as he stood in her office door–

way. There was no good purpose in letting Keith squirm. Eliza decided to go ahead and let him off the hook.

"Keith, come in for a minute, and close the door."

Obediently he followed her instructions and took a seat in the chair she offered him.

"I think we have to clear the air here, Keith."

He nodded silently, keeping his eyes averted downward. His hands gripped the armrests and Eliza noticed the bitten fingernails. *Poor guy.*

"Look. What happened was wrong. You know that and I know that, Keith. But you are a strong producer and have worked very hard to make sure that our stories are solid. On a professional level, I value you very much. But that's it."

He raised his head and looked up at her pathetically.

"God, Eliza, I can't tell you how sorry I am. I didn't sleep at all last night worrying about it. I don't know what I was thinking. Something like that will never, ever happen again. I swear to you," he said solemnly.

The lines of Eliza's mouth were set firmly as she stared at Keith, assessing the sincerity of his words.

"All right, then. Let's move on."

CHAPTER

77

She had agonized about it all weekend and finally made up her mind. Abigail was going to go ahead and give the Victoria's Secret gift to Eliza. But she didn't have the courage to bestow it face-to-face.

She kept the small pink shopping bag tucked beneath her desk all day and waited. After the *Evening Headlines* were over and the studio and offices on the second floor cleared, Abigail took the back staircase that led from the tiny hallway next to the Fishbowl up to Eliza's office. The door was closed and locked, so she looped the shopping-bag handles over the knob and prayed that it would be safe there until morning.

Abigail walked swiftly down the long corridor toward the elevator, her heart pounding, feeling heat rising to her face. She didn't realize hallway security cameras were recording her every move.

CHAPTER

78

It was a cool, crisp September morning, the first that felt like autumn was coming. Paige welcomed the opportunity to wear the knee–length red leather skirt and new black turtleneck she had gotten on sale at T. J. Maxx for next to nothing. She stopped in the restroom as she got off the elevator. She checked herself in the mirror and rearranged the cloud of curly dark hair that framed her face, twisting it up and clipping it to the back of her head.

I'm feeling more comfortable in my job, Paige thought with satisfaction as she strode down the hallway, past the producers' empty offices. She had her routine established, getting in between nine and nine-thirty, before most of the staff wandered in about ten. By the time Eliza arrived, her messages had been checked, the mail had been sorted and there was fresh coffee brewing in the little kitchen.

As she neared the office door, Paige spied the pink bag, recognizing its provenance immediately. Paige took it from the doorknob and let herself into the office, placing the shopping bag on her desk. It would be cool if it was a present for her.

But the small envelope that was taped to the box was marked *Eliza.*

Paige put the box back into the bag and carried it into her boss's office, leaving it on the desk.

After starting the coffee, Paige punched in the numbers on the phone to get messages.

"Hello. This is Samuel Morton. Sarah's dad. I will be in New York

next week and I was wondering if I could come by at some convenient time to express my thanks in person and to drop off a small gift
from Sarah."

Eliza's heart sank as she read the gift card, inscribed in block
letters.

> You are bright, beautiful and I wish that we could get to
> know each other more fully. I hope you will be open to hearing
> from me.

There was no signature.

Eliza lifted the lid of the box and looked with alarm at the silk
slip. It was such a personal gift. So inappropriate from someone she
didn't know.

Or did Eliza know the gift-giver?

She buzzed out to Paige and asked her to get Keith Chapel on the
telephone.

"Keith, there was something waiting for me when I got to work
this morning."

"Yes?"

"Do you know what it was?"

"No. Should I?"

"I certainly hope not. Are you sure you didn't leave a gift for me?"

"Yes, I'm sure, Eliza," he promised fervently. "I didn't leave anything for you."

If Keith hadn't, who had? Someone had been able to come right
to her office and drop off the bag. It must have been a KEY employee.

As she played with her charm bracelet, Eliza shivered at the thought that occurred to her. *What if someone from the outside had gotten into the Broadcast Center?*

"Hi, Eliza. What's up?"

"Joe, I feel a bit ridiculous calling you with this, but with every-thing that's been happening, I thought I should."

"What is it?"

"Someone left a gift for me here at the office last night."

"What was it?" asked the security chief.

"A silk slip."

"Great," he responded sarcastically. "Any card?"

"Yes, but it's not signed."

"Okay. Ask Paige to bring it all down to me, and please don't worry, Eliza. It's easy enough to find out who it was. We'll just check our tapes."

CHAPTER

79

After lunch, Susan Feeney pulled out the contents of the curbside mailbox, recognizing with pleasure the plastic-wrapped October issue of *Martha Stewart Living*. With the exception of Christmas, Halloween was Susan's favorite holiday and Martha was always good for another creative idea or two.

Susan loved to sew, and the attic held her extensive collection of outfits she had made for the children and for James and herself to wear to masquerade parties they had attended, starting even before they were married. The carefully marked cardboard boxes held the costumes of a monk and a nun, a pirate and a harem girl, Dracula, Zorro, a French maid, a go-go girl and Uncle Sam and the Statue of Liberty. Susan and James had won the prize for best couple's costume when they wore those patriotic outfits to a local Halloween party the year before. She would always dress up and trick-or-treat around the neighborhood with the kids. One year she had gone as a pregnant clown and nobody knew who she was.

She was having fun planning what this Halloween would bring. Last year Kelly and Kimberly had been a pair of little yellow Twinkies, while James had insisted on being Batman. This year, Kelly would be a bumblebee, while Kimberly was going as a ladybug. Susan had both of their costumes almost done. She had suggested that, in keeping with the insect theme, James could be a spider. But James had a mind of his own. He didn't want to be a spider or a devil or prizefighter, the other options his mother suggested. Susan was trying to be patient, but if he didn't decide soon, she was going to make the decision for him. There was a thin line between allowing and encouraging a son to steer his own course and raising a spoiled brat.

Turning from the mailbox, Susan heard a child's voice call from across the street.

"Mrs. Feeney, can James come over to play?"

Janie Blake, buttoned up in a bright red sweater, was standing in her driveway holding a leash with her golden puppy pulling on the end. Mrs. Garcia was standing guard behind her.

"James is inside watching a video, Janie. If it's all right with Mrs. Garcia, you're welcome to come over to our house for a while."

Janie turned to her caretaker and handed her Daisy's leash. In the child's mind, the decision was made, but she went through the polite motions. "It's okay, right, Mrs. Garcia?"

The housekeeper nodded. "Yes, *muñequita*. It's all right. I come over for you in a while and pick you up and walk you back home."

She held the child's hand and escorted her across the street.

James was engrossed in the *Popeye* video when Susan brought Janie downstairs to the playroom. The little girl took a seat on the sofa beside him. With both daughters upstairs napping, Susan decided to take a few minutes and sit down and relax. She flipped through the pages of her magazine, noting a recipe for Boston baked beans she would try, and another for Halloween lollipops, if she got ambitious enough and found the time.

That was the thing about Martha Stewart. It was fascinating to watch her television show or read her magazine and see all the things that could be done to make life nicer and more gracious, but Susan wondered if more people might be living vicariously through Martha's projects than actually had the time or inclination to do them.

She looked up as she heard James and Janie laughing at Robin Williams's antics as Popeye on the television screen. The hairless sailor with the bulging biceps and contorted face was eating his spinach and getting out of an improbable jam and the kids loved it.

"Hey, James! I have a good idea. How about being Popeye for Halloween?"

Her son burst from his seat on the couch. "Yeah!"

Janie sat quietly.

"Do you know what you're going to be for Halloween yet, Janie?" asked Susan.

Janie shook her head silently.

"Would you like to be Olive Oyl? You can ask your mom and if she says yes, I'll make your costume, too, and you and James can trick-or-treat together."

The thought was a real hit. Janie beamed. She knew it was going to be all right with Mommy. Mommy didn't sew. Mommy was always at work.

CHAPTER

80

Decades of experience in the security field had left Joe Connelly little surprised by anything. But the tapes recorded outside of Eliza's office last night did not show what he had expected.

A light-haired woman dressed in dark slacks and a turtleneck had hung a bag on the door at eight P.M. Joe didn't recognize the woman, but the best thing to do would be to call Eliza down to see if she did.

Eliza stared intently at the grainy image Joe had isolated on the monitor in the security office.

"It looks like Abigail Snow. She does promos for the broadcast."

"Has she ever come on to you in anyway?"

"Never."

Joe flipped off the screen.

"I'll call her in and talk to her."

A pained expression crossed Eliza's face. "God, Joe. I don't want to embarrass her. I don't know Abigail well at all, but she seems to be a very nice woman. I can't believe that she is any kind of threat."

"Well, how do you want to handle it? I wouldn't ignore it, Eliza. She should know in no uncertain terms that you aren't interested. You don't want anybody fantasizing that there's something developing between you when there isn't."

Eliza considered his words and made up her mind decisively.

"I'll talk to her myself, Joe."

"You're sure? I'd be glad to do it for you."

"No," she said resolutely. "I should do it myself."

Eliza left ten minutes earlier than usual to go down to makeup, stopping at the promotions office. Abigail was inside conferring with a co-worker.

"Abigail, may I speak with you for a moment?"

"Sure, Eliza. Come on in," Abigail answered enthusiastically, gesturing to a chair.

The co-worker took the cue and excused himself.

"Did you want to see the FRESHER LOOK promo I did for the story on commuter relationships?" Abigail offered.

"Gee, I can't right now. I have to get to makeup. I'm sure it's wonderful, though. Your promos always are." Eliza crossed her long legs and leaned forward in her chair.

Abigail's heart raced.

"Well, what is it you wanted to talk about?"

"Actually, Abigail, someone left a gift for me at my office last night and I think it might have been you."

Abigail's face flushed.

"Was it?"

"Yes."

Eliza wanted to flee the room as soon as she saw the hopeful expression on Abigail's face. An expression that would surely turn to mortification when she heard what Eliza was about to tell her. It was a delicate situation. Eliza didn't relish the idea of hurting Abigail, but she had to nip this thing in the bud.

"I'm not interested, Abigail. I'm sorry."

The woman didn't respond the way Eliza had expected she would.

"How do you know you aren't interested?" Abigail asked, almost too calmly.

"What?"

"Have you ever thought about it before?"

"That's really none of your business, Abigail. But the answer is no."

"You might find that you like it."

"I don't think so."

"You never know until you try."

"Look," said Eliza firmly. "I didn't come down here to get into a discussion about sexuality. I just wanted to let you know that I'd appreciate it if something like this didn't happen again."

She rose to leave.

"Eliza, just think about it, please. Many women marry and have children before they realize their true feelings. At the very least, consider what it is about it that makes you so uncomfortable."

"I'm not uncomfortable, Abigail. I like to think of myself as an open-minded person, but I know myself, and I know that I'm not sexually attracted to women."

Eliza sank into the chair, let out a long groan and told Doris about the exchange with Abigail.

"I knew she had the hots for you, baby," said Doris as she swirled her brush around in a pot of blush.

"You did? Why didn't you tell me?"

"Like you haven't had enough to worry about?" Doris stood back and stuck out her leggings-clad hip. She held up her fingers and pulled them back one by one. "Let's see. You're getting threatening phone calls. You're getting threatening letters. Your boyfriend cheated on you. And let's not forget your house was just robbed."

Eliza laughed in spite of herself. "Oh, yeah, and I have another happy thing I forgot to mention. Keith Chapel came on to me in Dallas last weekend."

Doris's bronze-painted mouth dropped. "You're kidding! Keith always seemed kind of Caspar Milquetoasty to me. I wouldn't have thought he had it in him to try to get it on with anyone, much less the anchorwoman. That was pretty gutsy."

Eliza shrugged as Doris removed the makeup smock. "Gutsy, stupid or desperate. Which one?" Eliza stood up and smoothed out her skirt. "On that happy note, I'm off to deliver the evening news to eight million people who would never suspect the chaos that is my life."

CHAPTER

81

So close and yet so far.

She was as close as the television screen.

She was as close as her picture in a magazine or newspaper.

She filled the thoughts that ran through the brain during the day and appeared vividly, hotly, in dreams at night.

She was always there, yet never there.

Envy. That's what pulsed through the veins, watching Eliza sit next to the woman she interviewed on the airplane. Oh, to be that close to Eliza Blake, feeling the warmth of her arm in that cramped seating space. To be flying with her to some exotic spot where they could be together.

Please, Eliza. . . . If I could only get that close to you.

CHAPTER

82

Eliza rushed from the studio as soon as the Thursday-evening broadcast was over. Back-to-School Night started at seven-thirty and she was having the driver go directly to HoHoKus Public School. Even if there was absolutely no traffic on the West Side Highway she was going to be late.

But, like most evenings, there was traffic. Lots of it. By the time Eliza hurried into Mrs. Prescott's kindergarten classroom, the teacher had finished her presentation. The parents were already up from the cramped positions they had taken in the pint-sized seats at the tiny desks and were milling around the room, searching for their respective children's crayoned artwork tacked to the walls.

"Mrs. Prescott, I'm Eliza Blake, Janie's mother."

"Of course, Ms. Blake," the diminutive, middle-aged teacher extended her hand. Mrs. Prescott wasn't that much taller than her students. "It's so good to meet you. My husband and I watch you every night."

"Thank you," said Eliza, a bit uncomfortably. She didn't want the focus to be on herself. She was here to talk about her daughter. "How is Janie doing?"

"Very well, very well," said Mrs. Prescott. "She seems to be adjusting nicely. I understand you just moved in a few days before she started school?"

"That's right. It was all very rushed."

"And you have a new housekeeper?"

"Yes, Mrs. Garcia," Eliza confirmed. "So far, so good. Janie and she are getting along famously."

Mrs. Prescott nodded. "Yes, she seems very nice when she picks up Janie every day. Janie seems happy to go with her."

"That's good to hear."

"Janie tells me that you had a robbery?"

Eliza was starting to feel uncomfortable, and guilty, as the teacher listed the litany of changes and traumas Janie had been through of late. "Yes, unfortunately, we did," she answered.

"Janie told me she was sad because some pictures were stolen."

Janie hadn't said a word to her about it. *Oh, God.*

"Yes, family pictures that were in frames."

"Some of her father?"

What was this? The inquisition?

Eliza nodded.

Mrs. Prescott bit the corner of her lip and Eliza sensed a growing reticence.

"You look like you have something on your mind, Mrs. Prescott. Please, tell me what it is."

"I read in the newspaper about what happened over the summer. Janie has been through quite a lot for such a little girl. I just want you to know I'm sensitive to that."

Eliza could feel other eyes watching her in the crowded classroom. It was at times like this that she yearned for anonymity. She was relieved when another parent approached to speak with the teacher.

The classroom bulletin boards had headings. The first was, "What I Did Over the Summer." Eliza was relieved to see Janie's depictions of the Newport seashore rather than a stick figure of Mrs. Twomey holding a gun.

The "Harvest" bulletin-board artwork was pretty universal. All the kids had drawn big orange pumpkins.

"My Family" was another heading. Eliza's heart sank as she looked at the five-year-olds' rudimentary drawings that clearly showed two big parents with assorted numbers of children. Basic all-American families. When she got to Janie's picture, she saw that her daughter had drawn a big mommy, and a little girl, with a tiny yellow blob next to her which Eliza supposed represented Daisy. There had still been lots of space remaining on the construction paper. In the corner, Janie had drawn her tiny version of KayKay and a white-haired Poppie holding hands. It was a lopsided arrangement. But that was family as Janie knew it.

For the first time, Eliza was glad that Larson had dropped off that dog.

She felt a tap on the shoulder and turned to see Susan Feeney smiling at her. Eliza made an effort to wipe the concern from her face.

"Hiya, Susan. How are you?"

"I'm fine. But what's wrong with you? You look so down."

Eliza gestured to the bulletin board.

"What?" asked Susan.

"Look at all those pictures and then look at Janie's."

Susan stared at the drawings. "Oh, you mean the mommy–daddy thing?" She patted Eliza on the arm. "Don't worry, in a couple of years half those parents will be divorced."

Eliza tried not to laugh. "That's not exactly what I had in mind."

"Forget about it, Eliza. Everything *looks* like Ozzie-and-Harrietland out here. But knock on just about any door: every family has its problems. You love Janie and she knows it. She is a very secure little girl. She'll be fine."

"I hope so," Eliza said, liking Susan more and more.

Susan held out a pad of paper. "Come on, sign up for something. Get involved. You'll feel better."

Eliza scanned the sheet. Class Mother. Forget it, there was no way she could take that on. Bake Sale. Well, she could have Mrs. Garcia bake something but that didn't warrant any real involvement on her part. Brownie Leader. Nope—had to be home after school for that. Book Sale. Again, it was during the week. Halloween Parade.

"What do you have to do for Halloween Parade?" Eliza asked.

"Get donuts and cider and be here at school the Saturday morning before Halloween when the kids finish their march from town in their costumes."

Eliza scribbled her signature on the line. "I can handle that." She handed the pad back to her neighbor. "And, Susan, thanks again for making Janie's costume. I really appreciate it."

The guilt never ended.

CHAPTER

83

Why had she ever agreed to do this interview with the *Record*?

Eliza didn't want any more publicity. But KEY News liked it. With the amount of money the company was paying her, Eliza felt obligated to hold up her end. The *Record* had a large circulation in northern New Jersey. Louise Kendall would certainly see the article and that meant Range would, too.

With notebook and pen in hand, the newspaper reporter sat in Eliza's office Friday morning.

"Why did you choose to move out to Bergen County?"

"I thought it would be a good atmosphere in which to raise my daughter. We loved living in the city, but I wanted Janie to have a backyard with a swing set and the whole works. I also wanted her to go to public school and Bergen County has a strong system."

"Your situation with your housekeeper got a lot of coverage. I suppose that had something to do with your decision?" the reporter prompted.

"It did. But I'd very much appreciate it if you didn't stress that in your article. We are trying to put that behind us."

The reporter nodded noncommittally.

"How are you liking HoHoKus?"

"It's a beautiful town. Very charming. And it's a fairly easy commute to New York."

"Have you met many people yet?"

"We've only been out here a few weeks, but the people that I have met have been very welcoming and friendly."

"Are you getting involved in any local activities?"

Eliza smiled. "Funny you should ask that, I just signed up last night to work at the HoHoKus Public School for the Halloween Parade. And I intend to continue my involvement with Fragile X syndrome fundraising efforts with my friend Louise Kendall, who, by the way, was also my Realtor. Last June I was privileged to be asked to speak at the Fragile X fundraising ball at the Park Ridge Marriott. Next year Louise is organizing it at Tavern on the Green. I'll be attending and helping in any way I can."

"Now, where exactly do you live in HoHoKus?" asked the reporter.

Eliza was uncomfortable. "You know, the last thing I want to do is make your job more difficult and I certainly wouldn't want to edit you in any way, but I'd rather you didn't put that in the article either. You know, for security reasons."

Too many nuts out there.

CHAPTER

84

Janie was excited about having supper and a sleepover at James's house Saturday night and Eliza was thrilled that she didn't have to feel guilty about going out to dinner.

Louise had said to dress casually, so Eliza picked a long-sleeved tunic top and a pair of black slacks. Her jewelry selection was limited. She still had the gold hoop earrings, and her grandmother's charm bracelet she had worn in Dallas. She thanked heaven again that the thief hadn't gotten that.

She left the house lights blazing, methodically set the alarm system, got into her station wagon and drove the few miles north to the Bear's Nest luxury condominium development. The uniformed security guard stopped her at the gatehouse.

"I'm going to Mrs. Kendall's."

"Your name, please?"

"Eliza Blake."

There was no name recognition on the guard's face as he checked his clipboard. *Nice change.*

"Go ahead in, miss."

Maybe she would have been smarter to move to a place like this, Eliza thought as she drove through the quiet streets. It would be comforting to have a security guard checking to see who came and went. But there were no big fences around the complex, and even if there were, if someone was determined to get to one of the townhouses, there was little anyone could do.

Range answered the doorbell, a drink in his hand.

"Here she is," he smiled broadly, bussing her on the cheek. "Come on in. Louise is out on the deck. It's still warm enough to have one last cocktail out there."

It was just getting dark and Louise had lit votive candles in tiny lanterns perched along the deck rails. They sipped their drinks and chatted animatedly about the upcoming presidential election until Louise let out a scream.

"What?" asked Range, alarm on his face.

"Oh my God, I think I just saw bats fly by!"

Range settled back in his seat and smirked. "Don't worry, honey. Eliza can tell you all about bats. There's nothing to be concerned about. Right, Eliza?"

"Well, she can tell me about it inside, because I'm getting out of here." Quickly Louise carried her scotch and soda through the French doors into the living room and the other two followed her.

Eliza explained the FRESHER LOOK research she was doing, but Louise remained unconvinced. "I don't care. Bats creep me out and nothing is going to change that. Let's talk about something more pleasant."

"Okay," agreed Eliza, changing the subject. "I got a good plug in for Fragile X yesterday," she offered brightly.

"How so?"

"The *Record* is doing an article on my move to the area. I told the reporter I would be working with you on fundraising for FRAXA."

"Thanks, Eliza, that's great. Every little bit helps. And even better, Range tells me that this week's FRESHER LOOK piece is on Fragile X. That should do a lot of good in getting the word out. I'm so glad you're doing that story."

As Louise excused herself and went to the kitchen to check on the roast, Range wanted to hear more about the newspaper interview.

"Do you think it was wise to publicize the fact that you've moved out here?" he asked. "You know, with those threats and all? Why let anyone know where you live?"

Eliza's eyes popped. "Range Bullock, I can't believe it! You are the one who always wants all the publicity you can get for the show. I thought you'd be pleased."

"All the publicity in the world won't help the ratings if you aren't around to sit in the anchor chair," he blurted.

Eliza's face sank.

"I'm sorry, Eliza. That didn't come out right."

"What didn't come out right?" asked Louise, hearing the tail end of the conversation as she returned to the living room.

"Range is worried about some threats I've been getting."

Louise took a seat in a crewel-covered armchair. "I know he's worried, and I am too. I remember when Bill used to get those crazy letters. I know he didn't even tell me about most of them, but there were a few over the years that even shook him up. They were truly blood-chilling."

Eliza played with the charm on her bracelet. "It really is one of the downsides of this business, isn't it? You do your job and report your story, but you never know exactly who is watching or how they are going to respond."

"Maybe we should do a story on that," suggested Range.

Eliza looked at him as if he were crazy.

"I'm serious, Eliza. I think it's a good story."

"No way, Range. I'm not the least bit interested in telling the country what's going on with me as far as all of this is concerned." She was adamant.

There was a silent pause in the room. Louise got up and took Eliza's glass to refill it.

"Did they ever find out what happened to Linda Anderson, Range?" Louise asked as she stood at the butler's-table bar and dropped fresh ice cubes into the crystal, double-old-fashioned glass.

"God, I don't know. I never heard anything."

"Who's Linda Anderson?" Eliza inquired.

"She was an anchor for Garden State Network. She was quite

good, and very attractive. We were considering hiring her when she disappeared." Range squinted. "That must have been about five years ago now. What made you think of her?"

Louise handed the refilled glass back and looked into her guest's face. "Well, I think Linda Anderson looked a bit like you, Eliza. Didn't she, Range?"

Startled, Range stared at his anchorwoman. "You're right. She did."

CHAPTER

85

Now this was the type of thing she had envisioned when she had made the move out of the city. It was a sunny, clear Sunday afternoon, and the pin oaks and maple trees were just beginning to color in the gold, orange and red hues that would only get brighter in the weeks to come. Eliza and Janie, holding Daisy on a leash, along with Susan and James with their Buddy, meandered around the pond.

"Watch out for the goose doo," Susan warned as the kids ran ahead with the dogs. "Those geese," she sighed. "I walk around this beautiful pond for an hour every day. It's one of the things that sold me on the neighborhood. But I spend most of my time concentrating on not stepping in the goose droppings."

"They should be flying south somewhere soon, shouldn't they?" asked Eliza.

Susan shrugged. "I don't know. It seems like they stay around forever. They're pretty to look at when they're in the water, but I can't stand all the mess they leave behind. Speaking of mess, have you heard anything from the police about the robbery?"

"Nada," Eliza replied. "And to tell the truth, I'm not really expecting to. The patrolmen who came that night weren't too encouraging."

"What do we pay our taxes for?" asked Susan angrily. "They should be doing something about this."

Eliza hesitated before going further with the conversation. She didn't want to throw around accusations, but for the last week she had been nagged by her suspicions about Larson Richards. She would explode if she didn't confide them to her neighbor.

"Gosh, Eliza," Susan answered when she heard Eliza's worry that Larson still had a key and could have let himself into the house. "I know Larson is desperate for money, but I can't believe he would resort to burglary."

"What do you mean, he's desperate for money?" Eliza pressed.

"I told you about that pizza-business deal of his."

"Yes."

Susan looked at Eliza. "I shouldn't really be breaking this confidence, but I guess it doesn't matter now that the Richardses are dead."

"What 'confidence'?"

Susan began slowly at first and then her story poured out. "The Richardses had lent Larson a great deal of money to keep his business afloat. Mrs. Richards was quite worried about it and asked him to sign notes for the loans. But as he came back for more and more, she finally told him that they didn't want to pour any more cash down the rathole."

"How did Larson take it?"

"Not well. Mrs. Richards was crying one day when she came over and told me about it. You wouldn't believe the horrible things Larson said to his own mother. He told her that if she didn't help him, he would never speak to her again. That she and Mr. Richards would be dead as far as he was concerned."

"Nice son," Eliza observed.

Susan's eyes welled with tears as the sun glistened on her dark hair. "Mrs. Richards said she didn't want to lose her only child and was reconsidering giving Larson more money."

"Did she?"

"I don't know. Right after that, that damned gas heater backed up and the Richardses were killed by the carbon monoxide."

CHAPTER

86

"A Mr. Morton is in the lobby to see Ms. Blake."

"Tell Mr. Morton I'll be right down."

Paige hung up the phone. An interview with one of the presidential candidates had opened up and Eliza had hastily taken the morning shuttle to Washington. Paige hadn't been able to reach Samuel Morton to cancel his appointment.

Not bothering to take the elevator, Paige rushed down the stairwell and the long corridor that led to the Broadcast Center lobby. Waiting at the guard desk was a tall, attractive man with dark hair and graying sideburns, carrying a medium-sized shopping bag. Paige knew her clothes and would bet that was a Zegna suit he was wearing, a suit that cost over two thousand dollars.

"Mr. Morton," greeted Paige, extending her hand, "I'm Ms. Blake's assistant, Paige Tintle."

"Nice to meet you." The man shook her hand firmly.

"I'm so sorry to have to tell you this, but Ms. Blake had to go out of town unexpectedly this morning. She is very sorry, and told me to tell you she hopes you can reschedule another time to meet."

Paige could see the disappointment on Samuel's face.

"If you'd like, I could give you a little tour of our operation now," Paige offered.

Samuel was very pleasant and showed a lot of interest over the half hour that Paige escorted him through the news facility. When they got upstairs to Eliza's office, Samuel gazed through the windowed wall down at the newsroom.

"I wish Sarah could have seen this," he murmured wistfully. "She would have loved it."

"I'm sorry, Mr. Morton." Paige couldn't think of anything else to say.

As they exited the office to go back down to the lobby, Samuel suddenly remembered the shopping bag he carried. He extended it to Eliza's assistant.

"I'll be in town all week, and I would very much appreciate a chance to see Ms. Blake personally, if her schedule permits. But just in case we can't get together, would you please give her this for me?"

CHAPTER

87

The weekend dinner conversation had stuck with him and Range was not giving up on his story idea. As executive producer it was his prerogative to assign any piece he wanted. After the morning editorial meeting, he called Keith Chapel down to the Fishbowl.

"See what you can find out about the disappearance, about five years ago, of a Garden State Network anchorwoman named Linda Anderson."

Keith scribbled on his notepad. "Are you thinking about this as a FRESHER LOOK?"

"I'm not sure yet," Range answered. "See what you come up with. Let me know and then we'll talk to Eliza about it."

Keith nodded and turned to leave the office.

"Wait a minute, Keith." Range pulled open his desk drawer and extracted a black videocassette box. "I searched around and found this audition tape that Anderson submitted when she was trying to get a job here. Take a look and see what you think."

Later, the producer popped the cassette into the viewing machine. The woman who appeared on the screen delivering dated New Jersey news reminded Keith of the woman who appeared on the dozens of other videotapes scattered around his office.

CHAPTER

88

That guy was loitering across the street from the Broadcast Center again.

By rights the security chief knew he should call the police and have them talk to the man, but Joe Connelly itched to get out there and confront him face-to-face. There had been more letters and still no response from the FBI. Connelly was tense, and determined that nothing would happen to Eliza Blake on his watch.

Taking two uniformed security guards along with him, Connelly pushed through the revolving door, waited for a break in the traffic and jaywalked across the wide street. The sweatshirt-clad man stared at him defiantly as he approached.

"Excuse me, sir. I'd like to know your name and why you've been hanging around here."

The man looked at him disdainfully. "I don't have to tell you my name, and the last time I looked, this is a free country and these are public sidewalks."

"Listen, clown. Move along and don't come back. Do you hear me? If I see you out here again, I'll call the police."

"Oh. I'm scared."

Connelly felt like slamming the sarcastic son–of–a–bitch in the face. Instead he motioned to one of the guards, who speedily pulled a camera from his pocket and snapped off a couple quick shots of the tough mug.

"Hey! You can't do that," the loiterer protested, lunging for the camera.

The guard pulled back, the camera safely out of Meat's reach.

"Why not call a policeman?" Connelly dared triumphantly. "Now get the hell out of here and, I'm warning you, don't come back."

CHAPTER

89

What a lucky little boy!

Sure, he had something called Fragile X syndrome and he was forced to live a life with mental retardation, speech problems and anxieties. He might never drive a car or learn to read or write, and it was a cinch he was never going to learn to do long division, but, just because he had some lousy genetic condition, he got to be close to Eliza.

It was heartwarming to watch Eliza talking so gently to the boy as he flapped his hands up and down. No wonder the kid was flapping. Being near her was damned exciting.

The thought of having pictures together with Eliza to watch over and over on the television screen at night would ensure sweet dreams. But then again, there were those pictures together with Linda Anderson and watching them over and over again didn't lead to peaceful nights. If only Linda hadn't resisted. It was her own fault, really. Linda had only herself to blame.

All that time spent working to get closer to Linda. Slowly bringing her to the point where she could be comfortable and confide her hopes and fears.

Fear. That was the problem. When Linda had sensed she was being followed, she had called the police, confiding that she had done so to a person she had thought she could trust. A person not content with the existing contact between them. A person who knew her schedule and hid in wait for opportunities to see her more.

Of course, when the police were escorting Linda, nothing happened. The stalker lay low until Linda cried that the cops were off the case.

The wait to be with her again had been excruciating, that October five years ago. The pressure had mounted until it was unbearable. At Linda's door, that last night, her mouth had quivered and her eyes bulged in frightened recognition.

It didn't have to have ended the way it did. If only she had been able to accept the love she was offered, she wouldn't have been dragged, struggling, through the woods. If only she had listened and been open to the life they could have had together. Instead she had begun to scream. There had been no choice but to silence her. The sound of the snapping of her neck was still haunting.

Linda's body had had to be stowed in the car trunk until provisions were ready to get rid of it... taking it to a place that would be deserted on an early-November night.

It wasn't supposed to end that way.

It could be different with Eliza. It could be wonderful between them.

Eliza wouldn't make the same mistake Linda Anderson had.

If she did, she'd suffer the same fate.

Please, God, don't let it be that way.

CHAPTER

90

Eliza turned the pages of the blue leather–bound scrapbook, reading the letters that had been neatly mounted on each thick page. In spite of his grief Samuel Morton had taken the time to organize all the letters that Eliza had penned his daughter, and had written sensitively about what he remembered of Sarah's response to receiving each one.

What that man must be going through!

"Paige," Eliza called through the intercom, "will you see if you can get Samuel Morton on the phone for me, please?"

As she waited for the buzzer to ring, Eliza stroked the cover of the scrapbook, looking at the picture of the smiling young girl with braces on her teeth, wearing a yellow soccer uniform.

"Mr. Morton is on line three, Eliza."

She took a deep breath and pressed the button on the telephone console.

"Mr. Morton? This is Eliza Blake. I wanted to apologize for not being here when you came in earlier this week. And I want to thank you so much for this wonderful remembrance of Sarah. That was so thoughtful of you."

"I'm so glad if you like it. It was a therapeutic thing for me to work on and, please, don't worry about having to cancel our meeting, Ms. Blake. I know how busy you must be."

She liked the sound of his deep voice.

"How are you doing, Mr. Morton?"

"Please, call me Samuel."

"Fine, if you'll call me Eliza."

"Done," he agreed. She could sense a slight smile on the other end of the telephone line. "Actually, I'm doing a bit better now that I'm here in New York. I needed to get away from home for a while."

"I can certainly understand that. Do you know people here?"

"Yes, actually, I do. I used to live up here, so I'm looking up some old friends."

"That's good. Sometimes it helps to just go through the motions of getting out with people and socializing a little bit, even though you really don't feel like it. If you sit in by yourself and think too much, it doesn't get you anywhere."

"That's certainly the truth," Samuel agreed. "But you know, even the best of friends are busy and have lives of their own. Plus they only have so much patience for a man who may break out in tears at any moment."

Eliza remembered well the dinners with friends after John died and the embarrassing knowledge that they—no matter how loving and well-meaning—were somehow uncomfortable being with her. She wished there was something she could do to help this man.

"I don't suppose you'd like to go out to dinner with me, Eliza. It would be a great pleasure."

She thought for a moment about making a lame excuse, but she couldn't bring herself to do it. She rubbed the leather scrapbook. What would it hurt to take a couple of hours and spend it with a man who could sorely use a little company?

"Sure, that would be lovely. I have to ask that we keep it an early evening, though."

"Wonderful." She heard the enthusiasm in his voice. "You just name the time and place."

"How about tomorrow night, right after the broadcast? I could meet you somewhere at seven–thirtyish?"

"Fine. And the place?"

"Why don't I leave that to you, Samuel? Just call my assistant tomorrow and let Paige know."

Eliza hung up the receiver and thought about Mack. She hadn't been out to dinner alone with a man since Mack had left for London. While she didn't think dinner with Samuel qualified as a date, Eliza wished Mack knew that she would be dining with someone else.

CHAPTER

91

Florence Anderson was only all too happy to talk to Keith Chapel when he called. No one wanted to hear her talk about Linda anymore. The police no longer paid attention to her. Nor were they doing any-thing, as far as Florence could see, to find out what had happened to her daughter. She could tell they thought she was a nuisance by the tone in their voice when she called the station house. She hated that they were resigned about the case.

She was angry. If it had been any one of *their* daughters, they wouldn't be giving up. Those cops stuck together like white on rice. If one of their own had disappeared, you could bet your sweet life, they would have found out what had happened by now. She vented her frustrations to the KEY News producer, unaware that he was thinking how good all her rage would be on television.

"The police started out all right," Florence admitted. "In the days right after Linda disappeared, they searched all over the place, with dogs and helicopters and boats. They kept saying that they hoped they wouldn't find anything. They hoped she was alive."

The woman paused. "Well, they didn't find anything. Now, all these years have gone by and I know in my heart Linda is dead. I would be satisfied just to know what happened to her. I would just like to find whatever is left of my daughter and bury her in peace. You can't imagine what it's like, not knowing...." Her voice trailed off.

"You're right. I can't imagine," Keith answered quietly. "Mrs. Anderson, would you be willing to be interviewed if we came out to you with a camera crew?"

"Mister, I'd stand naked on Broadway if it would help find out what happened to my Linda."

CHAPTER

9 2

"You must have connections. What did you have to do to get a dinner reservation here on such short notice?"

Samuel smiled but did not answer Eliza's question as they sat in the neutral-toned dining room at Jean Georges, the four-star restaurant in the luminous Trump Hotel. The austerity of the dining room, while comfortable, was low-key, putting the focus on food. Tables were reserved weeks in advance. The waiters bent over the tables, carving and pouring, intent only their guests' pleasure.

The last touch was put on each dish after it arrived at the table.

Eliza ordered the young garlic soup which arrived as a delicate bowl of purple chive blossoms. When the waiter ladled the soup over the blooms, the intoxicating aroma of garlic wafted into the air. Samuel's asparagus arrived looking tender but naked. But as the waiter dressed the spears with creamed morels, the stalks were transformed.

"I'm sure you've eaten here many times before," Samuel said.

"Actually, no, I haven't. I've been meaning to, but just haven't gotten around to it."

Samuel nodded. "I know how it is. A fabulous place can be in your own backyard and you never get around to going there."

"Something like that. I try not to go out to dinner too often, you know, with a young child at home. I like to get home to her after work."

The moment the words were out of her mouth, Eliza could have bitten off her tongue at the thoughtlessness of her remark. Here she was, prattling on about her daughter, when Samuel had just lost his.

He was gracious in his response. "Of course. Your time with your daughter must be very precious to you. I apologize for keeping you from her tonight."

"Please, this is my pleasure," Eliza insisted. "Janie is quite happy tonight. She just got a new Disney DVD and at this moment she is most likely happily munching away on popcorn, content that Mrs. Garcia will let her stay up a little later tonight."

"Mrs. Garcia is your nanny?"

"Nanny–slash–housekeeper. She's wonderful."

"Good help is hard to find. I remember when Sarah was little, after her mother died, I went through a slew of caretakers. I soon realized that one was stealing from us. Another actually had her boyfriend come over and sleep in my bed while I was away on business."

"How did you find that out? Did Sarah tell you?"

Samuel's face reddened. "I'm embarrassed to tell you. You'll surely think less of me."

Eliza waited and, finally, Samuel continued.

"I had a funny feeling about this young woman. Call it instinct or intuition. But I was leaving Sarah with her all day long and a few times I had gotten home earlier than I was expected and found the boyfriend there. One afternoon, I even thought I smelled marijuana."

Eliza groaned.

Samuel continued his explanation. "So on a weekend when this young woman was away, I searched her room." He looked sharply at Eliza to gauge her reaction. He found no judgment on her face.

"You found drugs?" she asked.

"No, but I found her diary, and I read through it. She described the whole thing. How they had slept in my bed, how weird it had felt, the fun they'd had in my shower. All while my Sarah was sleeping in the room next door." Samuel sat back in his chair. "You must think me truly awful."

Eliza stopped to consider. Ordinarily she would recoil from such an admission, but she could appreciate the force that would drive a parent to resort to desperate measures to ensure a child's safety.

"I can certainly understand why you did what you did. I might have done the same thing," she admitted candidly.

They talked about Samuel's work in contract law while they anticipated the waiter's arrival with their identical entrées. Pure white halibut surrounded on one side with a bright red comfit of tomatoes, on the other side, delicate green ribbons of zucchini. Lifting a sauce boat, the waiter completed the creation with an aromatic, sherrylike Château–Chalon sauce.

"Mmmm, this is fabulous," Eliza said after taking the first bite.

Samuel nodded in agreement. "We have wonderful fish in Sarasota, and wonderful restaurants, too. Have you ever been there?"

"Never. But I've heard great things about the city. I'd be afraid, though, that I wouldn't want to go to work if I lived near the water. I love the beach."

"Me too. There is something about the water that is so soothing. I had Sarah's ashes sprinkled in the Gulf of Mexico."

Suddenly Eliza didn't taste the perfect food in her mouth. Her face

must have registered her distress as Samuel began to apologize profusely.

"Please, forgive me, Eliza. That just popped out. It's hardly dinner
conversation."

Poor guy. It was all so fresh.

On the sidewalk in front of the restaurant, a paparazzo stood
poised, hoping for a celebrity to appear. After dinner, as Samuel escorted Eliza out to the car waiting for her on Central Park West, the
photographer got what he wanted.

The next morning, the *Daily News* carried a picture of two surprised faces with a caption that read, NEW LOVE FOR ELIZA BLAKE.

CHAPTER

93

Saturday morning brought an embarrassment of riches as Drake
brought in the morning newspapers to his master as he had been
trained to do. First Jerry scanned the pages of the *Record*, catching his
breath as he saw the large colored picture of Eliza Blake that domi-
nated the front page of the "Local" section. He read the article quickly,
his heart racing as he realized that Eliza's house was now only a few
miles from his own in Upper Saddle River. Eliza and her young
daughter were now his neighbors!

He read the article over and over again before taking a pair of scissors from the drawer and cutting precisely along the black edging that outlined the story. Then he carefully folded the printed paper and slipped it into the drawer of the bedside table.

The *New York Times*, the paper that was supposed to bring the world to the reader's door, bored Jerry after what he had read in the *Record*. He turned the pages matter-of-factly, noting that it looked like the Yankees were on their way to the World Series again this year. Jerry used to love playing baseball.

But the *Daily News* sent him seething.

NEW LOVE FOR ELIZA BLAKE.

He stared at the grainy picture. Eliza couldn't be interested in that uptight-looking guy who stared like a deer caught in the headlights at her side. Jerry steamed about it all morning and into the afternoon, eating almost an entire box of Devil Dogs. Then, pumped by all the sugar in his system, he spent half an hour lifting his hand weights. Up and down, up and down. The pressure grew as perspiration broke out on his forehead. Finally, at two o'clock, he could contain himself no longer.

He dialed the New York number and waited as he was transferred to Eliza's office.

"I read about you in the papers today, Eliza. I'm glad that you came to your senses and moved out of the city. You'll like it much better out here." Jerry's voice cracked as he continued. "But you better not be taking up with that stiff. He looks *way* too boring for you. I can give you the excitement you need, baby. Give me a try."

He was about to hang up, but there was something else he thought he should add. Something that would make her know for certain that he was not fooling around.

Jerry hissed out his last words, as Drake began to bark in alarm. "Listen to me, Eliza. Listen to me good. Because if you don't, I'm going to come and take your little girl."

CHAPTER

94

Abigail felt satisfied after she finished her early Sunday-morning session with her trainer. She wished she could show off the washboard abs she'd worked so hard to get. If only Eliza would give her the chance.

By the time Abigail showered and dressed, the gym was starting to get crowded. She stuffed her sweats into her bag and hurried out. Monica Anderson bumped into her on the sidewalk. Abigail said hello and muttered something about being late to meet a friend for brunch. But Monica was determined to have a conversation.

"Abigail, guess what?" Monica didn't wait for an answer. "KEY News is doing a story on Linda's disappearance. My mother is all excited. She's convinced a national news story will bring new attention to the case. Maybe someone out there will see it and come forward with some fresh information."

"That's great, Monica," Abigail answered without enthusiasm.

"My mother and I thought that you might have had something to do with KEY doing a story on Linda. Did you suggest it?"

She could lie and Monica would probably never find out. But why bother?

"I wish I could say I did, Monica, but it wasn't me who came up with the idea. Who is doing the story?"

Monica bit her lip as she tried to recall the name her mother had mentioned. "I can't recall the producer Mom spoke to, but he did say that the story was being done for the *Evening Headlines*. Eliza Blake might be coming to our house for an interview."

As Abigail walked down Broadway, she wondered why the Linda Anderson story was being done now, after all this time. Why would the *Evening Headlines* want to dredge all that up again? It was old news.

But the fact that Eliza would be doing the story on Abigail's old friend's disappearance struck her as destiny. Another sign that Eliza's and Abigail's lives were meant to be intertwined.

OCTOBER

CHAPTER

95

Finally, a promising break. Promising, but most alarming.

Paige had listened to the call first thing Monday morning and transferred it downstairs immediately. "Don't mention it to her, Paige," the security chief instructed. "I'll talk to Eliza about it."

Saturday afternoon was not an extremely busy time for the switch-board at the Broadcast Center. Records of calls made around two o'clock would help the telephone-company computers winnow down the suspect list.

Connelly listened to the call again and made entries on his computer.

The caller had said he lived near Eliza's HoHoKus home.

The caller read the northern New Jersey newspaper as well as New York City's *Daily News*.

The caller had a dog.

The caller had taken it to a new level now. He had threatened Eliza's daughter.

Beads of perspiration broke out on Joe Connelly's creased forehead.

"I think it's time we get a security team guarding your house."

Eliza gripped the armrests of her office chair, stunned at the enormity of what Joe had just told her.

Janie.

She was at school right now. Some maniac could walk right in with a machine gun and take her. Or worse. How many times had she reported a story like this? Eliza couldn't catch her breath and she closed her eyes tight, as if the darkness would make the terror that filled her go away.

"This is no time to panic, Eliza."

Joe was right. She couldn't clutch now. She had to keep her wits about her. Janie's life could depend on it.

"I'll make the phone calls and set things up," she heard Joe say. "We'll have security on your house by this afternoon."

Eliza nodded numbly. "I should call the school and Mrs. Garcia," she murmured.

"I can do that," offered Joe.

With every fiber of determination that she possessed, Eliza straightened in her chair. "No, I'll call."

Some sick lunatic was not going to take over her life.

CHAPTER

96

To hell with that security jerk. Meat didn't have to bother anymore with going into New York and camping out on the sidewalk in front of the Broadcast Center anyway. Eliza had moved into his own backyard.

Well, almost his backyard. HoHoKus may have been in the same county as Moonachie, but it was a world away in terms of lifestyle. The *Record* called it an "upscale" community. Meat's hometown certainly wasn't that.

He dressed carefully, selecting his only pair of khaki pants and that ridiculous sweater with the polo player embroidered on the front. When his mother had given the maroon sweater to him last Christmas in an attempt to spiff him up, he had sworn to himself that he would never wear it. Now he was glad that he hadn't tossed it. The sweater was just the type of thing those HoHoKus swells wore.

He drove his beat-up Escort north on Route 17 and watched for a HoHoKus exit. Taking the Hollywood Avenue ramp, he crossed back over the highway, noting the names of the intersecting streets. Lloyd, Elmwood, Lakewood, Fairview. After he drove less than a mile, he turned left into the HoHoKus business district.

Business district! That was a laugh. What a sleepy little burg this was. Cruising slowly along the main drag, he craned his neck, looking for the local barbershop. He needed a haircut. But, more importantly, the town barber always knew the local gossip.

Meat spotted the red-and-white-striped pole and continued down the block, parking in a spot he was certain could not be seen from the barbershop. When he walked to the front door, he saw the sign. CLOSED.

What an idiot! It was Monday. Of course the barbershop was closed. Meat cupped his hands, pressed them to the window and gazed through. Though no lights were on, he could see someone inside. He tapped on the window and hastily concocted his story.

"Hi there. I just moved into town and my in-laws are coming to see the house for the first time today. My wife sent me out for a haircut and she'll kill me if I don't come back with one. Any chance you could possibly take me?"

The barber glanced at his watch. "Well, I'm going to play some golf, but my tee time isn't until after lunch. I guess it's all right. Come on in."

"You're a lifesaver, pal," said Meat as he headed to the barber's chair.

"Good thing I left my wallet here, or you never would have caught me in today." The barber switched on the overhead lights. "Where did you move to?"

"We bought a house on Lakewood."

"Lakewood? I don't remember hearing about any house on Lakewood being on the market."

Meat thought quickly. "It was a private sale."

"You're lucky. Everything that comes on the market here lately is snapped up before the Realtors even get a chance to show it." The barber snapped the giant bib around Meat's neck.

"Yeah. My wife had her heart set on this town. She was beside herself when she read in the paper this weekend that Eliza Blake had moved in, too. Do you know where she lives?"

The barber took out his sharp scissors and began to snip. "She bought the Richardses' place on Saddle Ridge Road. A big brick colonial."

"I'll have to take my wife for a drive-by. Is it the only brick colonial on the street?"

The barber stopped combing and cutting to consider. "I'm not sure. I know there's been some new construction over there recently. But Eliza Blake's house is on the right-hand side when you turn in from East Saddle River Road. It's right where the road bends."

CHAPTER

97

A tall vase with two dozen perfect pink roses arrived at the Broadcast Center on Monday afternoon. When Paige brought up the cellophane-wrapped arrangement from the lobby and placed it on Eliza's desk, her boss barely looked up.

"Do you want me to read the card?" Paige asked.

"Go ahead," Eliza said dully.

Paige slipped open the small white envelope. " 'Thank you for helping me realize that there is still enjoyment left to be had. Samuel.' "

The assistant looked expectantly at her boss, hoping the romantic gesture would boost her spirits.

"That's nice," was all Eliza could muster. She rose from her chair and walked over to the window, wrapping her arms around herself. "God, Paige, I just want this day to be over so I can get home."

"Are the security men there yet?"

"Yes. I just talked to Mrs. Garcia. Two of them are on watch outside."

"And Janie?"

"She's fine. She doesn't realize what is going on."

"That's good," said Paige.

Eliza pounded her clenched fists against the glass in desperation. *Why can't the phone company and Joe Connelly catch these nuts?*

CHAPTER

98

The pouch destined for the London bureau was picked up by a courier at the Broadcast Center by five P.M. each weekday in order to make the night flight to the U.K. At four-thirty, Abigail hurried to the Traffic Desk carrying a gray interoffice envelope marked for Mack McBride and dropped it in the bright yellow mesh shipping bag along with all the other envelopes and small packages already inside. You were supposed to register your entry on the clipboard that hung beside the pouch, but Abigail didn't bother.

Why not share the misery?

On the other side of the Atlantic, Mack would open the envelope and find only the copy of the *Daily News* picture. He would never know who had sent it his way.

What could it hurt? If Mack knew Eliza was already seeing someone else, that she was moving on, perhaps it would discourage him from trying to make things right between them again.

Abigail had not given up. Despite Eliza's protestations, Abigail hoped she might still come around. She did not want Mack coming back into Eliza's life.

CHAPTER

99

Another call came in after midnight. Against Joe's advice, Eliza demanded that he play it back for her. Her face paled as she listened to the whispered words.

"Eliza, you are beautiful, even without your makeup. I dream of waking up beside your scrubbed face each morning. Your daughter can join us in our bed and we will all snuggle together."

Without her makeup? Who had seen her without her makeup? Was he looking in her windows, watching her as she played with Janie out in the yard? Had he seen her come into the Broadcast Center one morning when she hadn't had time to apply her makeup?

Eliza felt physically ill. She ran down the hallway and vomited.

She had to do her job. She had to.

Keith wanted to go over the FRESHER LOOK shooting schedule. Could they go to the Bronx Zoo this weekend, interview the bat expert there and get man-on-the-street sound bites about how people felt about bats? The weather was expected to be good over the Columbus Day holiday weekend and there would be plenty of zoo-goers.

Eliza tried to think. There was absolutely no way on God's green earth that she was going to leave Janie this weekend.

"I'll do it, Keith, but I'm bringing Janie with me," she said firmly.

If the producer was surprised, he didn't show it. Actually Keith hoped that he would be as devoted to his baby when it finally arrived.

"Sure, Eliza. That sounds great. I hear they have some Halloween things going on there. Janie should love it." Keith looked at his clipboard. "Now, about the Linda Anderson story. We can go out and interview Mrs. Anderson next Tuesday. Will that work for you?"

Eliza was having a hard time thinking past this afternoon. "Check with Paige. If I'm open, fine."

Keith's research had convinced Range that the Linda Anderson story would make good TV. Though Eliza had been uncomfortable when Range insisted that they do it as a FRESHER LOOK, she now felt almost compelled to face it head-on. Linda Anderson had resembled Eliza, she had a similar job and, because of Linda's high profile and large audience, the police thought almost anyone could have become obsessed with her.

People who had known Linda for years were called in and questioned after she disappeared. Co-workers, friends and acquaintances. The police conducted over four hundred interviews and followed up on twelve hundred leads. In the end, though, the authorities were convinced that an obsessive fan had targeted Linda as an object of desire. The very phenomenon that had helped Linda in her career— the fact that even if you had never met her, you felt you knew her— had led to her death. And all the investigations, manhunts and cadaver dogs had turned up nothing.

CHAPTER

100

With James in school and her housekeeper keeping an eye on the girls, Susan tied up the laces on her running shoes, determined to get her exercise. She did some stretches against the side of the house and started briskly down the driveway. The dark gray sedan was parked in front of Eliza's again this morning. One man was sitting in the car and another was patrolling the property.

Susan's heart went out to her new friend. She had always thought it must be so exciting to be a celebrity. Now she realized that being famous had a terrible downside as well. She was more appreciative than ever of her own secure little world.

Susan nodded at the man in the car and trotted down the slight incline that led to the quiet road that circled the pond. Then she picked up her pace. She was on her fifth lap when she noticed a beat-up blue car pulling to a stop in front of the wooded lot on the far side of the pond. When she circled round the next time, the car was still there, but there was no one in it.

Meat had driven by the brick colonial and spotted the gray sedan. He didn't dare go back for a second look. That was a cop car, he could smell it.

He parked the car in the spot he had found when he'd cased the neighborhood on Monday morning after his conversation with the barber. The space, edging the woods, was not in front of anyone's house, so unless he left it there for an extended period of time, nobody was going to be calling the police to report it. Good thing he had come then, before those bastards were posted in front of Eliza's house.

That morning reconnaissance mission had been rewarding. The wealthy neighborhood was peaceful and landscaped with lots of trees and thick hedges. It had really been no big accomplishment to hide among the bushes and sneak round the back of Eliza's house to case things out.

That cabana was pretty neat. He could live in that place—it was nicer than his apartment. But the tree house was the place he had chosen for his viewing spot. If he could get in there at night, he would be able to peer through the slot in the boarded wall and look into Eliza's lighted windows.

That was still the plan, but the security guards would make it a little more difficult to execute. Difficult, but not impossible.

He looked forward to it, really. The tree house brought to mind his bat house. And just like his furry friends, Meat, when the time was right, would come out to feed.

Larson Richards was eager to meet his potential investor for lunch at Marcello's at the HoHoKus Inn. *It better go well today*, he thought as he drove to the Sheridan Avenue restaurant. He had barely met payroll this week, and if he didn't get a large cash infusion in the coming days, he wasn't going to be able to pay his workers on the fifteenth of the month. That would be the beginning of the end.

If the lawyers and accountants and secretaries he had on staff didn't get their checks, they would sense the ship was sinking and bail. They would tell their spouses, who would tell their friends, and the word would be out that Richards Enterprises was failing.

The digital clock on the Mercedes dashboard told him he had some time to spare. It was only eleven forty-five. Impulsively he turned left onto Lloyd Avenue. Eliza's daughter should be getting out of kindergarten about now.

He still hoped that he could get on Eliza's good side. If he could gain her trust, he might be able to persuade her to invest with him. Her warning not to come to the house anymore flashed through his mind. She hadn't said anything about going to the school. If he could get Janie to like him, Eliza might come around. At this point he was desperate and anything was worth a shot. Hell, even that gas-pumper Augie was nagging him.

Larson parked the car behind the row of SUVs and station wagons that waited for their treasured passengers. He didn't notice the gray sedan parked behind the white Volvo.

Within a few minutes the young students began running from the school building to their mothers and nannies. He spotted Janie walking out, her hand held by a very short woman who brought her directly to the caramel-skinned housekeeper.

Larson started to get out of the car, but thought better of it. Maybe this wasn't the time. He could tell the Guatemalan woman had not liked him when he had visited the house. The last thing he needed was the foreign housekeeper complaining about him to Eliza.

Better to wait for another chance.

So that's how it worked.

The security car followed the maid when she went out to pick up the kid.

That could be his window of opportunity. When they were all out, he could sneak into the tree house with his gear and wait.

It was a long time between noon and night. And what if the security guys checked out the tree house every time they came back? Meat hid in the bushes and waited for the cars to return. The maid took the kid in the house and the security guys sat out front and ate their lunch in the car. Every twenty minutes or so, one of the men got out of the car and walked around the property, coming close but never discovering Meat. At four o'clock a new pair came to relieve them.

Meat waited another hour, knowing the owner would be ticked off that he was late for work. He was going to be more ticked off when Meat told him he was taking Friday night off. No matter how much the boss moaned, Meat was determined not to work, because in the five hours that Meat had hidden in the bushes behind Eliza's home, no one had ever climbed up to check the tree house.

CHAPTER

101

"Don't ask me why I did it, Doris. I just did."

"Feeling sorry for a guy is no reason to ask him to dinner at your home, especially with all you've got going on right now."

Doris was absolutely right, but when Samuel had called and asked if they could get together again, Eliza had blurted out all that had been happening. He had shown so much concern that she was genuinely touched. And though she hated to admit it to herself, she was relieved as well. Eliza knew it was that "man as protector" thing that was instilled in women as they grew up. She didn't care, though. At this point she liked the idea of a man in the house on Friday night.

She hadn't told KayKay and Poppie about the threat to Janie, knowing they would be wild with worry and would insist on coming out to stay with them again. What if Paul had a heart attack or something from the stress of it all? It wasn't fair to keep depending on them so.

"What's Janie going to think about a new man coming to the house?" Doris asked as she outlined Eliza's lips.

"I hope she'll be fine with it. I'm bribing her by telling her that if she is on her best behavior, she can come with me to the Bronx Zoo on Saturday."

Doris rolled her eyes and Eliza laughed for the first time in days.

"Whatever works, honey, whatever works."

The whole time he was in Israel, Mack thought about calling Eliza. He never got around to it. He could blame it on being too busy, or too preoccupied with the developing events he had been assigned to cover. But he knew in his heart he was simply a coward. Why was he able to suit up in a flak jacket each day and drive into warring territories, yet unable to pick up the telephone and try to work things out between them?

She hadn't responded to the long letter he had written her, begging for forgiveness. But he knew Eliza had been seeing his face, at least, as he reported from the Middle East.

As each day passed, the situation just got worse and worse as their estrangement grew. Now, safely back in London, lying on his back in his hotel, Mack realized that it might be too late ever to put things back together again. The newspaper clipping lay on the bed beside him.

She was seeing someone else.

Why shouldn't she? He had cheated on her—all bets were off. He wasn't there for her, now, when she needed him. Eliza didn't know that he had been calling Joe Connelly on a regular basis for updates on the threats. He'd asked Joe not to tell her.

If he had any guts at all he would march into Marcy's office in the morning and tell her that he needed to fly back to the States. He could get on a plane and be in New York tomorrow night.

Mack picked up the newspaper clipping and stared at it again. The guy looked decent enough. Maybe this man would treat Eliza better than he had. She deserved that.

CHAPTER

1 0 2

The night was chilly and Meat was glad that he had been smart enough to bring his down ski jacket and gloves with him. His knapsack held a couple of bologna-and-cheese sandwiches on hard rolls, a thermos of coffee and several cans of beer. He could pee in the empty beer cans when nature called.

The house was ablaze with lights and, from his perch in the tree, Meat had a front-row seat on the action inside. It was like looking at a giant dollhouse and being able to see what was going on in every room at one time.

First there was all the chitchat in the kitchen, as Eliza tried to play the happy homemaker, pouring glasses of wine and tossing the salad. The guy with her looked like a doofus, the type who would have a closetful of those dumb preppie sweaters.

As far as Meat could tell, this wasn't the guy he had seen Eliza with in *People* magazine over the summer. He had made a point, after seeing that magazine picture, of watching the news for Mack McBride. He wanted to see what Eliza saw in him. Meat had noticed that McBride had been reporting from the Middle East lately. Nope. The guy in there with her tonight wasn't McBride.

What kind of mother was she? Going from one guy to the next and bringing him home when there was a little kid in the house? *Slut.*

The saccharine scene of the three of them gathered around the dining-room table made Meat nauseous. The guy was sucking up to the little girl, big time. Turning to talk to her and listening to her and laughing at the things she said. But the worst was yet to come.

Eliza and the child left the room and the guy sat for a while sipping his wine at the table. A light behind a small window upstairs clicked on and Meat could see yellow tiles on the walls. He saw Eliza's mouth moving as her head tilted downward. The little kid was probably brushing her teeth or something.

Meanwhile the guy rose from the table downstairs, went into the kitchen and poured himself another drink. He looked out the window and then opened the back door and walked out to the pool. In the darkness of the yard, Meat couldn't see much, but he thought the man knelt down and swished his hand in the water. *Strange duck.*

The bathroom light clicked off, and a few minutes after that, another light went off upstairs. The kid must be in bed now. Moments later, Eliza reappeared in the kitchen, stuck her head into the dining room and then turned around and went back into the kitchen where she realized the back door was open.

Meat heard her call out, "Samuel?"

"I'm out here, Eliza, admiring your pool."

"Here, let me switch the lights on out there."

The backyard was suddenly flooded with light, and Meat crouched lower in the tree house. He needn't have bothered. They weren't paying any attention to him.

"I've got to get the pool company over to cover this up," said Eliza as she walked out with her arms wrapped across her chest against the night chill. When she got to the pool, the guy put his arm around her. They talked in hushed voices and Meat couldn't hear what they were saying.

But his eyes saw it all. Meat watched as the man leaned over and kissed Eliza, and the rage within him grew as Eliza wrapped her arms around the man's neck and kissed him back.

Tramp. It didn't matter that the man didn't stay the night.

The dinner guest left a little after eleven. Half an hour later, the upstairs lights flicked off. Just after midnight, as the security guards were changing shifts out front, Meat quietly climbed down from the tree house.

He stole along the edge of the bush-lined property and through the backyards of three neighboring homes that led to the street that circled the pond. His rubber-soled shoes padded silently across the macadam toward his car.

There was a ticket on the window.

Damn!

CHAPTER

103

"All right, come. You can hang out with the other elephants."

The moment the words spewed from his mouth, Keith knew he had crossed the Rubicon. Even if their marriage survived, Cindy would never, ever, let him forget what he had just said to her in exasperation.

The stunned expression on his wife's puffy face quickly dissolved to hurt.

Here come the tears.

"Damn it, Cindy. I'm sorry. But you push and push."

"I just wanted to spend the day with my husband. What am I supposed to do, hang around this apartment by myself all day?" she sobbed.

Keith looked at her bloated ankles peeking from beneath the bathrobe stretched tightly around her protruding belly. Her once-lustrous blonde hair was limp and dull. Her skin was blotchy and there were dark circles under eyes from lack of sleep. Keith felt sorry for Cindy, yet at the same time he was repelled. He was embarrassed at the thought of bringing her along to the zoo.

He thought of how uncomfortable it would be for both him and Eliza. His wife standing there in the advanced stages of pregnancy, while both of them knew he had made that pass. There was no way he wanted Cindy to come along on this shoot.

"Look, Cindy. This isn't going to take all day. I'll be back by mid-afternoon. We'll do something together when I get home. I promise."

But Cindy's initial hurt had progressed to the next stage.

"Don't bother," she said angrily. Cindy lumbered into the bed-room and slammed the door.

CHAPTER

104

Meat's eyes were glazed from a night of fitful napping in his car. He had driven from his woodside spot into the HoHoKus business district and pulled into a gas station. There were several cars parked at the side of the station. His Escort slid in next to them. Just another car, waiting to be serviced. There he stayed until the morning light.

He bought a Taylor ham–and–fried egg sandwich on a buttered roll and a cup of coffee at a deli and ate his breakfast in the car. He chewed and wondered what Eliza was going to do today.

Meat gulped his hot coffee and considered his options. If he went back to his spot and parked, the police might come sniffing around. Cruising the neighborhood would be risky. If he passed by the house, those thugs parked out front would be sure to notice. He needed to find a spot from which to view the house without the guards seeing him.

Then it occurred to him. The new mansion that was being built down the street. The construction workers wouldn't be there on Saturday. He could pull right into the garage. Even if someone saw his dusty old car, they would assume it was only a laborer's.

He turned onto Saddle Ridge Road, his tired eyes spotting the back of the gray sedan up the street ahead. Meat pulled into the dirt driveway of the uncompleted house and slipped into the garage. He got out of the car and walked up the makeshift wooden ramp that led up to what looked like it would be the new kitchen. He wandered around until he found the main staircase, went upstairs and turned in the direction of Eliza's home. In a corner bedroom, he found a spot that gave him a clear view.

He watched and waited until, finally, the payoff. Eliza shepherded her little girl into the station wagon. A little boy came out of the house across the street and got in as well. The Volvo pulled out of the driveway and the gray sedan followed behind.

Meat brushed the sawdust from his pants and sped downstairs to get to his car.

CHAPTER

105

Samuel paced back and forth in the bright morning sun at the entrance of the World of Darkness. He was thrilled that Eliza had asked him if he wanted to meet her at the Bronx Zoo and spend the rest of the day there after she finished her shoot. It was so kind of her to include him. Samuel hoped Eliza wasn't just feeling sorry for him. Pity-dating was not what he had in mind.

The warmth of her mouth as she had returned his kiss last night by the swimming pool had not been rooted in sympathy, he was sure of it. There had been an urgency to it. Samuel felt he could have pushed for more. Though he desperately wanted to go further with Eliza, he didn't think it would be wise. It was too early.

He spied Eliza and two skipping children rounding the path. Three men followed, laden with camera gear. Several yards behind were two more men. The security detail, Samuel surmised. Eliza kissed Samuel lightly on the cheek.

"Good morning." She greeted him with a smile. "I realized after you left last night that I should have told you to meet us later. I hope you won't be bored stiff while we get our work done."

"Not at all," Samuel protested. "I'm very interested in seeing how the television–news world works."

Eliza turned to the others and made introductions.

"You already know Janie, and this is her friend, James."

Samuel bent down to shake the boy's hand.

"And this is producer Keith Chapel, cameraman B.J. D'Elia and soundman John Dolan."

"Gentlemen," Samuel nodded. Hands were shaken all around. Samuel noticed that Eliza ignored the security men.

"What did you want to do first, Keith?" Eliza asked.

"I thought it would be good if we went inside and took a look at the exhibit while the crew sets up out here. We can ask people what they thought of the bats when they come out."

"Fine. Let's go." Eliza walked back to the security men and suggested they wait outside. She didn't need them hovering over them inside. It would ruin the experience for the kids.

This was really too good to be true.

Meat mingled among the other visitors and watched as Eliza and her retinue gathered in front of the World of Darkness. He knew the exhibit well. He had been here dozens of times before, in his quest to learn all he could about bats. The zoo offered all sorts of hands-on educational programs. It was here in the Bronx that he had first held a little brown bat in his own hands.

The juxtaposition of his two passions, right before his eyes, was unbearably exciting.

Look at Eliza! Could those jeans be any tighter?

Five pairs of eyes squinted, adjusting from the bright daylight to the pitch-black of night as the three adults and two children entered the World of Darkness pavilion. The sprawling room was designed to re-create a nightlike environment that would coax out of hiding various species of the animal kingdom that otherwise would never have been seen. Janie and James squeezed Eliza's hands with trepidation at first, but within minutes they broke away, running to the glass cases that lined the walls.

"What are these, Mommy?"

Eliza read the dimly lighted plaque at the base of the window and grimaced as she stared at the subterranean world behind the glass. "Naked mole rats." Pale, bald, tubular creatures huddled together in masses in their tunnels. Janie and James were mesmerized as they pressed their faces to the glass.

Just walk in calmly with all the others.

Meat sauntered right past the security guards and the camera crew, up the ramp and into the World of Darkness.

It didn't take long for his eyes to get adjusted.

"Janie, James! Don't run off," Eliza commanded. "Stay with me."

The children had beelined to the next window.

"Ewww! Bats!" Eliza heard Janie's voice.

"Cool!" exclaimed James.

It took awhile to make them out, but Eliza, Keith and Samuel stared right along with all the other visitors at the thick clusters of dark bats that hung from the tree limbs. From time to time, one of the bats would spread its wings, revealing its distinctive, eerie silhouette.

It was more than Meat could take.

Eliza was standing right in front of the bats. The two guys and the little kids were with her and there were other visitors in the large, dark room, but he could contain himself no longer.

Eliza held back for just a minute as the others moved on, re-reading the information on the mounted plaques. She felt the warmth of a hand against her neck and at first she found it surprising yet pleasing, thinking Samuel might be reaching out to her in the darkness, like a high-school kid at the movies with a date. But as the voice whispered hotly into her ear, Eliza instinctively recoiled in fear.

"Why do you insist on dressing like a slut? Learn from these bats and be a good example for your daughter."

"Mommy, Mommy! Come see this." Eliza could hear Janie's voice in the split second it took for her to scream out.

In the shadowy darkness, Samuel and Keith found her and wrestled Meat to the floor.

CHAPTER

106

Joe was in his backyard putting away the lawn furniture in the shed for the winter when his wife called out from the house. The office was on the phone.

Ten minutes later Connelly was driving to the Bronx precinct house. When he got there half an hour later, he immediately recognized the scruffy man in the holding cell. It was the same guy who had been camping out in front of the Broadcast Center. Only now the man had a name and a hometown. Cornelius Bacon of Moonachie, New Jersey.

The Bronx cops had already called the Moonachie Police Department. They knew the guy. He was a bartender at one of the local gin joints. He was a strange one. Kept bats in his backyard.

Bats. The letters to Eliza ran through Connelly's quick mind. "VAMPIRE BATS SUCK BLOOD. . . . LEARN FROM THE BATS. . . ."

Just for fun, Connelly had asked the arresting officer to call the Moonachie police again and ask if they knew whether the suspect had any nicknames. The answer came back and Joe heaved a deep sigh of relief. Thank God they had caught this guy.

Joe didn't even want to think about what had almost happened. But he had to. The security guards had been right there, yet this animal had gotten to Eliza.

And the phone lunatic was still out there somewhere.

CHAPTER

107

When Eliza arrived at work Monday morning, Paige greeted her with the news that *Entertainment Tonight* had called and wanted to see if she would do an interview about the episode at the Bronx Zoo over the weekend.

"Absolutely not," Eliza replied. "That's the last thing I need. More publicity. I don't want anyone else out there getting any crazy ideas."

"The producer told me they are doing the story whether you talk with them or not. They know that our camera crew got pictures. They want to know if they can have a dub of those, too, and credit KEY News for their usage," Paige said timidly.

A deep sigh heaved from Eliza's chest. This whole thing was getting to her. She noticed she had selected the most conservative suit she owned to wear this morning. She felt vulnerable and exposed.

"Not if I have anything to say about it," Eliza said with determination. "And I'll be damned if I'll supply their sound bites for them." She would go to Yelena Gregory if she had to, but the chaotic video the crew had shot outside the World of Darkness was not going to make air. Janie crying and holding on to her mother, James Feeney's solemn little face. Hell would freeze over before Eliza would let that tape be seen. She didn't give a fig in this case about the journalistic truth or the public's right to know. Was she being a hypocrite? Perhaps. But she didn't care.

Paige scribbled a note on her pad and glanced at the call log. "Mr. Connelly has called twice this morning already."

"Okay. Get him on the phone for me, please, Paige." Eliza walked toward her office and turned to her assistant. "And Paige? Happy Columbus Day. I'm sorry I had to make you come in to work today."

"This guy Meat's fingerprints cleared. The criminal judge set a measly one-thousand-dollar bail and his mother came over and got him out. But at least the civil court judge issued a temporary restraining order against him until the case goes to court. He can't come within five hundred feet of you."

"All this happened on a holiday weekend?" Eliza asked incredulously, pulling tensely on the telephone cord.

"Yeah. These things can be arranged when you put the pressure on."

"How long until it comes to court?"

"Don't know for sure. It might be a couple of months."

Eliza digested his words but felt no less worried. "And who's to say that he'll obey the restraining order?"

Connelly hesitated. "We don't know for sure. But we still have the security detail on you, Eliza."

Neither of them said what they were thinking.

The security detail had been there at the zoo, too.

CHAPTER

108

The familiar opening theme of *Entertainment Tonight* blared and the announcer teased the upcoming stories.

"KEY News anchorwoman Eliza Blake stalked at the Bronx Zoo."

A publicity photo of Eliza filled the screen.

The story reported that thirty-two-year-old Cornelius Bacon had been arrested for harassing the network anchorwoman while she was at the zoo over the weekend with her daughter and a KEY News crew. Bacon was a bartender at the Like It Rare steakhouse in Moonachie, New Jersey. The *ET* camera was there when Bacon showed up for work on Sunday night. The suspect walked brusquely past, covering his face with his jacket.

How dare this Bacon? Eliza wasn't his. Eliza belonged to another.

The legal system didn't always take care of things the way it should. There were other ways this guy could be dealt with to make sure he didn't get to Eliza again.

CHAPTER

109

Gray-haired Florence Anderson was a survivor and much of what she had been through showed in her gaunt face. Deep lines creased her forehead and the area that led downward from her nose to her mouth. Frown lines. She hadn't had much to smile about over the last five years. Yet the clear blue eyes that peered from the hollowed sockets sparkled with heated determination. Florence welcomed the KEY News crew into her home.

As Eliza and Florence shook hands, their eyes locked in mutual understanding.

"I saw *Entertainment Tonight* last night," Florence said. "I'm so sorry."

"Thank you."

"I'm so glad they got that nut. But I can't understand how they let him out of jail."

Eliza shrugged. "That's how it works, I guess. He made bond and he's out there until we go to court."

"That sucks," Florence spat.

Eliza almost laughed at the incongruity of the words coming from the older woman's mouth, but Florence was absolutely right. It did suck.

The crew set up in the living room, a shrine to Florence's daughter. Pictures of Linda Anderson hung on the walls and sat in frames on the tables. Linda as a baby; Linda as a toddler; Linda as a little girl in her Brownie uniform; Linda in a bathing suit, holding a trophy; Linda in cap and gown; Linda holding a microphone, doing an interview in front of a courthouse; Linda sitting behind an anchor desk. Eliza felt a chill as she looked at the pictures that documented a life that was too close to being her own.

She wondered how Florence Anderson could stand being surrounded by all these reminders of her missing daughter each day. If anything ever happened to Janie, Eliza didn't think she could bear looking at her pictures. If anything ever happened to Janie, she would get a hose, attach it to the tailpipe of the Volvo and run it back into the car and sit there, inhaling deeply until peace came.

Don't go there!

Keith suggested that Mrs. Anderson sit on the sofa for the interview. Eliza knew he selected the spot because the pictures of Linda would hang on the walls behind her in the shot. A tiny black microphone was clipped to the edge of Florence's blazer.

"Tell me about your daughter, Mrs. Anderson."

"Linda was everything a parent would want," Florence began. "She was a sunny little baby, had a great personality, did well in school, never gave her father—God rest his soul—and me any real trouble. That's not to say she was a goody-goody, mind you. She liked to have fun and she did the usual things in high school that kids do." Florence smiled wryly as she remembered. "One time we had to go down to the police station and pick her up. She had been stopped with a bunch of other kids riding around in a car. They'd been drinking."

Eliza nodded as Florence continued.

"But basically she was just a good, decent kid. Ever since she was a teenager she wanted to work in TV. But this isn't what Linda had in mind when she said she wanted to be on television."

Eliza could identify with that, too. "I understand that her career was really on the rise. I'm told there was talk of Linda being hired by KEY News."

"Yes, an agent had approached her and submitted her audition tape and there was actually an interview set up. Linda was so excited about the possibility of going to work for one of the big networks."

Florence slumped a bit and looked down at the wringing hands in her lap. "But everything happened before Linda went in for those interviews."

"Linda must have been very good. Agents don't usually do the approaching. You have to do the approaching and convince them to take you on."

"She was good," answered Florence softly. "I know I'm her mother and so I'm biased. But people said that when you met Linda, you felt like you knew her. That came across on TV as well."

"Can you tell me about the period right before Linda disappeared?" Eliza asked gently.

Florence paused and then straightened resolutely. "Something was wrong. Very, very wrong. Linda thought she was being followed. She called me crying about it a few times. I wanted her to move home and live with us until everything straightened out. If only she had." The tortured blue eyes looked imploringly at Eliza.

"Linda went to the police?" Eliza led.

"Of course she did. In fairness to them, they put a police escort on her for a while, but while they were around, nothing happened. They said they couldn't go on escorting her forever. Linda said she wasn't going to live in fear. She started taking a self-defense course at her health club. But I guess she wasn't strong enough or skilled enough to save herself."

"And after Linda disappeared? What happened then?"

"In the beginning, the police went all-out. They searched everywhere, interviewed people who knew her, questioned old boyfriends, spoke to her co-workers. The story was on the Garden State Network every night. People tied yellow ribbons around trees. There was a reward offered for information, but nobody came forward with anything. But if you ask me, as time went on the police gave up. One of the detectives called me into the station and told me that the more time went by, the less chance there was of finding out what had happened. He said the police thought it probably was a mentally disturbed viewer who had become obsessed with Linda and since there were so many people who could have seen Linda on television, the suspect pool was limitless."

"Thank you, Mrs. Anderson," said Eliza, reaching out to pat the woman's hand. "I appreciate you talking to us so candidly. I can only imagine how difficult it is for you."

"It's worth it if it can somehow help to figure out what happened to my daughter. I want whoever did this to Linda to be caught."

The cameraman took some reversal shots of Eliza making small talk with Mrs. Anderson to be used later in the editing room as cut-aways. Next he videotaped close-up shots of some of the framed pictures of Linda.

As the group was leaving the house, Florence asked a question as an afterthought.

"Do you know Abigail Snow? She works at KEY."

Eliza looked at her sharply. "Yes, I know Abigail. She works in our promotions department."

"Would you please tell her I was asking for her? She and Linda were good friends when they worked together at Garden State Network. They took that self-defense course together. But after Linda disappeared, Abigail got her job in New York and we lost touch. My other daughter, Monica, sees her at the gym once in a while." Mrs. Anderson sighed. "Yes, Abigail and Linda were great pals."

On the way back to the Broadcast Center, Eliza and Keith rode in the backseat of the crew car and discussed the interview.

"Can you imagine what life has been like for that poor woman?" Eliza asked, staring out the window.

Keith shook his head.

"It's a parent's worst nightmare. Just wait until your baby is born, Keith. The fear of losing that child will be beyond anything you can imagine."

"That certainly gives me something to look forward to," he said glumly.

Eliza looked at her producer sitting beside her, biting anxiously at the side of his thumbnail. Her disdain for Keith's behavior in Dallas had turned to pity. Here he was, going out to make his living in a very pressurized environment each day, clearly unhappy at home. With a child on the way, he was truly forced to join the world of adults. Big responsibilities and no turning back. It was easy to feel trapped.

Eliza wanted to tell him that she understood, but she refrained. He might misinterpret what she said and think she was reaching out to him. Better to keep the personal side of things out of their relationship.

"You know, Keith, I've been thinking. Maybe we should do a FRESHER LOOK on the loss of a child."

"Sure, Eliza, whatever you say." There was no enthusiasm whatsoever in Keith's voice.

CHAPTER

110

Samuel waited for the light to change and strode across Fifth Avenue at Fifty-seventh Street. He was very concerned about Eliza. That nut at the zoo, all the threatening calls, the gift of lingerie, the burglary at her home. Samuel was on a mission to make her feel better and, in the process, to ingratiate himself as well.

He entered the cavernous street-level floor of Tiffany's and perused the dazzling display cases, spending a good deal of time looking at the rings. The diamonds, sparkling in their near-perfection, were cut in all carat weights and shapes. Solitaire, marquise, emerald, pear, oval, even heart-shaped. Samuel spotted a large emerald-cut white diamond beautifully set in platinum. If it came to it, as Samuel hoped it might, that ring would be perfect for Eliza.

Samuel spent another forty-five minutes in the jewelry store, looking for an appropriate gift among the treasures. Finally he found it. Eighteen-karat-gold-and-diamond earrings, designed by Elsa Peretti in the shape of starfish.

Perfect. They would remind Eliza of the sea, their shared love.

"Samuel! I was going to call you."

"That's certainly good to hear."

"You might not think so when I tell you why."

"Oh?"

"I'm going to be working on a piece about..." Eliza tried to find the right words and then decided it was best to be direct. "Well, it's a piece about parents who have lost a child. I was wondering if you could help me out with it."

Samuel didn't know what to say.

"I know I'm putting you on the spot, Samuel," Eliza apologized.

"Gee, Eliza, of course I'd want to help you in any way I could. What exactly did you have in mind?" he asked cautiously.

"Well, we're calling Sloan-Kettering to see if we can get permission to shoot in their pediatric unit, and we're trying to find some parents who are going through the painful process with their children right now. But I was thinking you might be willing to be interviewed from the other side of the loss."

"It's awfully fresh, Eliza."

"I know it is, Samuel. But that's one of the reasons why what you would have to say would be so strong."

Eliza heard a long silence on the other end of the phone.

"Samuel?"

"I'm here, Eliza," he answered wearily. "Can I think about it and give you my answer a little later?"

"Of course."

"Are we still on for Saturday night?"

"We are if you don't mind going out to New Jersey again. I'm going to have Mrs. Garcia come and stay with Janie and I'll make a reservation at this restaurant I've been hearing such great things about. It's called Esty Street."

CHAPTER

111

Augie hadn't had a house to hit since Eliza Blake's and he was getting desperate. He still had a few of Eliza's things to take into New York. The New Jersey fence hadn't offered close to what Augie felt the jewelry must be worth. Those were quality pieces.

Even if Augie got a couple grand for them, it wasn't enough, though. He wanted the money he had invested in that bogus business deal of Larson's. But on the rare occasion that Larson took Augie's call, that son-of-a-bitch always gave him the runaround.

"Soon. Soon."

Augie was sick and tired of "soon." He wanted his money and he wanted it now. But his hands were tied. The papers Augie had signed stated that the money was committed to Richards Enterprises until the deal came to completion. Then, and only then, would the payoff come due.

What the hell was he supposed to do in the meantime? What if there never was a completion of the deal?

Augie dialed the telephone.

"Larson Richards, please. Augie Sinisi calling."

"Mr. Richards is in a meeting, Mr. Sinisi."

"Well, get him out of his damned meeting or I am going to drive right up there and pull him out myself!"

"Just a moment, please."

Augie smiled knowingly as he heard Larson pick up the phone less than a minute later. Larson didn't want a greasy car mechanic coming up to his plush office building.

"Hey, guy. How's everything?"

"Don't 'Hey, guy' me, Larson. I want my money and I want it now."

"Augie, Augie. You know that's not the way it works," Larson answered with exasperation. "The deal isn't done yet."

"Well, when the hell is the deal *going* to be done?"

"These things take time, Augie. Sometimes unforeseen things happen. Complications."

"Complications? I'll give you complications."

"Are you threatening me, Augie?" Larson's tone was smooth.

Augie knew better than to fall into that trap. He tried to steady himself.

"No, Larson. I'm not threatening you, but I need my money."

"Business a little off, is it, Augie?" His voice was condescending and Augie hated him for it.

"Something like that."

"That's something I can help you with. My car could use a tune-up."

Augie's first reaction was to scream with rage at this smug jackass, but he controlled himself as he thought of a better plan.

"All right, Larson," he said in a conciliatory tone. "I'll pick the car up at your office in the morning and have it back there waiting for you by the end of the business day. Just leave your keys with the receptionist."

CHAPTER

112

Before he left the Broadcast Center for the weekend, Joe called his contact at the phone company.

"Have you gotten anything yet on those calls?"

"Joe, I told you. I promise to call the minute we have anything. Even then I can't tell you who it is and where the calls are coming from."

"Yeah, I know, I know. But if you call me the second you've got it, I'll get the NYPD to call you right away so they can get the guy."

"Got it."

"Why is this taking so long, Fred?"

"Come on now, Joe. You know how this goes. It takes as long as it takes."

Connelly took off his black-rimmed glasses and rubbed his strained eyes.

He was getting too old for this.

Starting with the *Entertainment Tonight* story on Monday and watching Eliza on the *Evening Headlines* every night, it had been a long, tense week and even Lori's therapeutic massages hadn't lessened the strain Jerry was feeling. The massages were supposed to alleviate pain, discomfort, muscle spasms and stress. Jerry was suffering from all of them.

He couldn't shut his mind off. He wished he could, but he couldn't. Living with the knowledge that Eliza resided so close by was driving him to distraction. He needed a release.

As Lori packed up her case of oils, Jerry knew for certain that he would make another call tonight.

CHAPTER

113

Tiny white lights glittered from the trees out front and a massive spray of fresh snapdragons, lilies and white roses in a large crystal vase greeted them as they entered the restaurant.

"Welcome to Esty Street." Owner Scott Tremble smiled warmly and escorted Eliza and Samuel to their table against one of the mirrored walls of the tasteful dining room. Eliza could feel the eyes of several diners on her as she took her seat. She spotted Larson Richards sitting at one of the tables, but, thankfully, he wasn't looking in her direction.

"How does it feel to have people looking at you everywhere you go?" Samuel asked.

"Not as good as some might think," Eliza said as she opened her heavy white napkin and spread it across her lap. "It goes with the territory and you get used to it, but you're always aware that anything you do, or anything you say, or even the way you look might be commented on later. Sometimes I ache for anonymity."

"It's a bit like living under a microscope, I'd suppose."

Eliza shrugged. "I shouldn't complain. I chose this. Most people in my profession would give anything to be in my shoes."

The waiter arrived to take their drink orders and another brought hot, crusty rolls to the table. Eliza broke off a piece, dipped it into a tasty pesto, and ate it appreciatively.

"So far, so good. This bread is wonderful."

They pored over the autumn dinner menu and both agreed they couldn't decide what to order, everything sounded so good. Braised duck ravioli with butternut squash and toasted pecans, and sautéed crabcakes with roasted spaghetti squash, crispy shallots and a cranberry glaze, made the cut as appetizers. For entrées, Eliza ordered the braised lamb shank with sweet potato *pierogi* and baby carrots, Samuel the grilled filet mignon of beef with roasted-garlic mashed potatoes and rosemary *jus*. Everything tasted even better than it sounded. Though sorely tempted, they passed on the fabulous dessert menu, but ordered coffee.

Eliza had avoided the subject all evening, waiting to bring it up now.

"Have you given any thought to my request, Samuel?"

His face looked pained. "I have, Eliza. Believe me, I have. But I'm just not ready to talk about losing Sarah yet. And I certainly can't do it for a national audience. I hope you'll understand."

He reached out across the table and put his hand over hers and looked earnestly into her eyes.

"Of course I do, Samuel. I shouldn't have asked you. It was terribly insensitive of me. I'm so sorry."

"There's nothing to be sorry about. I know that you had all the right intentions. I've always been interested in how these things came to be. What made you want to do this story at this particular time? Was our relationship and Sarah the catalyst?"

"Actually, I'm doing a story on another parent who lost a child. The story is about stalking and a newswoman who disappeared five years ago. But when I interviewed her mother, I got to thinking how horrible it was to lose a child—no matter what the age. You and Sarah came to mind."

Eliza reached over and brushed back a strand of hair that had fallen across Samuel's forehead as her other hand held his. Agony was written all over the poor man's face.

"I'm so sorry, Samuel. About everything," she whispered.

She could see that he was trying to shake himself out of his suddenly morose mood. Eliza watched as Samuel pulled a small pale-blue box tied with a white satin ribbon from his jacket pocket and placed it on the table between them.

"For you, Eliza. I hope you like it."

She tugged at the end of the satin bow and opened the unmistakable Tiffany box.

"Oh, Samuel! They're beautiful!"

"I hoped you'd like them. We have to restock that jewelry collection of yours."

"They're exquisite," said Eliza, holding the diamond starfish earrings in her hands. "Exquisite . . . and much too extravagant." This was starting to get out of hand.

"No, it's not. You don't know how much our time together has meant to me, Eliza. When I came to New York, I thought my life was over. Being with you makes me want to believe in the future."

Even if Eliza had been inclined to invite Samuel in, the gray sedan was standing guard in front of the house and Janie was sleeping inside. Samuel didn't push it.

"I'll call you," he said after he kissed her good night.

Eliza let herself into the house and called out quietly for Mrs. Garcia. The housekeeper was in the den watching television.

"How was she?"

"*La muñequita* was tired tonight and went to bed right when I tell her."

"Good. I'm glad. Any phone calls?"

"*Sí*. Señora Blake called after Janie was sleeping. Her grandma say she calls tomorrow. And Señor McBride called, too."

By the way her heart pounded at that news, Eliza knew she wasn't over Mack yet.

CHAPTER

114

Larson drove home from Esty Street with a sinking feeling. Those investors who had so happily eaten on his dime tonight were not going to bite on putting money into his business. He could feel it.

He clicked the electronic door opener, slid the Mercedes into the garage and walked dejectedly into the house. The light was blinking on the kitchen Caller ID box. Larson picked up the receiver and punched in his code. There were no new messages.

Yet the flashing red light indicated someone must have called.

Larson pushed the review button. Carmine Carelli had called. Twice.

Of course Carmine had left no message. He was too smart for that.

Jesus. Why had he gotten involved with that crowd? They didn't fool around. He was going to come home one night to find some thug waiting to break his legs. And that would be the *best*-case scenario.

He grabbed a beer from the shelf in the refrigerator. Larson was about to close the door when he sensed something was amiss. All the contents of the shelves had been pushed to the side.

Panic seized him as he opened the freezer compartment. The boxes of frozen peas and asparagus that he had so neatly arranged were a jumbled mess. He rifled beneath them frantically.

The frosty metal strongbox was gone.

Why had he saved that last letter from his mother? He had sold her jewelry, destroyed the promissory notes.

But he had kept that damned letter.

Sentimentality was for fools.

CHAPTER

115

That character from Moonachie wasn't going to get much more than a slap on the wrist for what he had done to Eliza at the zoo. Even if Cornelius Bacon served some jail time, he would be out too soon.

That wasn't right.

He could get to Eliza again. That couldn't be allowed to happen.

Eliza was too precious. She had to be protected.

Bacon had to be stopped.

CHAPTER

116

He worried about it all weekend. The phone trap wasn't working fast enough. Joe went to work earlier than he normally would on Monday morning, booted up his computer and clicked into his AB-ERRANT BEHAVIOR file.

Connelly scanned the entries, unsure of what exactly he was look-ing for. The caller must have said something that Joe could work with, something that might give him a clue to the identity of the harasser.

"Eliza, you are beautiful, even without your makeup."

That was something to follow.

The security chief was waiting in Eliza's office when she arrived.

"I want you to think of anyone who has seen you without your makeup."

"God, Joe. Where would I begin? Some days I come into the office without putting on any makeup. Anyone here could have seen me without it."

"All right. Outside of the Broadcast Center," Connelly pushed.

Eliza tried to recall the nearly impossible. Where had she been without makeup?

"Offhand, I remember a morning that the guy who sold me my

house unexpectedly brought Janie a puppy. He saw me without my makeup."

Joe wrote down Larson Richards's name. "Do you have his phone number?"

"Paige probably does, on the Rolodex."

"Good. I'll have it checked out. Anyone else?"

The memory of Keith Chapel in the Dallas hotel gym flashed through Eliza's mind, but she couldn't bring herself to single him out. Besides, Keith worked in the Broadcast Center. He should just be considered along with everyone else.

Eliza shook her head. "No one comes to mind right now."

"Well, keep thinking about it, Eliza. Call me if you remember anyone at all."

CHAPTER

117

The letter was written in flowery script on pale pink stationery.

Dear Larson,

I can't tell you how upset your father and I are at the recent turn of events between us. As your mother, I am heartbroken that you could say the things you said to us when you were here.

We have loved you and raised you since the joyous time you were born to us, working hard to nurture you and afford you every possible opportunity. For you to turn on us like this hurts us beyond anything that words can describe.

You said that we would be dead to you if we didn't give you more to bolster your business. I can't believe that it's come to this, especially since we have already helped you so much financially. Obviously you care more about your business than you do about our comfort. That's a painful realization for us.

We will not be threatened, Larson. If you feel that you must cut yourself off from us, so be it. But I pray that you will think about all this and come to your senses. Dad and I love you very much and would be willing to forgive and forget what you said in anger.

I want you know that everything we have will eventually be yours anyway, Larson. No matter whether you cut us off or not.

Love,
Mother

Augie looked at the date at the top of the paper, folded up the letter and stuck it in his pocket. A trip to the public library was in order. If a back issue of the *Record* confirmed what he suspected, Mrs. Richards had written this letter to her son just before she and her husband died.

CHAPTER

118

"I don't know how I feel anymore, Mack. And I don't think any of this can be resolved on the telephone. If you do come back for Thanksgiving, maybe we can talk then." Eliza glanced at her watch. She should be down in makeup. "I have to go."

Staring at her reflection in the mirror, Eliza frowned.

"God, I look awful."

"No you don't, sweetie," Doris reassured her, "and when I'm through with you, you'll look dynamite."

"Well, you better get out a tub of concealer. Look at those bags!"

Doris gently patted the white cream on the gray circles beneath Eliza's eyes.

"You didn't sleep well again last night?"

"No. I fall asleep by midnight, but I'm wide awake at two. I lie there and think and worry, watching the clock and only getting more anxious that I won't be able to fall back to sleep and then I'll be exhausted the next day. It's a vicious cycle."

"You've got a lot on your mind, honey. No wonder you can't sleep. Think you should get some sleeping pills?" Doris suggested.

Eliza shrugged. "Maybe. But I want to avoid that if I can. I'm afraid I'll go into a deep sleep and won't wake up if something happens and

Janie needs me. Besides, I'm so busy right now, I don't have time to get to the doctor."

"I have some at home," Doris offered. "I'll bring them in tomorrow. You can try them if you want and see if they work for you."

The makeup artist's handiwork could only do its magic to a point. Eliza still looked tired.

"Try to rest up this weekend, Eliza. Turn your mind off."

"How can I do that, Doris? Let's not even go into the guards outside my house and the kooks out there, wherever they are. Mack called."

"What did *he* want?" Doris asked dourly.

"Someone sent him that picture of Samuel and me in the newspaper."

"Good. I wish I'd thought of that."

A half-smile formed on Eliza's painted lips. "He wants to try to work things out."

"How do you feel?"

"Conflicted."

In the president's office, Yelena Gregory watched the *Evening Headlines* with concern. Eliza wasn't looking her usual luminous self. In a perfect world perhaps it wouldn't matter what the person delivering the news looked like. But this was the real world. Presentation counted right up there with content if you wanted to get good ratings.

She could well understand the strain Eliza was under. Yelena had been keeping abreast of the security problems. Joe Connelly had reassured her just this afternoon that something should be coming from the phone company soon on the threatening calls.

It damned well better.

CHAPTER

119

Susan Feeney had outdone herself. The Olive Oyl costume she had put together was spectacular. Janie wriggled in excitement, wearing a shirtwaist dress with Peter Pan collar, striped tights and black shoes. Susan had fashioned a turned-up nose of putty and found a black wig which she had swept back and pinned into a tight bun. The creation was adorable.

James wore a white sailor suit and hat, biting hard on a corncob pipe at the corner of his mouth and carrying a can of spinach. Rolling back the sleeve of the shirt, Susan had drawn an anchor tattoo on her son's arm.

The plan was for all of them to go into town together to the kick-off point of the Halloween parade. Eliza would break off and go to the school to be ready with the cider and donuts for the kids and their parents, while Susan would stay with Janie, James, Bumblebee Kelly and Ladybug Kimberly. The mothers, but not their children, were aware that the security guards would be following along nearby.

The scene in downtown HoHoKus was something straight out of a Norman Rockwell painting as scores of children assembled in their Halloween regalia—witches and monsters, magicians and devils, pumpkins and princesses. While the most creative costumes were clearly homemade, Eliza noted with relief that many were obviously the store-bought kind. Not everyone was Martha Stewart out here, after all.

The kids marched along happily in the October morning sunshine. Eliza trained her video camera on their procession and promised to make a copy of the tape for Susan, who had her hands full with Kelly and Kimberly. When they reached the halfway point, Eliza broke away.

The trestle tables in the schoolyard were all set, covered with plates of cinnamon and powdered-sugar donuts and jugs of apple cider from nearby Demarest Farm. Eliza was stacking paper cups when Larson Richards approached.

"I figured I could find you here with Janie this morning. I didn't know you'd be manning the refreshment stand."

"Just want to do my small part, Larson," she answered in a dismissive tone. She continued arranging the cups, hoping he would get the hint and leave.

Instead he pressed a folded piece of paper into her hand.

"What's this?"

"The combination to the safe."

"Too little, too late, Larson. You probably heard, I've already been robbed."

"I did hear and I'm sorry I didn't get this to you sooner." How could he tell her that he had been holding on to the combination as a reason to seek her out again?

She ignored his apology.

"I was wondering if I could talk with you, Eliza."

"About what?"

"An investment opportunity I think you might be interested in."

"This is hardly the place, Larson," she answered shortly.

"Oh, I know that. I know that," he answered nervously. "But I was hoping that we could get together over the weekend sometime and talk."

"I don't think so, Larson. I'm not looking to make any investments right now."

"This is really a great opportunity, Eliza," he insisted.

She looked at him squarely. Though she hadn't gone to the police about it, Eliza still had her suspicions about the possibility of Larson being the one who had robbed her home. And if Joe Connelly found out that it was this slimeball who had been making the sick phone calls, she would personally find him and scratch his eyes out, for threatening not her, but her daughter.

"Look, Larson. I'm not interested. Period, the end. Please leave me alone."

He skulked away angrily. Eliza Blake was an ungrateful bitch.

CHAPTER

120

Another Saturday night.

It was after two A.M. when Meat finished cleaning up. He pulled the large, heavy-duty plastic garbage bag from its container and tied a knot at the top. Then he put on his jacket and turned off the lights in the bar.

The bats are gone now until next year, he thought as he went outside and the frosty night air blew against his face. Meat laid the garbage bag down on the cement and rifled through his pockets for the keys to lock up.

The dark green Dumpster was at the back of the building, next to Meat's car. He always parked there so he could hop right in after his last duty was completed. He sauntered across the deserted parking lot. Deserted, save for the one other car that sat waiting, headlights off.

At first Meat didn't hear the car rolling toward him. But he did hear it when it began to accelerate. He turned to face the direction of the sound. The headlights flashed on, blinding him. He dropped the garbage bag and raised his arms to shield his face from the glaring light.

The car careened into him and then over him, braking to a stop after nailing its target. Then the driver put the car in reverse and backed up over Meat's crushed body, finishing the job.

CHAPTER

121

"God forgive me, Joe, but I'm relieved." Not wanting Janie to hear the conversation, Eliza whispered on the phone extension in her bedroom.

"I feel the same way, Eliza. At least that's one we don't have to worry about anymore. I knew you wouldn't mind if I called you at home to let you know."

"'Mind'? Are you kidding? Now I won't have to worry if my skirt is too short tomorrow," she joked lamely.

"We're not out of the woods yet, Eliza," Joe warned, "but I know I'll sleep a little better tonight than I have been lately."

"Do the police have any idea who killed him?"

"Nothing so far, but in my book, whoever it was did us a favor."

When Samuel called that evening, Eliza tried to keep her voice even as she told him about Meat's demise.

"Good. I'm glad," he said adamantly. "I don't know what I would do if something happened to you."

Eliza was troubled. It was clear that Samuel was falling for her, hard. And she guiltily acknowledged to herself that she had encouraged him. She had wanted to have a man with her during this tense time and, out of her own need, she had used him. Not maliciously, but she had. She had told herself that she was helping him through a tough time, but the fact was he had been helping Eliza through hers.

Samuel was a lovely man, but the timing just wasn't right. He was coming off the harshest blow of his life and it was natural he would be grasping for something or someone to hold on to. She, on the other hand, still had not resolved her feelings about Mack. This wasn't the way to start a solid relationship. Plus, she had to admit, they didn't exactly have wild chemistry between them. Samuel was pleasant to be with, but she felt no excitement at his touch. Eliza knew she needed that, to go forward.

She had to tell him. But how could she? She didn't think Samuel could take another hurt right now. The longer she waited, though, the harder it would be.

CHAPTER

1 2 2

For once in his life Augie Sinisi had the upper hand. He strode confidently into the marble-floored lobby of Richards Enterprises.

"I'd like to see Mr. Richards, please."

The prim receptionist eyed Augie's overalls. "Do you have an appointment, sir?"

"No. I don't. Just tell Mr. Richards that August Sinisi wants to see him. I have some very important information for him."

Within minutes Augie was sitting in Larson's office.

"This better be good, Augie. I'm very busy."

"I know, Larson. You're a busy guy. Very busy." Augie's smug smile signaled trouble.

"What is it, Augie? What's this information you have for me?"

"I just thought you'd be interested to know that the police could be getting an anonymous tip about your parents' untimely death."

"What the hell does that mean?" Larson said sharply.

"You know damn well what it means, Larson."

Larson's mind raced. *The strongbox. Augie's got the letter. Careful. Careful.*

"You know, Augie, my house was broken into over the weekend."

"Gee, that's too bad."

"If someone had something that had been stolen from my house, that could mean that person was a thief. That person could get into a lot of trouble for that, especially if it turned out he had been breaking into other houses, too."

"Yeah, I guess he could. But not as much trouble as someone who offed his parents."

Larson absentmindedly fingered the paperweight that sat atop the latest financial report of Richards Enterprises as he considered Augie's words. "Yes, that's true. But neither person would want to go to jail, would they?"

"No. And nobody would have to, either. If I get my money out of your company and get something extra as, you might say, a little dividend, nobody has to go to jail. The police don't need to know anything."

CHAPTER

123

"We've got it, Joe."

"Yes!" Connelly wanted to kiss his contact at the phone company right through the phone line. "Is it that Richards number I gave you last week?"

"No, but it *is* a phone in New Jersey. You know I can't tell you who. Have your NYPD detective call me."

Northern New Jersey was so close to New York City that it was acceptable practice for NYPD detectives to drive out to local Bergen County police departments when necessary. Detectives Ed Kane and

Kenneth Sheehan entered the Upper Saddle River police station and showed their badges to the sergeant at the desk.

"What can we do for you?"

"We need some help. We have a phone subscriber out here who's making threatening calls. We want to go the house and talk to the guy," Kane said.

"What's the guy's name?" asked the sergeant.

Sheehan looked at his pad. "Walinski. Jerry Walinski. Know him?"

"Sure. I know the poor son-of-a-bitch. We all do."

The unmarked sedan with New York plates pulled into the driveway behind the Upper Saddle River Police squad car. The detectives and two patrolmen walked up to the front door and rang the bell. A dog barked warningly from inside.

Jerry Walinski answered the door in his wheelchair.

Joe wanted to deliver this news face-to-face.

Jerry Walinski was not going to be doing Eliza or her little girl any harm.

"It's pitiful, really. The guy is a paraplegic. He was in a car accident a few years ago and he'll never walk again. But he did get a huge insurance settlement for his suffering and a lifetime loss-of-wages."

"What about his seeing me without my makeup?" Eliza asked.

"He made it up. Imagined it. The cops said he had pictures of you all over the place. Videotapes, too. He has a lot of time to sit around and think."

Eliza digested the information. "What do we do now?"

"Well, we can prosecute."

Eliza's face crinkled with distaste. "I don't know, Joe. The thought of dragging a paraplegic into court doesn't turn me on."

"My guess is, we could reach some sort of plea bargain, with the stipulation that Walinski get psychiatric counseling. He wouldn't have to do any time."

"Fine. That sounds like the way to go." Eliza nodded, satisfied. "So we're all clear now? I mean, with Bacon dead and Walinski taken care of?"

"It sure looks that way," Joe smiled. "I think we can take the security off your house now."

CHAPTER

124

Eliza stared into the TelePrompTer and read the lead-in to the last piece of the broadcast.

"For hundreds of years, bats have fluttered through our subconscious as symbols of evil and darkness. But research is casting a new light on bats as perhaps the most highly specialized of all mammal groups. With Halloween approaching, we thought we'd take a FRESHER LOOK at our misunderstood creatures of the night."

As she watched the story on the monitor, Eliza had to hand it to Keith. He had done a first-rate job. The piece began with video he had culled from the San Antonio affiliate. Shot at dusk, it showed literally millions of Mexican free-tailed bats, the largest concentration of warm-blooded animals in the world, flying from the wide, dark mouth of the Bracken Cave. The long black column of bats looked like a tornado spinning across the Texas sky as the bats left to consume the two hundred tons of insects they would eat that night.

The first sound bite came from a leading authority on bats.

"Bats are really among the gentlest of creatures. They've just had bad press. The only bats that people see are the ones that are sick or dying. If you find one lying on the ground someplace, naturally the bat opens its mouth and bares its teeth. It's trying to scare you away. Of course, you should never pick up a bat lying on the ground. You should never try to catch a bat or keep one in captivity. But if people could just see bats as they really are, they'd find them just as comical and cute as other animals.' "

It was a long sound bite as sound bites went, but it worked.

Keith had gone back up to the Bronx Zoo and videotaped the public's reactions, which they had had to forgo after the Meat episode. Eliza winced as she watched the snippets of interviews done with zoo-goers exiting the World of Darkness.

"They're creepy," a woman said.

"They're neat," said a teenaged boy.

"I find them fascinating," a man said.

Fascinating, useful, beautiful or strange, Eliza knew that, as long as she lived, she would associate bats with Cornelius "Meat" Bacon.

Eliza felt an enormous weight lift from her shoulders as the Town Car let her off in front of the house. The security sedan, parked for so long at her curb reminding her of a funeral car, was gone.

The aroma of Mrs. Garcia's *arroz con frijoles* greeted Eliza as she opened the front door. She heard Janie chirping from the kitchen.

"*Pollito*, chicken.

"*Gallina*, hen.

"*Lapiz*, pencil.

"Y *pluma*, pen.

"*Ventana*, window.

"*Puerta*, door.

"*Maestra*, teacher.

"Y *piso*, floor."

This is what Eliza had longed for. The homecoming to a secure, well-tended nest. Her daughter singing happily. How lucky she was! Eliza walked over the freshly vacuumed rug in the hallway, toward the kitchen. Janie ran into her mother's arms and Eliza hugged her precious child.

Eliza kissed the top of Janie's head and tried to push an unsettling thought from her mind. The FRESHER LOOK piece that was being prepared for next week's broadcast. Halloween. The fifth anniversary of Linda Anderson's disappearance.

Florence Anderson didn't have her daughter to hug tonight.

CHAPTER

125

Abigail wasn't particularly in the mood for dressing up for Halloween again this year, but she had to put something together. It was tradition. There was no way her friends would let her out of going to the annual Greenwich Village parade. They would drag her if they had to.

It would be quite an event. It always was, as hundreds of gay men and women used their very creative energies to come up with the most fabulous and imaginative costumes. Abigail had gone each year since she'd moved into the city and enjoyed it, to a point. It was fun being a part of the decked-out group that gathered on Houston Street and marched up Sixth Avenue. But Abigail always found herself thinking of the night as a tragic anniversary.

Five years. How had the time gone by so quickly?

And still Linda's disappearance went unsolved.

But that might change soon, with the national exposure the case was about to receive. Keith had given her a heads-up on next week's FRESHER LOOK, bringing the tapes to her to dub for the promo.

"I knew Linda Anderson," she had told him.

"Oh, yeah. Her mother mentioned something about that when we were out there. You worked with her?"

"Yes. We got to be good friends."

She thought she could read Keith's mind. *No, Linda wasn't gay—though I wished she had been,* Abigail was tempted to snap. But she had said nothing.

CHAPTER

126

Eliza slipped out at lunchtime and took a cab to Bergdorf Goodman. She wanted to pick out the birthday present herself. Paige was working out to be the most competent, conscientious assistant Eliza had ever had. Eliza was impressed with how the young woman had handled all the anxiety that had been swirling around her. It was a bonus that Paige had such a winning personality. Eliza was very happy with her and she wanted to show it.

She had noticed that Paige was a clotheshorse, dressing stylishly on what Eliza knew was not a big salary. As Eliza went in through the store's Fifth Avenue entrance, she headed for the sweater section.

The cashmere collection was extensive, a cornucopia of colors and styles. Eliza had trouble deciding between a jewel-necked black one and a cornflower-blue turtleneck. She loved the blue, and thought it would look terrific on Paige, but the black might be more practical. She bought both. Paige was more than worth it.

Eliza stopped in the children's department and picked out a new winter jacket with matching hat and mittens for Janie and then scooted over to the hosiery section and bought a dozen pairs of pantyhose for herself. She was satisfied with her forty-five minutes of power shopping when she went out again into the Fifth Avenue sunlight. As she stood on the corner of Fifty-seventh Street, waiting for a cab in the crowded lunchtime traffic, Eliza glanced across the street in the direction of Tiffany's.

He didn't see her, but Eliza thought she recognized Samuel's tall, lanky frame coming out of the store. *Yes, that was him,* she confirmed as the figure walked to the corner and waited for the light to change. Samuel was carrying a small blue shopping bag in his hand.

Eliza was relieved when a yellow taxi glided to a stop. She quickly got into the backseat of the cab. She didn't want to see Samuel right now. Saturday night would be soon enough to tell him what she knew he wouldn't want to hear.

She certainly hoped that the bag he was carrying didn't hold something else for her.

CHAPTER

127

Cindy's obstetrician said she thought they were still a few weeks away from delivery, and first babies sometimes came a little late. But Cindy had been having those Braxton Hicks contractions and Keith was nervous.

He was always nervous. He lived his life that way.

Range said he understood, but Keith got the feeling there was some resentment there. Keith was worried about taking time off after the baby was born. He was doing all he could to get ahead of the game. He wanted to shoot as many elements as possible for the upcoming FRESHER LOOKS.

Tiredly, Keith made himself call Sloan–Kettering to confirm that Dr. Lieber, the head of pediatric oncology, would be available for an interview on Monday morning.

If only Cindy could hold off until he got that piece in the can.

CHAPTER

128

Eliza hustled Janie and James into the car on Saturday afternoon and drove over to Demarest Farms to pick out their Halloween pumpkins. The three of them stood in the long line and waited for the hayride that took them to the patch behind the acres of apple and peach orchards. The kids searched intently for just the right pumpkins, selecting bright orange orbs they could barely carry. Afterwards, back at the big red barn, Eliza picked out an apple pie and a quart of vanilla ice cream for dessert that night.

Eliza had given a lot of thought to how she wanted to handle things with Samuel.

She was going to make dinner herself and, after Janie went to bed, quietly talk to him about everything. She hoped that they could continue their relationship as friends. She hoped he would understand. She hoped he wouldn't be too hurt.

Mrs. Garcia had done the shopping and everything was ready for her to start cooking. Thick pork chops, sweet-and-sour red cabbage, large baking potatoes. A good, hearty fall dinner.

As she pulled the station wagon out of the crowded parking lot, Eliza noticed that the gas gauge was near empty. Mrs. Garcia had forgotten to fill the tank. Eliza steered the car toward the gas station.

"What the hell are you wearing?" Augie demanded as a preening Helene swaggered into the station office.

"You were holding out on me, Sugar." Helene wrapped her arms around her husband's wide girth. "I found this in the bottom of your drawer. This, and those other things. They're beautiful, Augie. Were you going to surprise me?"

Sex or no sex, Augie verbally let loose on her.

Eliza half listened to Janie and James discuss how they were going to carve their pumpkins, but mostly she thought about Samuel as the high-test poured into the Volvo's tank. She was staring at the doorway to the station's office when a tall, thin blonde wearing a heavy turtleneck sweater and tight-fitting black leather pants walked out.

That's not a happy camper, Eliza thought, looking at the sour expression on the woman's face.

The woman passed by the car and the autumn sunlight reflected off a pin on the neck of her sweater.

Eliza went slack-jawed as she recognized the sapphire-and-diamond pin that John had bought before he died. The gift to commemorate Janie's birth.

She grabbed a pencil and an old gas receipt from the glove compartment and scribbled down the license-plate number of the car as the woman tore out of the lot.

She handed Janie the *New York Times.*

"Here. You and James spread this out on the kitchen table. Then go get your markers and draw the faces you want on the pumpkins.

I have to go upstairs for a minute. When I get back, we'll carve the pumpkins. Don't you dare go into the drawer and get the knife until I come back. Understand?"

The children nodded solemnly.

Eliza ran up to her bedroom and called the HoHoKus police.

CHAPTER

129

Eliza came down from tucking in Janie for the night to find the jewelry box waiting at her place at the dining-room table.

"What's this?"

"Open it and see. Even if the police do get your jewelry back, I hope this will be something that you'll cherish as I cherish you, Eliza." Samuel smiled contentedly.

Eliza felt like a louse. "Samuel. I can't. I have to talk to you."

"Open it first," he urged. "Then we'll talk."

Uncomfortably, Eliza lifted the lid of the blue box. Inside was the companion necklace to the starfish earrings.

"It's beautiful, Samuel. Absolutely beautiful. But I can't..."

"Here, let me put it on you," he interrupted. He stood behind her and fastened the gold clasp and then turned Eliza by the shoulders to face him.

"It looks wonderful on you."

"I can't accept it, Samuel."

"Of course you can," he insisted. "I want you to have it. It's as if it was made for you."

"Oh, Samuel. You dear, sweet man. You've been through so much. I wouldn't want to hurt you for anything in the world."

The happy expression on Samuel's face changed as he began to get the picture.

That idiot Helene!

He'd been enraged when Helene had showed up with that pin at the station today. Now the cops were at his door with a search warrant.

Augie thought fast. Most everything he had stolen was gone. Fenced. Just the few things of Eliza's he hadn't gotten rid of yet. Now he was glad that Larson's strongbox had only had some papers in it.

All they could pin on him was the Blake burglary.

Augie demanded to call an attorney. A good lawyer might be able to get the charges dropped in exchange for information about a double murder.

"I'm so sorry, Samuel. But I hope, when you think about it, you'll realize that I'm right. This isn't the time for us, but I do hope we can still be friends."

Friends. Even to Eliza it sounded so lame.

Samuel tried valiantly, but couldn't conceal the hurt on his face. Stricken, he walked slowly to the door.

"Here. You must take this with you." Eliza handed the jewelry box to him.

"No," he shook his head. "Please. Keep it. For all you did for Sarah and for me."

CHAPTER

1 3 0

The hallways of Memorial Sloan–Kettering brought it all back.

How many times had she walked the polished floors of the mammoth hospital complex, unable to distinguish if she was nauseous because of the early stages of pregnancy or because her young husband lay in fevered pain in his hospital room dying?

But Eliza had never been to pediatrics.

The hospital staff tried to make the surroundings as happy as they could. But it was what it was. The afflicted children, many in wheelchairs, soldiered through their treatments. Their hairless heads made them look older than their years. Little, old, bald boys and girls, fighting for their young lives.

The camera recorded Dr. Lieber as he escorted Eliza through the hallways.

"The problem, as you know, is that children grow so quickly. So do their cancer cells."

"When you finally know that nothing is going to help a child, how do you help the parents?" Eliza asked.

"We have counselors on staff. But despite the best efforts, I really don't know how much counseling helps. How can you make something like this better? The only thing is, sometimes the child has been through so much, that the parents just want it to be over for them. Over for the child, I mean. The parents almost never want to give up."

Eliza thought of Samuel. "I have a friend who just lost his daughter to cancer. In fact, she came here for treatment."

"What was her name?"

"Sarah Morton."

Dr. Lieber shook his head. "I can't place the name. But I'm not surprised. There are so many kids. How is your friend doing now?"

"Not well," Eliza answered, thinking of Samuel's face as he left her house Saturday night.

"It takes a long time."

The crew took pictures in the pediatric lounge, careful to shoot from the back of the bald heads or from an angle so that the youthful identities would not be recognizable. No faces could be shown in the piece unless the parents signed release forms.

There was one little girl whose face could be taped. Her parents had agreed to be interviewed for the story. The mother was stoic as she told the story of what they had been going through over the past two years. The father asked that the camera be turned off when he started to break down.

Dr. Lieber met up with them again when they were finished shooting. He handed Eliza his card.

"Call me if I can be of any other help. I was thinking about your friend, Ms. Blake. If you'd like, have him call me and I will be happy to arrange counseling for him if he wants."

After the broadcast that evening, Eliza called Samuel. When she heard the initial hope in his voice she wondered if she had done the right thing.

"I just wanted to see how you were doing."

"Oh," he said dully. "I'm fine. Please, don't worry about me, Eliza. That would make it worse."

"I am worried, Samuel. You've been through too much. I wanted to tell you that I interviewed a doctor at Sloan–Kettering today and he said that he would set up some grief counseling for you if you wanted it."

"No, thanks. This is something I have to work through on my own."

"A little professional help wouldn't hurt."

"What is a therapist going to tell me that I don't know already? Sarah's dead." His voice was morose. "Thank you for thinking of me."

The phone clicked in her ear.

She thought about Samuel as the car crawled up the West Side Highway. At the George Washington Bridge, Eliza pulled Dr. Lieber's card from her wallet and tapped in the number on her cellular phone pad. She got his answering machine and left a message.

"Dr. Lieber, this is Eliza Blake. I am very worried about that friend of mine I was telling you about today. Would you please give me a call when you can?"

She left both her office and home phone numbers.

CHAPTER

1 3 1

It was amazing. One minute you thought you had the worst problems imaginable. The next, those problems paled by comparison to new ones. Larson's financial worries were far from his mind when he got the call.

The police wanted him to come in and talk.

CHAPTER

1 3 2

"I'm sorry, Ms. Blake. I didn't get your message until this morning."

Eliza realized that most people did not get apologies from doctors who hadn't returned non-emergency phone calls made after office hours only the night before. That was the power of KEY News. Phone calls were returned. Promptly.

She described her phone call with Samuel to Dr. Lieber.

"I'm not a psychiatrist, Ms. Blake, but it sounds like your friend definitely needs some help. Would you like me to have someone here call him?"

Eliza weighed the offer. Was she doing this out of guilt? Would Samuel be angry with her? That shouldn't matter to her if his well-being hung in the balance. But he might shut down totally, feeling alienated that she had broken his trust. She wasn't sure what to do. She wanted to do something to help him.

"Yes, Dr. Lieber," Eliza decided. "I think that might be a good thing. I can't get through to him."

Samuel's phone call came that afternoon.

"I know what you're trying to do, Eliza. I know that you mean well. But please, forget about me. We can't be friends—not now, any-way. I have to move forward alone for a while."

CHAPTER

133

Mischief Night or Cabbage Night. Whatever it was called, the night before Halloween brought out adolescents eager to have what they considered harmless fun decorating their neighborhoods with bars of soap, smashed eggs and toilet tissue.

A group of teenagers made its way along Larson Richards's street, soaping up the windows of cars stupidly left in driveways. If the own-ers weren't smart enough to put their cars away tonight, they de-served to come out in the morning to find their windshields a mess.

There was no car in Larson Richards's driveway and the house was completely dark. The kids snickered as they ran up to the sprawling ranch. It was easy to soap every single window when they were all on one floor.

They proceeded sneakily on to the next house, unaware that a Mercedes-Benz was idling in Larson's closed garage, carbon monoxide filling the passenger cab.

Live by the sword, die by the sword.

CHAPTER

134

Janie hopped out of bed on Halloween morning, eager to go to school in her Olive Oyl costume. Susan and Mrs. Garcia would take the kids around trick-or-treating in the afternoon. Eliza promised her daughter that she would get home as quickly as she possibly could after work so they could give out the candy together to the nighttime trick-or-treaters.

Doris had outdone herself again this year. She had spent hours painstakingly taping long, thin adhesive strips to a black tunic and skirt. Then she had carefully measured and marked boxes along the tape, numbering the corners of some of the boxes with a fine-tipped pen. She had bought a pair of inexpensive black sunglasses and painted sporadic squares on them with Wite-Out. She used her expert skills, coating her face with white pancake and drawing, with the help of a ruler, horizontal and vertical lines. She donned a pair of black opaque tights and pulled her flowing mane of hair up into a ponytail, tying it with a man's tie—a tie printed in the design of a crossword puzzle. The inspiration for her costume.

She left her apartment early, bound for the ABC studio. The *Regis* producers loved her costume and wanted her to come inside and be on the show. But she couldn't win a prize, they warned her, since she had won last year.

Bummer.

Doris headed for the Broadcast Center, eagerly anticipating the reaction she would get there.

Florence Anderson awoke before dawn and lay alone in her bed. It was the day she dreaded all year long.

The first year after Linda's death, she hadn't even been able to open her door to the children who came begging. The next year, she had managed to give out packages of M&Ms. Without nuts. Those had been Linda's favorites.

Now, and every year since, a big bowlful of the chocolate candy packages sat ready on the table in the foyer. Life had to go on.

And maybe, just maybe, Florence allowed herself to hope, the piece that was scheduled to air on tonight's *KEY Evening Headlines* might jog someone's memory and lead to some closure to the pain she had been living with for the past five years.

CHAPTER

135

Keith called from the editing booth.

"It's done. Do you want to come down and see it?"

"Sure. I'll be right there," answered Eliza.

She took the stairs down two floors to the hard-news editing center, passing half a dozen small rooms with sliding glass doors until she reached Joe Leiding's booth. Keith got up and offered her his chair.

"Are you happy with it?" she asked as she took the seat.

"Yeah. I think it's pretty good. See what you think," Keith said. He stood at the back of the booth and began gnawing at his thumbnail as Leiding hit the PLAY button. The piece opened with a clip of Linda Anderson wrapping up the last news broadcast she ever anchored. Then Eliza's narration began.

"Linda Anderson did not know, as she signed off from the Garden State Network on the night before Halloween five years ago, that it would be her last time reporting from the anchor chair. She thought she had everything to look forward to."

Mrs. Anderson's careworn faced appeared on the screen. "People said that when you met Linda, you felt you knew her. That came across on TV as well."

"Indeed, the audience responded to Linda Anderson," Eliza's track continued. "She had a loyal following in New Jersey and there was interest on the other side of the Hudson River as well."

Sound-bite Florence Anderson: "An agent had approached her and submitted her audition tape and there was actually an interview set up. Linda was so excited about the possibility of going to work for one of the big networks."

Eliza's voice picked up the story. "But Linda Anderson never went for that network interview. After she finished her late broadcast, she left the studio and was never seen again."

Florence Anderson: "In the beginning, the police went all-out. They searched everywhere, interviewed people who knew her, questioned old boyfriends, spoke to her co-workers." Mrs. Anderson's voice was still heard, but file tape of pictures was edited over to illustrate her next words. "The story was on the Garden State Network every night. People tied yellow ribbons around trees. There was a reward offered for information, but nobody came forward with anything. But if you ask me, as time went on, the police gave up."

"That's a charge the police deny," narrated Eliza.

"Linda Anderson's file is still open here and will be until this case is solved," said a detective Keith had interviewed at the police station. "There's a national preoccupation with celebrity in this country, and though we've searched and investigated every possible lead, the fact is that anyone with a television set could have targeted Linda. That's a pretty broad range of suspects."

That was the end of the edited package. Keith handed Eliza the script she was to read on camera, coming out of the piece.

"Before she disappeared, Linda Anderson told her family and friends that she thought she was being followed. Stalking is illegal in all fifty states and while it is the celebrity stalkings that receive media coverage, the most common victims are not news reporters or movie stars. The largest number of stalking victims are ordinary people on whom another person, for whatever reason, becomes fixated. The advice from law enforcement professionals? If you meet someone who makes you feel uncomfortable, act on your feelings. Get away from that person and break off any future contact."

"What do you think?" asked Keith.

"It's good, Keith. I just wish we had a little more time to tell the story in greater depth."

"Believe it or not, Range wanted us to edit out ten or fifteen seconds. I told him there was nothing left to cut."

Eliza nodded. She well understood the executive producer's preoccupation with time. "Nice job, Joe," she complimented the editor as she rose to leave. Eliza noticed the box that contained Linda Anderson's audition tape lying on the console table. She picked it up.

"Can I take this with me?" she asked. "I'd like to take a look at it."

It was eerie how much Linda reminded Eliza of herself.

CHAPTER

136

The door to the makeup room was open, but no one was inside.

Doris was probably strutting around the halls in that crossword-puzzle costume, Abigail thought as she walked in and inspected the contents of the giant makeup case on the counter. Shelves of foundations, creams, eyeshadows and lipsticks. Abigail glanced at the wall clock. Eliza would be coming down any minute to be made up for the broadcast. Abigail wanted to avoid a potentially uncomfortable meeting.

She picked up one of several containers of dark pancake makeup. It was exactly what she needed. If Doris were there to ask, Abigail was sure she wouldn't refuse her. Abigail would bring it back tomorrow.

She stuffed the plastic container into her pocket.

Eliza was sitting in the Fishbowl, reading through scripts, when Keith arrived out of breath.

"Cindy's water broke! I've got to go."

"Good luck, buddy," called Range, barely looking up from his computer screen.

"Yes, Keith. Good luck," Eliza wished him. "Make sure and call and let us know as soon as the baby's born. You've got my home number," she reminded him.

"I will," said Keith. He turned and ran across the studio.

Range turned to Eliza and smirked. "Can you imagine having that nervous Nellie in the delivery room with you?"

"It's better than no one at all, Range."

Remembering the circumstances of Eliza's delivery, the executive producer, for once, had nothing to say.

CHAPTER

137

Why was Eliza doing this story?

Why dredge up all that misery again?

Linda's face smiled from the television screen. She had been so beautiful, so full of life. If only she hadn't resisted.

Why would someone spurn the possibility of true love?

Linda had. Now Eliza was.

CHAPTER

138

Eliza stuffed Linda Anderson's audition tape in her carry bag, on the off chance that she would have time to look at it at home. Something was always coming up at the office and she wanted to take fifteen minutes and view the tape without interruption.

She said good night to Paige, delighted to see the blue cashmere turtleneck was so becoming on her assistant, and hurried down to the waiting car. Traffic wasn't too bad and in forty-five minutes she was home. It was just eight o'clock.

The HoHoKus police had set a loose curfew of nine P.M. Then they would cruise neighborhoods, telling trick-or-treaters to head on home. Eliza had promised Janie she could stay up until then so they could give out the Butterfingers together.

The doorbell rang only sporadically. Two pirates and a young Tinkerbell, escorted by their parents who waited on the street out front. Some teenaged girls, laughing and wearing their cheerleading uniforms. A group of adolescent boys, with no costumes at all, as far as Eliza could tell. Baggy jeans, oversized flannel workshirts and untied Timberlands were probably what they'd worn to school today.

In between the callers, Janie sorted through the candy she had collected with James on their afternoon foray through the neighborhood. The packages of gum were definite keepers. So were the M&Ms, Snickers bars and Milk Duds. Anything with coconut Janie offered to her mother.

At nine on the dot, Eliza announced that it was time to go to bed. No more trick–or–treaters would be coming tonight.

A dark–faced scarecrow stood in the crowd of revelers on Sixth Avenue in New York City's Greenwich Village. In the mayhem of hooded ghosts and goblins and men dressed as women and women dressed as men, Abigail was surrounded by life, but felt totally alone.

The story on Linda tonight was haunting her. All of Linda's lost promise. Five years had gone by and still it was so sad.

Abigail didn't want to pretend she was having a good time. Not tonight.

She hung back on the congested sidewalk as the rest of the group surged forward. It was easy to slip away from her friends.

Eliza tucked Janie into bed and went to her own room to change into a loose–fitting sweater and pair of jeans. Then she came downstairs and went to the kitchen. The refrigerator held the dinner Mrs. Garcia had left for her, but she wasn't in the mood to eat a big meal this late. Instead she took out a wedge of cheddar cheese and sliced off a few pieces on the cutting board. She tossed a handful of crackers onto the plate and poured a glass of white wine, ready to look at the audition tape.

In the den, she was pulling the black plastic box from her bag when the doorbell rang. *A late trick-or-treater,* she thought as she went to answer the door, leaving the tape on the desk.

"Samuel!" she said with surprise. "Come on in."

Jimmy Willis crouched behind a tree and waited as the police patrol car passed.

Tough. This curfew was stupid and he was determined to hit a few more houses before he went home for the night. His mother was already ticked off at him for being hauled into the station last night after the cops caught him egging the neighbors' house. She had forbidden him to go out tonight, but it had been a cinch to sneak out anyway. Might as well have some good loot in his bag for his pains—and the grounding that was sure to come.

The fourteen-year-old waited until the red taillights were out of sight. He came out from his hiding place and continued down Saddle Ridge Road.

Samuel looked like he had lost his best friend as he sat on the sofa in her den. Eliza's heart went out to him.

"I can't eat. I can't sleep. I feel terrible without you in my life."

The phone rang, buying Eliza time. *Saved by the bell.* What was she going to say to make him feel better?

"Excuse me, Samuel." Eliza walked over to the desk and picked up the receiver. A proud new father was on the other end of the line.

"Congratulations, Keith! That's wonderful. How is Cindy?" Eliza could feel Samuel watching her as she listened to Keith's response. She picked up the audition tape and began to fiddle with the box.

"C-section? Oh, that's too bad. But better that than something happening to the baby."

Absentmindedly Eliza clicked the box open and then closed it again.

"Nine pounds? Wow! That's a big fella. Have you named him yet?"

Keith told her his son's name, but it did not register. Eliza had opened the box and looked at the label affixed to the video cartridge.

Under Linda Anderson's name was that of her business representative. The agent was named Samuel Morton.

Abigail scrubbed the brown makeup from her face and changed into sweats. While she didn't want to be part of the Halloween craziness on the streets, she didn't want to sit in all by herself, either. She went out to see if she could find a quiet bar.

The tiny eyes were clamped shut, the rosebud mouth opened, emitting a tiny yawn. Perfect ears, perfect nose and, wrapped snugly beneath the cotton receiving blanket, perfect fingers and perfect toes.

Robert Keith Chapel, his son.

Keith gazed at the miracle that lay in his wife's arms.

Cindy looked up at her husband and their eyes locked in mutual understanding.

It had all been worth it. Now they could move forward, together, as a family.

Cindy had been through so much and Keith hoped she could forgive him for the way he had behaved and, eventually, he hoped he would be able to forgive himself.

Eliza tried to remember. Hadn't she told Samuel about the FRESHER LOOK she was working on? Yes. She had, that night at dinner at Esty Street. He hadn't remarked on it.

She wanted desperately to give Samuel the benefit of the doubt. She didn't think she had mentioned Linda Anderson. Maybe he hadn't made the connection. But even if she hadn't mentioned Linda by name, the case she had described to Samuel should have provoked a response from him about the anchorwoman he had represented.

Eliza's spine stiffened. She needed time to think. Perhaps it was another Samuel Morton. She took her seat across from Samuel.

"Where were we?" she asked.

"I was telling you how miserable I am without you. Please, Eliza, isn't there some way you'll reconsider? We can go slowly. I promise, I won't push things. But I need to know that we can still see each another."

"We can, Samuel, as long as you know that it will be as friends."

That was not the answer Samuel wanted. He winced as though Eliza had struck him.

"Come," she urged, rising from her chair. "Let's go into the kitchen and get you a drink."

She had just finished filling his glass with wine when the telephone rang again. "I don't want to let it go," she apologized. "It might wake Janie."

Samuel nodded glumly.

"Ms. Blake? This is Bob Lieber from Sloan–Kettering. I hope you don't mind that I'm calling you at home."

"No, not at all. How are you?"

"Concerned. I'm here in my office working late tonight. Our counseling department ran your friend's daughter's name through our computer."

"Yes?"

"Over the last six months, no one named Sarah Morton has been admitted to this hospital."

One more house and that was it. Jimmy was going to stop press-
ing his luck. *That TV newswoman should be good for some decent candy.*

He tossed away his forbidden cigarette and walked up to the
brightly-lit colonial, pushed the bell and waited. The door didn't open.

Someone was home. Jimmy knew it.

He lifted the door knocker and slammed it insistently.

"Don't answer that."

"It will just take a minute, Samuel."

"I'm telling you, Eliza. Don't answer it."

She wanted to run to the front door and fling it open, escaping
into the dark night. But Janie . . . Janie was upstairs. She couldn't leave
her little girl behind.

Eliza was stunned at the depth of Samuel's deception. There had
to be a mistake. No Sarah Morton had been in the cancer hospital.
Why had Samuel lied about that? She couldn't think of a reason.

And then the truly awful fear occurred to her. *What if there never
had been a child?*

But she had seen the girl's picture on the album of letters Samuel
had given her. There was a definite resemblance between the child
and Samuel.

A visceral fear rose.

What if Samuel Morton had been Linda Anderson's killer?

Who did this woman think she was? Would it kill her to open the door and throw out a piece of candy into his pillowcase? His mother thought it was so cool that this big shot had moved to town. Jimmy was unimpressed.

Jimmy tried the bell one more time and waited until he heard a car coming up the street. *Cops.* He ducked behind the bushes beneath the front window.

By the time the police sedan passed, Jimmy had made up his mind. If the homeowner didn't give him a treat, he would give her a little trick. He pulled his weapon from the pillowcase.

He peeked into the front window and looked into the living room. Seeing no one inside, he did a good soap job on the small panes.

But he was still ticked off. He went to the other side and peered into the library. Again, no one there. Angrily he smeared the glass.

Why not finish the job? Emboldened, Jimmy walked quickly to the backyard. The lights were on in the kitchen and from the side window he could see a man and a woman.

He should hightail it out of there.

But what Jimmy saw mesmerized him. He recognized the woman from TV. She was standing with her back to the counter. The man was pacing up and down. While the man wasn't looking, the anchorwoman picked up a knife from the countertop and slid it under her sweater, into the back of her jeans.

She had to get Samuel out of the house. She couldn't let him know what she suspected and she had to get him away from Janie.

Eliza pretended to take a sip of her wine. "Samuel, maybe I've been wrong. Maybe we *can* work things out. I'm so confused. I have to think." Eliza ran her fingers through her hair.

Samuel looked at her hopefully.

"Let's go for a walk around the pond and clear our heads," she suggested.

"And leave Janie?"

"She'll be okay for a little while. We won't go far. Come on." She reached out and took his cold hand. "Some fresh air will do us both good."

Holy cripes!

Where were the police when you needed them?

Jimmy ran down Saddle Ridge Road and, for the first time in his life, he prayed he would run into a police car.

He didn't.

They said it happened this way sometimes.

You met someone and, instantly, you knew.

Abigail studied the face of the young woman who sat on the bar stool beside her. For the first time in months, she didn't think about Eliza.

The pond was peaceful in the reflected autumn moonlight.

Eliza used all her willpower not to recoil as Samuel put his arm around her shoulders. Better there than around her waist.

"Do you really think we can work things out?" he asked softly.

"I'm sure we can," she lied.

Why doesn't a car drive by? Please, God. Let somebody come. Please, please, please.

Samuel stopped walking and turned her toward him.

"I love you, Eliza." He lifted her chin and leaned forward to kiss her. She kissed him back. Her life depended on it.

"And just where have you been, young man?" Jimmy's mother demanded angrily.

"Mom! Mom! We have to call the police!"

"Don't you think we've had enough of the police lately?"

"You don't understand, Mom."

"I understand perfectly well. I'm sick and tired of your antics. I told you not to leave your room. Now, you're grounded."

Jimmy pounded up to his room and flopped onto the bed. He should let the whole thing go, but he couldn't. He picked up the phone extension and called information and then asked the number for the HoHoKus police.

His adolescent voice cracked as he began to tell his story.

"Who is this?" demanded the desk sergeant.

"Jim Willis."

"The kid who was in here last night?"

"Yeah. But don't worry about that now. I'm telling you, you better get over to that anchorwoman's house on Saddle Ridge Road. This guy and her were in the kitchen and I saw her sneaking a big knife behind her back. It looked real scary in there."

"Yeah, kid, sure. Happy Halloween."

Eliza didn't close her eyes but watched as Samuel opened his, midway through the kiss. He pulled his mouth from hers.

"What's wrong?" he asked.

"Nothing. Nothing's wrong."

"Why are you looking at me like that?"

Eliza's right hand moved to the back of her jeans.

"You know, don't you, Eliza?"

"Know what?"

Her hand felt for the handle of the knife.

"About me."

"What *about* you, Samuel?" She couldn't keep her voice from quivering now. Why didn't someone come? If she screamed, no one might hear her and Samuel would know that she was on to him.

"Don't lie to me, Eliza. I can tell you're lying now. I have watched you for far too long. I watched you in the mornings when you were anchoring *KEY to America*. I've watched you these past months on the *Evening Headlines*. I've taped you and watched you over and over again. I can tell when you are lying."

"Lying about what, Samuel?"

"You know there is no Sarah, Eliza. I know you do. Don't play coy with me. I made her up to get to you."

"But I saw her picture," Eliza answered. "She looks just like you."

"That was a picture of my brother Leo's daughter."

Eliza gripped the knife handle.

"I had to find a way to reach you, Eliza. I knew we were meant for each other, and I hoped you would come to see it, too. It was going so well. We were getting closer. You were confiding in me. But you blew it. You ruined it."

Eliza's mind raced.

Linda had thought she was being stalked but when the police began escorting her, no one had bothered her. Had Linda confided in her agent, unwittingly alerting Samuel that it wasn't safe to follow her while the police were protecting her?

"I hoped it wouldn't have to come to this." Samuel looked at the gleaming pond. "But you love the water, just as I do—just as Linda did. The water is a tranquil, final resting place. I think so often of Linda. How wonderful to be at rest in the vast Atlantic Ocean."

"Is that where Linda is, Samuel?"

He shrugged. "Why not? I guess I can tell you—you won't be telling anyone now. Yes, Linda's tomb is off the coast of Sandy Hook. I like to think she's at peace near the place where we had walked so happily together."

"Surely Linda's body would have washed up somewhere, Samuel." Eliza tried to keep her voice steady.

"Give me some credit, Eliza. I took Linda from my trunk and strapped her to a good strong air raft and tied some weights on for good measure. Then, just before I launched Linda's funeral bed into the dark sea, I made a small slit in the raft. I watched in the moonlight as Linda floated out and then sank beneath the waves."

Eliza's decision was made. In one quick movement she thrust the knife up into Samuel's side.

The police sergeant would bet a week's pay that the Willis kid was lying. The teenager would get some perverse thrill having a squad car rush out on a false alarm.

But what if the kid was telling the truth? There'd be hell to pay if it got out that they hadn't followed up on this.

He had better send a car out.

Samuel cried out in pain as he lunged for Eliza's neck. His grip had the strength of a crazy person. Eliza struggled to break free but he was too strong.

What could she do?

She managed to knee him in the groin. Eliza felt his hands loosen and she was able to break away. But the force of her blow had not been great enough to bring him to his knees. She ran as fast as she had ever run in her life, hearing the leather-soled shoes pounding on the macadam behind her. Despite the bleeding wound in his side, he was gaining on her.

Then she heard Samuel groan as he slipped and fell to the pavement. The goose droppings gave her precious extra seconds.

Should she run to the Feeneys'?

That would leave Janie alone. If she could just get into the house, she could call the police. But Samuel was so enraged, he could easily force himself inside.

Instinctively she went back to be near her child. Eliza locked the door behind her and ran to the phone. The emergency numbers were glued on the receiver. She dialed as fast as she could and after only one ring she heard, "HoHoKus Police."

The squad car got the radio call and obediently headed toward Saddle Ridge Road.

"It could be a prank, but you better check it out anyway."

The car was blocks away from Eliza's house when the second call came on the radio.

"Suspect armed and dangerous. Sending backup."

Eliza waited, afraid to look out the window. Where were the police? Where *were* they?

If Samuel got in, she would face him herself.

With what? She cast about frantically.

She went to the fireplace and grabbed the iron–and–brass poker.

The wound ached painfully as Samuel lurched to the back of Eliza's house and pulled back the heavy pool cover. Eliza would come to her end in the water after all. Then, with all the strength of a madman, he picked up one of the large rocks that lined the garden and smashed it through the kitchen door's plate–glass window.

Eliza was waiting for him.

The police car sped into Eliza's driveway. The patrolman ran up and banged on the front door and waited for an answer that did not come.

He pulled his gun, not knowing what he was going to be facing.

He had to wait for backup.

Samuel stepped over the shattered glass into the kitchen and listened carefully.

Where was she?

He stealthily walked through the dining room, the living room and into the den, leaving a trail of blood behind.

She must have gone upstairs to guard her baby.

With determination he climbed the stairs. When he reached the landing, he turned to check the hallway. Eliza's waiting eyes met his.

With all her instinctive maternal strength, she brought the poker smashing down on top of his head, the blow sending him careening backwards down the stairs.

Eliza stood motionless as she heard footsteps and then watched the blue-uniformed men crouch down beside the crumpled, bleeding figure on the floor below.

Janie slept through the whole thing.

NOVEMBER

EPILOGUE

A biting wind whipped across the choppy gray water at Sandy Hook, blowing the hair and coats of the people assembled at the shoreline. At the front of the group, Florence and Monica Anderson stood in the wet sand and listened as the minister read from his Bible.

"'The Lord giveth and the Lord taketh away....'"

Along with the other mourners, Eliza Blake and Abigail Snow walked to the water's edge and tossed pink carnations into the Atlantic Ocean.

Eliza waited her turn to speak to Linda's mother. "I'm so sorry, Mrs. Anderson." There was nothing else she could think to say.

Florence Anderson raised her arms and wrapped them around Eliza.

"Thank you, dear. At least I know what happened now. It's better this way."

Eliza pulled back and looked into the woman's sad, yet still-sparkling blue eyes. She prayed this mother would be able, finally, to find peace.

"Will you be able to join us for lunch?" Florence asked.

"Thank you, but I'm afraid not. I have to get back to work for an election coverage rehearsal."

Eliza offered Abigail a ride back to the Broadcast Center, expecting her to accept all too eagerly. But Abigail declined. She was going to lunch with her former co-workers from the Garden State Network who had come to the memorial service.

"Eliza, I just want you to know, I won't be bothering you anymore. I've found someone."

"I'm glad for you, Abigail. I really am."

Alone, Eliza walked across the sand to the waiting car. Her thoughts turned to Mack. He would be home in a few weeks for Thanksgiving. Maybe they *could* work things out.

Everyone made mistakes.

"As Linda Anderson's agent, Samuel Morton stood to make a tidy fee if he negotiated a network contract for his client. The police had questioned Morton along with all Linda's other friends and acquaintances, but they dismissed him as a suspect. He was an educated, polished, assured individual with no apparent motive. In fact, Morton only gained if Linda lived."

When Eliza returned to the Broadcast Center from the memorial service, Joe Connelly reeled off the information he had gotten from the local police detective in charge of the Anderson case at the time of her disappearance.

"And he could just move away like that?" Eliza asked. It didn't make sense.

"Sure he could. He wasn't accused of any crime. The police knew he'd moved to Florida about a year after Linda disappeared. It didn't look like he was fleeing. He was joining his brother's law firm and going to live in a beautiful city in a wonderful climate. Who was going to argue with that?"

"Did they ever check up on him with the Sarasota police?"

Joe nodded. "Yeah, they did. Though they didn't have to. But all reports were that Morton was a model citizen, big on philanthropy and heavy into the social scene."

God, you never knew. The urbane, sophisticated man sitting next to you at the black–tie fundraiser could turn out to be an obsessed madman.

"What about Samuel's brother? Did he know anything about all this?"

"The Sarasota PD doesn't think so. Leo Morton said he was worried about his brother's depression. He said Samuel wouldn't show up at work sometimes, explaining he just had to walk the beach. Leo was concerned about the behavior, but he never for a minute suspected that his brother was a murderer. Leo was there when the cops searched Samuel's townhouse. He seemed truly appalled when they found videotapes of Linda Anderson and you."

"Does he know that Samuel used a picture of his daughter and passed her off as his own?"

Joe nodded. "He does now. I hear he's livid about it."

"I would be, too, if someone used Janie's picture that way." Eliza tried to think of the future. "What happens now?"

"If your aim had been a little better, or if you'd been a little stronger, you wouldn't have to ask that question. But when his wounds heal, he'll stand trial. You'll have to testify. In some sick way, he'll enjoy that—being close to you one more time."

The police had recovered her engagement ring, the diamond earrings, the heirloom emerald bracelet and the treasured pin. The HoHoKus detective told her that keys to other robbed homes had been found in the service-station office. Augie Sinisi would be going to jail.

"You look positively serene tonight, honey," Doris commented as she airbrushed Eliza's fair skin.

Indeed, when Doris went into the control room for a last check of Eliza's makeup under the blazing studio lights, she noted with satisfaction that the anchorwoman glowed from the monitor screen. The stress had vanished from the beautiful face.

Janie was watching out the front window as the car headlights lit up the driveway.

"Mommy's home!" she cried out to Mrs. Garcia.

Janie greeted her mother with a litany of what had happened that day. They were learning about the pilgrims at school. Daisy sat on command. Mrs. Garcia had taught her two new Spanish words.

Eliza listened intently, luxuriating in the ordinary, precious details of which life was made. She bent down and took her little girl in her arms and held her close. Eliza vowed that she would never take anything for granted again, yet, inevitably, she knew she would. That was human nature.